THE URBANA FREE LIBRARY

W9-BCL-479

DISCARDED BY THE
URBANA FREE LIBRARY

The Urbana Free Library

To renew: call 217-367-4057
or go to "*urbanafreelibrary.org*"
and select "Renew/Request Items"

	DATE DUE	
JUL 0 8 2013		

CHILDREN

of the

JACARANDA TREE

CHILDREN
of the
JACARANDA
TREE

A Novel

Sahar Delijani

ATRIA BOOKS

New York   London   Toronto   Sydney   New Delhi

ATRIA BOOKS

A Division of Simon & Schuster, Inc.
1230 Avenue of the Americas
New York, NY 10020

This book is a work of fiction. Any references to historical events, real people, or real places are used fictitiously. Other names, characters, places, and events are products of the author's imagination, and any resemblance to actual events or places or persons, living or dead, is entirely coincidental.

Copyright © 2013 by Sahar Delijani

All rights reserved, including the right to reproduce this book or portions thereof in any form whatsoever. For information address Atria Books Subsidiary Rights Department, 1230 Avenue of the Americas, New York, NY 10020.

First Atria Books hardcover edition June 2013

ATRIA BOOKS and colophon are trademarks of Simon & Schuster, Inc.

For information about special discounts for bulk purchases, please contact Simon & Schuster Special Sales at 1-866-506-1949 or business@simonandschuster.com.

The Simon & Schuster Speakers Bureau can bring authors to your live event. For more information or to book an event contact the Simon & Schuster Speakers Bureau at 1-866-248-3049 or visit our website at www.simonspeakers.com.

Designed by Dana Sloan

Manufactured in the United States of America

10 9 8 7 6 5 4 3 2 1

Library of Congress Cataloging-in-Publication Data

Delijani, Sahar, 1983–
    Children of the Jacaranda tree : a novel / Sahar Delijani.—First Atria Books hardcover edition.
        pages   cm

    1. Iran—History —Revolution, 1979 —Fiction.   2. Domestic fiction.
I. Title.
    PS3604.E44425C48 2013
    823'.92 —dc23   2012047347

ISBN 978-1-4767-0909-3
ISBN 978-1-4767-0911-6 (ebook)

To my parents

1983

Evin Prison, Tehran

Azar sat on the corrugated iron floor of a van, huddled against the wall. The undulating street made the car sway from side to side, swinging her this way and that. With her free hand, she clasped on to something that felt like a railing. The other hand lay on her hard, bulging belly, which contracted and strained, making her breathing choppy, irregular. A heat wave of pain spouted from somewhere in her backbone and burst through her body. Azar gasped, seizing the chador wrapped around her, gripping so hard that her knuckles turned white. With every turn, she was thrashed against the walls. With every bump and pothole, her body was sent flying toward the ceiling, the child in her belly rigid, cringing. The blindfold over her eyes was damp with sweat.

She lifted a hand and wiped the moisture from her eyes. She dared not remove the blindfold, even though there was no one with her in the back of the van. But she knew there was a window behind her. She had felt the glass when she first climbed in. Sister might turn around and see her through this window, or they could stop so abruptly that Azar would not have time to put the blindfold back on.

She didn't know what would happen to her if they caught her with open eyes, and she did not wish to. At times she tried to convince herself that the fear that had crept inside her, cleaving to her, was not justifiable; no one had ever raised a hand to her, shoved her around, threatened her. She had no reason to be terrified of them, of the Sisters and the Brothers, no tangible reason. But then there were the screams that shook the prison walls, tearing through the empty corridors, waking the prisoners at night, cutting across a conversation as the prisoners divided up their lunch, forcing them all to a tight-jawed, stiff-limbed silence that lasted well through the evening. No one knew where the screams were coming from. No one dared ask. Shrieks of pain they were, this much they knew. For no one could confuse howls of pain with any other kind; they were cries of a body without a self, abandoned, crushed to a shapeless splotch, whose only sign of being was the force with which it could shatter the silence inside the prison walls. And no one knew when their turn would come up, when they would disappear down the corridor and nothing would remain of them but howls. So they lived and waited and followed orders under the looming cloud of a menace that everyone knew could not be eluded forever.

From a tiny opening somewhere above Azar's head, the muffled din of the city waking up intruded into the car: shutters rolling open, cars honking, children laughing, street vendors haggling. Through the window, she could also hear the intermittent sounds of chatter and laughter coming from the front of the van, though the words were not clear. She could hear only the guffaws of Sister at something one of the Brothers had just finished recounting. Azar tried to keep out the voices inside the van by concentrating on the hum of the city outside—Tehran, her beloved city, which she had neither seen nor heard for months. She wondered how the city could have changed with the war with Iraq dragging on into its third year. Had the flames of war reached Tehran? Were people leaving the city? From the noises outside, it seemed as if everything continued as always, the same chaos, the same din of struggle and survival. She wondered what her parents were doing at this moment. Mother was probably in line at the baker's; her father was probably getting on his motorcycle and leaving for work. At the thought of them, she felt like something was gripping her throat. She lifted her head, opened her mouth wide, and tried to gulp down the air seeping through the opening.

Her head thrown back, she breathed hard, so hard that her throat burned and she started to cough. She undid the tight knot of the headscarf under her chin and let the chador slide down her head. She held on to the railing, sitting stiffly, trying to bear the swaying and lashing of the car as another burst of pain blazed through her like the fiery end of a bullet. Azar tried to sit up; she bristled at the thought of having to give birth on the iron floor of a van, on these bumpy streets, with the shrill laughter of Sister in her ears. Tightening her grasp on the railing, she took a deep breath and tried to shut herself against the urge of erupting. She was determined to keep the child inside until they reached the hospital.

Just then she felt a sudden gush between her legs and held

her breath as the uncontrollable trickle ran down her thigh. She pushed her chador aside. Panic swept through her as she touched the pants carefully with the tips of her fingers. She knew that a pregnant woman's water would break at some point, but not what would happen after that. Did this mean birth was imminent? Was it dangerous? Azar had just started reading books on pregnancy when they came to her door. She was about to reach the chapter on water breaking, contractions, what she should pack in her hospital bag, when they knocked so loudly, as if they wanted to break down the front door of her house. When they dragged her out, her stomach was already beginning to show.

She clenched her jaw as her heart pounded violently. She wished her mother were there so she could explain what was happening. Mother with her deep voice and gentle face. She wished she had something of her mother that she could hold on to, a piece of clothing, her headscarf. It would have helped.

She wished Ismael were there so he could hold her hand and tell her that everything was going to be fine. He would have been frightened, she knew, if he had seen her in these conditions, sick with worry. He would have stared at her with his bright brown eyes as if he wanted to devour her pain, make it his own. There was nothing he hated more than seeing her in pain. The time she fell from the chair that she had climbed in order to pick grapes from the vine tree, he was so shocked, seeing her wriggling on the ground, that he almost cried, gathering her in his arms. *I thought you had broken your back*, he told her later on. *I would die if something ever happened to you.* His love made her feel like a mountain, unshakable, immortal. She needed that all-encompassing love, those worried eyes, the way in which, by taking it upon herself to reassure him, to calm him down, she always succeeded in reassuring herself too.

She wished her father were there so he could carry her to his car and drive like a madman to the hospital.

The van came to a stop, and Azar, shaken out of her thoughts, turned around sharply, as if she could see. Although the grumble of the engine had fallen silent, no door opened. Her hands crept up to her headscarf, tightening the knot, sweeping the chador over her head. Sister's gales of laughter once again burst forth. Soon it became apparent that they were waiting for the Brother to finish telling his story. Azar waited for them, her hands trembling on the slippery edge of her chador.

After a few moments, she heard doors open and swing shut. Someone fiddled with the lock on the back of the van. Clinging to the railing, Azar lugged her body forward. She was at the edge of the car when the doors were drawn open.

"Get out," Sister said as she fastened the handcuffs around Azar's wrists.

Azar found that she could barely stand. She lumbered alongside Sister, engulfed in the darkness enveloping her eyes, her wet pants sticking to her thighs. Soon she felt a pair of hands behind her head, untying the blindfold, and saw that she was standing in a dimly lit corridor, flanked by long rows of closed doors. A few plastic chairs were set against the walls, which were covered with posters of children's happy faces and a framed photo of a nurse with a finger against her lips to indicate silence. Azar felt a great lifting in her heart as she realized they had at last reached the prison hospital.

A few young nurses hurried past. Azar watched as they disappeared down the corridor. There was something beautiful about having her eyes out in the open, her gaze hopping hurriedly, freely, from the green walls to the doors to the flat neon lights embedded in the ceiling to the nurses in white uniforms and white shoes, fluttering around, opening and shutting doors, their faces flushed with the excitement of work. Azar felt less exposed now that she could see, and on equal ground with everyone else. Behind the blindfold, she had felt incomplete, mutilated, bogged down in a fluid world of physical vulnerability, where anything could happen and she could not defend herself. Now she felt as if, with one glance, she could shed the stunting fear that hacked away at her, that made her feel less than whole, less than a person. With open eyes, in the dim corridor surrounded by the bustle of life and birth, Azar felt she was beginning to reclaim her humanity.

From behind some of those doors came the muffled chorus of babies wailing. Azar listened carefully, as if, in their endless, hungry cries, there was a message for her, a message from the other side of time, from the other side of her body and flesh.

A nurse came to a halt in front of them. She was a portly woman with bright hazel eyes. She looked up and down at Azar and then turned to Sister.

"It's a busy day. We're trying to cope with the Eid-e-Ghorban rush, and I don't know if there's any room available. But come on up. We'll have the doctor at least take a look at her."

The nurse led them to a flight of stairs, which Azar climbed with difficulty. Every few steps, she had to stop to catch her breath. The nurse walked ahead, as if avoiding this prisoner with her baby and her agony, the perspiration glistening on her scrawny face.

They went from floor to floor, Azar hauling her body from one corridor to the next, one closed door to another. Finally, the doctor in one of the rooms motioned them in. Azar quickly lay down and submitted herself to the doctor's efficient, impersonal hands.

The baby inside her felt as tense as a knot.

"As I said before, we can't keep her here," the nurse said once the doctor was gone, the door swinging shut silently behind her. "She's not part of this prison. You have to take her somewhere else."

Sister signaled to Azar to get up. Descending stairs, flight after flight, floor after floor, Azar clasped the banister, tight, stiff, panting. The pain was changing gear. It gripped her back, then her stomach. She gasped, feeling as if the baby were being wrung out of her by giant hands. For a moment, her eyes welled up, to her biting shame. She gritted her teeth, swallowed hard. This was not a place for tears—not on these stairs, not in these long corridors.

Before leaving the hospital, Sister made sure the blindfold was tied hermetically over her prisoner's bloodshot eyes.

Back on the corrugated iron floor, the doors slammed shut. The van smelled of heat and violent suffering. As soon as the engine started, the chattering from the front picked up where it had left off. Sister sounded excited. There was a flirtatious edge to her voice and to her high-pitched laughter.

Back in position, Azar slouched slightly with fatigue. As the van zigzagged through the jarring traffic, she remembered the first time she took Ismael to her house. It had been a hot day, much like today. He smelled sweet, of soap and happiness, as he walked beside her down the narrow street. She wanted to show him where she came from, she had said, the house she lived in with its low brick walls, the blue fountain, and the jacaranda tree that dominated everything. He had been doubtful; what if her parents came back and caught him there? But he came anyway. *Nothing but a quick tour*, Azar promised, laughing, grabbing his hand. They ran from room to room, never letting go of that moment, of each other, of the perfume of the flowers that enfolded them.

She wondered where Ismael was, and if he was all right. It had been months since she'd had news of him, months when she did not even know if he was still alive. *No, no, no.* She shook her head repeatedly. She should not think about that. *Not now.* She had heard from some of the new prisoners that the men had also been transferred to the Evin prison. Most of the men. If they made it to Evin, it meant they had made it through the interrogations and everything else she did not dare think about at the Komiteh Moshtarak detention center. She was sure Ismael was one of those men. She was sure he was in Evin with her. He had to be.

Once again, the van came to a stop and the door swung open. This time, the blindfold did not come off. The sun shone feebly through it and into Azar's eyes as she faltered out of the van, tottering alongside Sister and Brothers into another building and then down a corridor. They must have entered the labor ward of another hospital, for soon the sounds of women moaning and screaming filled her ears. Azar felt a rush of hope. Maybe now they would leave her to the safe hands of the doctors. Maybe the agony would be over. The blindfold slid down a bit on one side, and from the opening, she watched eagerly the gray tiled floor of the long corridor and the metal feet of chairs along the walls. She felt the brisk passing of people, perhaps nurses, their soft shoes thudding down the hallway. Their bodies moving past raised a quick breeze to her face.

Soon their course changed, and they were going up another flight of stairs. The sound of the women's moans drifted. Azar cocked her ears and knew they were taking her away from the labor ward. The corners of her eyes twitched. When they finally came to a stop and a door opened, she was led into a room and told to sit down. She lowered herself onto a hard wooden chair, exhausted. Sweat dripped from her forehead and into her eyes as a rush of pain came back to claim her. *Soon the doctor will be here,* she thought, trying to console herself.

Yet, she quickly realized it was not a doctor she was waiting for when, from behind the closed door, came the slip-slap of plastic slippers approaching; the noise grew louder and louder. She knew what that sound meant, and she knew when she heard it that she had to prepare herself. She gripped the warm, sweaty metal of the handcuff and squeezed her eyes shut, hoping the slip-slap would stride right past her door and leave her alone. When it fell silent behind the door, Azar's heart sank; they were here for her.

The door squeaked open. From underneath the blindfold, she had a glimpse of black pants and a man's skinny toes with long pointy nails. She heard him dawdle across the room, pull a chair raspingly over the floor, and sit down. Azar's body grew tense against the ominous being that she could not see but felt with every molecule of her body. The child inside her pushed and twisted. She winced, clasped into her chador.

"Your first and last name?"

In a quivering voice, Azar gave her name. She then said the name of the political party to which she belonged and the name of her husband. Another stab of pain and she crouched over, a whimper escaping through her mouth. But the man did not seem to hear or see. The questions continued to roll off his tongue mechanically, as if he were reading from a list he had been given but knew nothing about. There was aggressiveness in his voice that stemmed from the deep and dangerous boredom of an interrogator who had grown tired of his own questions.

The room was very hot. Under the coarse layers of her manteau and chador, Azar's body was soaked in sweat. The man asked her the date of her husband's arrest. She told him that and whom she knew and whom she didn't. Her voice throbbed with agony as waves of pain blazed through her. *I must keep calm*, she told herself. *I mustn't make the baby suffer.* She shook her head against the image that continued to crop up in her mind: that of a child, her child, deformed, broken, a sight of irreversible agony. *Like the children of Biafra.* She gave a grunt. Sweat trickled down her back.

Where were the meetings? the man asked. How many of them attended each meeting? As she gripped the chair against the fresh all-encompassing stabs of pain, Azar tried to remember all the right answers. All the answers she had given from one interrogation to the next. Not a date, not a name, not a piece of information or lack of it should differ. She knew why she was here, why they had thought that now was the perfect time to interrogate her, to get at her. *Keep calm*, she repeated to herself while she answered. As she omitted names, dates, places, meetings, she tried to remain calm by imagining her baby's feet, hands, knees, the shape of the eyes, the color. Another wave of pain soared and crashed inside her. She writhed, shocked at its ferocity. It was pain she had never thought possible. She was losing herself to it. *Fingers, knuckles, nostrils, earlobes, neck.*

Where did she print the leaflets? She heard the man repeat the question. She tried to answer, but the contractions seemed to be swallowing her, not giving her a chance to speak. She lurched forward, grabbing the table in front of her. She heard herself moan. *Belly button, black hair, curve of the chin.* She took a deep breath. She felt like she was going to faint. She bit her tongue. She bit her lips. She could taste the blood blending into her saliva. She bit into her whitened knuckles.

But the outside world was quickly fading away as Azar's pain grew worse. She could no longer hear anything, nor was she aware of what was around her. The waves of pain had hurled her into a space where nothing else existed, nothing except an agony so acute and unbelievable that it felt no longer part of her but a condition of life, a state of being. She was no longer a body; she was a space where everything writhed and wriggled, where pain, pure and infinite, held sway.

She didn't know how long the man waited for her answer about the leaflets; it never came. She was only half-conscious when she heard him close what sounded like a notebook. She knew the interrogation was over. The sense of relief was almost dizzying. She didn't hear the man get up but did recognize his slip-slapping away. Soon she heard Sister's voice telling her to get up. Azar stumbled out of the room, down the corridor, flanked by Sister and someone who felt like a nurse. She could barely keep their pace. She lumbered along, bent almost double, breathing quickly. The handcuffs felt unbearably heavy on her wrists. They went down the flight of stairs. The sound of women's wails once again filled Azar's ears.

"Here we are," the nurse said as they came to a stop.

Sister unfastened the handcuffs and took off Azar's blindfold.

She climbed on a narrow bed in a roomful of nurses and a doctor. The wall on her right side was dazzled by the afternoon sun. In a lull between contractions, Azar sank heavily in her exhaustion, her arms lying slack on the bed, watching the smooth skin of sunlight as she submitted herself to the hands of the doctor checking her.

Sister stood next to the doctor, looking on in silence. Azar refused to look at her. She refused to acknowledge Sister's presence there, wished to forget it completely. Not only Sister but everything Sister's presence meant: Azar's captivity, her solitude, her fear, giving birth in a prison. She was now a foreigner, surrounded by people who saw her as an enemy to be tamed and defeated, who saw her very being as an obstacle to their power, to their own understanding of right and wrong, moral and immoral. People who loathed her because she refused to take what they offered as what she had fought for; people who saw her as their foe because she refused to accept that their God had all the answers.

Azar wanted to close her eyes and pretend she was somewhere else, in another time, another place, another hospital room, where Ismael was standing next to her, caressing her face, looking at her with concern, holding her hand and not letting go, and her parents were outside, waiting, her father pacing up and down the corridor, her mother clasping her hospital bag between tense fingers, sitting on the edge of the chair, ready to careen into the room when needed.

Here, she could thrust her hand out and it would come back with nothing. Emptiness. She was completely alone.

"The baby's turned." She heard the doctor's voice and looked down at her stomach. The taut lump that had appeared somewhere close to her belly button now looked as if it had climbed up to the space between her breasts.

The doctor turned to the two women behind her. "We have to push it down."

Azar's mouth went dry. Push it down? How? The women, who appeared to be midwives, moved closer, their wrinkled faces and hands reeking of the province, of remote villages at the bend of narrow muddy roads. They were holding torn pieces of cloth in their hands. Azar almost gasped with fright. What did they want with those torn pieces? What were they going to do? Gag her to keep her screams from reaching outside? The women looked at Sister, who grabbed one of the torn pieces of cloth and showed them how to tie Azar's leg. Azar winced at the touch of those moist, callused fingers tethering her to the bed railings. The women looked hesitant but eventually went ahead with the job. One of them grabbed Azar's legs, the other her arms. Azar jolted with a fierce thrust inside her. The lull was over; the pain had returned.

The doctor spread a blanket over Azar's legs and leaned forward in front of her. "Here we go."

After tying her down, the midwives interlaced their fingers and placed their hands somewhere close to Azar's breasts. Azar watched them, helpless with pain, as her heart pounded wildly in her chest. She was frightened of them, of what they would do to her, to her child. Was this even a proper hospital? Who were these women, and where had they come from? Did they know what they were doing?

She heard herself groan. The women took deep breaths to prepare themselves, like boxers gathering their strength before a fight. Then, wide-eyed and prim-lipped, with those hands that perhaps had squeezed the swollen belly of a cow or tugged at the trembling legs of a lamb, they gave the lump, her child, a hard shove.

For a moment, Azar froze with the excruciating violence of that shove. Then a scream, wild and unknown, burst from her throat. A scream so forceful her entire body shook with its echo. She lurched forward, struggling to push the women away from her stomach, her child. Would they squeeze the child dead? Strangle it? Azar couldn't move her hands but tried to thrust her neck forward to bite them as another lurch of pain dragged her back to the bed.

"Push!" the doctor demanded.

The lump was resistant. The women rammed their hands against it, their faces flushed with the pressure of those rough, interlaced fingers. Sweat glistened on their brows, along the lines of their noses. Their mouths twitched as they pressed.

Azar felt her body grow cold as another wail erupted through her. For a moment, she saw nothing. When her eyes cleared, she saw that one of the women was standing next to her. She was younger than the other, probably Azar's age, in her early twenties. Her almond-shaped black eyes shone gently. "It's okay," she whispered encouragingly, placing her cold hand on Azar's burning forehead. "We got the baby's head down; now you just have to push." As a fresh pain came, she said, "Your baby's almost here."

The woman smiled, but Azar looked at her with wild eyes. She didn't know what it all meant, what the girl was telling her. There was something inside her that was pushing ahead, out of her control. She tensed and released another scream.

"That's it, push. Another one."

Sister grabbed Azar's hand. "Scream! Call God! Call Imam Ali! Call them now, at least!"

The pain soared through Azar, cold and dark. She screamed and clasped the girl's arm. She didn't call anyone.

"It's coming," the doctor shouted. "Good girl, one more push!"

Something was being torn inside her. Torn open and apart.

With her last vestiges of strength, Azar gave one last push. Everything went black. From afar, she heard the weak cries of a baby fill the room.

The room was empty when she opened her eyes. A cold breeze wafting through the open window made her shiver. She was still tied down to the bed, and her legs had lost all sensation. Her damp hair lay pasted to her face; her feet hurt as if there was a layer of broken glass in them.

She had no idea how long she'd lain there. Hours, days, an eternity. Her eyes were eagerly, anxiously on the door. *Where have they taken my baby?* Soon the door creaked open and Sister sauntered in, gathering her black chador around her. Azar opened her mouth to say something, to ask of the child, but her lips were so dry that the corners of her mouth cracked. Behind Sister, the two midwives barreled in.

"Your daughter's in the other room," Sister said, as if she had read Azar's mind, seen the question on her sore lips. "I don't know when they're going to bring her here."

Azar closed her eyes. *It's a girl*, she thought. An exhausted but triumphant smile trembled on her lips, yet she felt anxious at the same time. She was not sure if she should believe Sister. What if the child was dead and Sister was lying? What if this was just another cruel trick? What if those cries she had heard in the room had died as soon as they erupted? She looked over at the young midwife, who smiled and nodded. Azar had no choice but to believe.

The midwives rolled Azar's bed out of the room, down the corridor, and into another room, where the window was closed. They untied her. There was something about these women's faces that reminded Azar of the mothers of the children she taught in the villages on the outskirts of Tehran in the first year after the revolution. Quiet, obedient, standing next to their poorly dressed children, accepting everything Azar said. Their eyes full of admiration, of deference verging on fear of the city girl who opened and closed books so easily, who spoke in perfect Farsi, who looked out of place in her city clothes in the classroom with its clay walls that constituted the entire school.

Azar's heart ached at the thought of those days, when she worked fervently for a new country, a better, more just country. How happy she had been, taking the bus back to Tehran in the evening. She had felt one with the city, seething and sizzling with excitement, with enthusiasm for what the present as well as the future held. She could not wait to arrive home, knowing Ismael would be expecting her in their tiny apartment. She remembered seeing the glow of the lamp in the living room seeping out through the curtains and the way it made her heart lift with joy. Night after night, that light, which meant Ismael was at home and she would soon be in his embrace, made her smile and her heart race as she rushed up the stairs. There would be the perfume of steamed rice filling in her nostrils as she entered the flat, and Ismael would come to her, pull her into his arms, and say, *"Khaste nabaashi azizam." May you never get tired.* She would make tea, and while they drank it together, sitting by the narrow window that faced the trees of the courtyard engulfed in the night, he would tell her of Karl Marx and she would read him the poems of Forugh Farrokhzad.

Merely a year had passed since the revolution, and both Azar and Ismael still burned with its fervent ecstasy. It brought tears of joy to their eyes, and their voices cracked, full of emotion, when they spoke of their triumph, the triumph of a nation in ousting the shah, the once untouchable king; it filled them with hope. And yet they knew something had gone wrong. The men with the severe faces and mouths full of rage and hope and relentlessness and God who had taken over the country, claiming to be the deliverers of righteous words and holy laws, made them bristle. *What is happening?* She would turn at times to Ismael, desperate. Gradually, it was becoming clear to all that these men considered themselves the only legitimate proprietors of the revolution, its indubitable victors. They purged universities of what they called anti-revolutionary activities, closed newspapers, banned political parties. Their words became law, and everyone else went underground, Azar and Ismael with them.

Azar drew her arms and legs in. A tremor had taken hold of her, and she could not stop shaking. The young woman left the room to bring a blanket and cover her with it. Azar coiled into a lump underneath it, straining to absorb the heat from its every corner. They left the room, closing the door silently behind them.

Azar pulled the blanket over her head and tried to breathe in the warmth. She closed her eyes and rocked her body side to side, waiting for the heat to take root, for the calm to settle in. She stayed there under the blanket for a long time, a shapeless heap.

Gradually, as the warmth began oozing through her body, Azar poked her head out and then her shoulders. Next to her, on the other side of the room, there was an empty bed with ruffled sheets and a dip in the pillow. The body seemed to have been removed recently. On the floor next to the bed, there was a plate, the rice and green beans on it half-eaten. When it caught her eyes, Azar realized how hungry she was. She had not eaten since the night before. Her eyes were fixed on the plate as she tugged her legs free from the blanket. This was her chance. That plate had to be hers. She tried to stand up, but her legs trembled and her knees gave way. About to fall, she grabbed the side of her bed and cautiously lowered herself to the floor. Her heart beat hotly in her chest as she steadied herself on the cold tiles and began to crawl forward.

The closer she got to the plate, the bolder she got, the more determined to guzzle up every last grain of rice. She was going to eat, and she was going to do it without Sister's permission. She was going to grab that plate and gobble everything up. To make it her own, part of her body, her being. She was going to possess it all, the rice, the beans, the plate itself. The thought even came to her to hide the plate somewhere and take it away with her, back to prison. She felt nauseated with hunger, with her brazenness, with the prospect of eating, with the fear of being caught before reaching that dish, that treasure, which was at that moment like life itself. She pressed her elbows against the floor and hauled herself over more quickly.

The rice was cold and dry, and as she gulped it down, she felt the sharp grains scratching her throat and thought of the buckets of food Sister would hand out to the prisoners at lunch hour. Her fingers worked fast, gathering the rice and the beans, lifting them to her mouth, her teeth that hurt, her tongue that could not taste anything. She chewed hurriedly, the grains spilling down her fingers. At any moment, this could all disappear and she could fall back into that reality where nothing was hers, neither to give nor to take. At any moment, Sister could walk into the room and take away the plate. But she could eat the food now. This was her moment.

The doctor in her white uniform smiled at Azar while checking her blood pressure. The bluish pouches under her eyes looked out of place in her round, welcoming face. Sister was standing on the other side of the bed, her arms free and unbound. She looked so comfortable in her black chador. They all did. Those Sisters. They walked, gestured, handed out buckets of food, tied blindfolds, locked and unlocked doors and handcuffs with such agility that it seemed as if the encumbering, slippery cloth did not exist, as if it weren't wrapped around them like the wings of a sleeping bat. Azar knew better than to ask Sister about her baby too many times. If she showed too much enthusiasm, Sister might take longer to bring the child to her just to spite her, just to make her suffer. Azar had to be good; she had to be patient.

"She has a tearing inside that could get infected." The doctor stopped inflating the cuff around Azar's arm. "She must stay for at least two days."

Sister tossed her head in a clumsy attempt to seem haughty. Azar could see somewhere in Sister's large eyes, in the thick fold of her lower lip and the missing tooth revealed in a rare smile, the poverty of the dust-blown peripheries, of languid afternoon gossip with the neighboring women on doorsteps, of watching boys play soccer in dusty streets and wishing for a color TV, of not continuing beyond fifth grade. And here she was, that woman of the poor peripheries, the queen of the plebeian, spreading her big black chador over the city and its privileged city girls. Sister was slowly learning to be proud of that poverty, just as she had learned to be proud of her chador.

"We have everything there," Sister asserted in a cold, flat voice. "We can take care of her."

Under the covers, Azar's bony hand edged across the bed. When she reached the doctor's leg, she pinched the flesh with all her might.

"We have to kill the bacteria inside her." The doctor looked directly at Sister. She betrayed no reaction to Azar's pinch. "That'll take a few days."

"No, we can do it there. We have everything. Doctors. Hospital. Medicine."

Azar wanted to shout out that they didn't, that Sister was lying, that they would leave her with the tearing inside her, that the infection would spread, that she would rot from the inside. She pinched the doctor's leg again, harder than before. Almost clinging.

"I'm telling you that she needs care, professional care, inside a hospital," the doctor insisted. She seemed to understand the meaning behind Azar's pinches. "We have to monitor her condition. She's been torn inside."

Sister hurled an angry glance at Azar, as if the tearing inside her had been her own fault. Azar's hand went limp on the edge of the bed. Sister beckoned to the doctor to follow her outside. Before the doctor moved away from the bed, Azar grasped her hand. "My baby?" she whispered.

The doctor placed a hand on top of Azar's desperate clasp. "She's fine. Don't worry. You'll have her soon."

Azar sat on the bed, staring at the door, waiting for the baby who did not come. She clasped her hands together, quivering with anger, frustration, longing, and fear. As the hours passed, she was beginning to lose patience. After nine long months of living with the child inside her, feeling it grow, protecting it, surviving with it, it seemed impossible that she still had not seen it, had not held it in her arms, did not know if it looked more like her or Ismael, did not even know for sure if it was alive. As the minutes crawled by and she watched the door, Azar felt the yearning for her child mounting inside her so powerfully that she could hardly breathe.

The afternoon sunlight was petering out, dragging its shadows against the walls. Azar clambered onto the windowsill to lift herself up and look through the closed glass. She wanted to know where she was. Through the sparse, grayish leaves of the sycamore trees, she saw a bridge clogged with afternoon rush-hour traffic. The sky was laden with smog; it was the last heat of the summer, and there was the edgy echo of car honks. She saw a flight of birds soaring through the sky, making a great loop and perching on the branches of the trees. The city looked different. Everything seemed to have been whitewashed, stainless, glossy. The white had been splashed on concrete buildings hurriedly, as if to hide something: blood, soot, history, the war, the unending war. It was a frenzied attempt to camouflage the devastation that breathed ever more closely down everyone's neck.

Although Azar had not been born here, Tehran had always been her home, where she had felt she belonged. She loved the city, with its traffic and its soiled white buildings and its overpowering chaos. She loved it so much that she'd once believed she could change its destiny. That was what she told Ismael when she informed him of her decision to continue her political activity. *This is not what we fought for, what we risked our lives for*, she said, *we cannot let them take everything away from us.*

Ismael came along with her, hand in hand, at every stage. *Whatever we do, we shall do it together*, he said. Whatever happened to them, it would be their shared destiny. He was quickly, readily infused with her fervor. He went with her to the underground meetings in stuffy rooms, helped her print leaflets, carry messages in cigarette packets, spoke of the future at his university. When it was time, when the persecutions began and it was too dangerous to keep contact with their families, they stopped calling and answering their parents' phone calls, stopped visiting them. They shed tears together, desperate, no longer certain what was the right thing to do. No longer having the strength to move forward and knowing it was too late to turn back. The door of their apartment became menacing, glaring at them askance, expecting responses to the unuttered questions that their parents impressed upon it with their persistent knocks. That was when they decided to move and hence wipe out their traces forever. It was easier that way. No one would be knocking on the door anymore. Cut off, they found it easier to pretend to forget.

Was it worth it? Azar wiped the strands of hair away from her face. Would Ismael ever forgive her for putting her fight before everything? Before him, their life together, the child growing in her womb? Would they be given a second chance?

The thoughts agitated her. She pressed her thin elbows against the windowsill and her forehead against the warm window. The traffic huffed and puffed slowly across the bridge. Although far from them, Azar could see the tiny, agitated faces in the cars, the restless bodies impaled on the motorbikes with not enough space to maneuver through the jam. Above the traffic, hovering overhead like a gigantic cloud, was a billboard with one of the maxims of the Supreme Leader written in careful, elegant cursive. *Our revolution was an explosion of light.* Painted next to it was the depiction of an explosion, like fireworks.

On the sidewalk, underneath the billboard, a man was standing and staring at the cars, dazed. He looked tired, much older than his age. The sun struck at his sallow, haggard face. When Azar saw him, her heart skipped a beat. She felt her face light up. She opened her mouth, flabbergasted.

"Pedar!" she screamed, banging on the window with her open palm.

Her father didn't hear her. Or look up. He put the bags down on the ground and slipped a handkerchief out of his pocket to wipe the sweat off his forehead. His wiry body looked hunched by something that was not age.

Azar's face twitched and twisted. Never in the months of prison had she felt her father to be so far, so unreachable. Never had she felt so alone, so afraid of what was to become of her.

"Pedar!" she cried out with the last vestiges of strength left in

her. Her voice was nothing but a throaty whimper. It barely trav-
eled beyond the thick glass of the window.

Her father picked up the bags and began walking away, never
lifting his head. Azar watched, wide-eyed, panting as his tall,
stooped body dwindled into the hazy afternoon light. He got on
his motorbike and rode away.

The traffic began moving. Azar's hand lay motionless on the
window, against the reflection of shabby leaves and empty nests
and a black billboard that spoke of light.

The next time the door swung open, Sister was alone. The child
was not with her. Neither were the midwives or the doctor. With
stunned eyes, Azar watched Sister carrying her clothes. She was
still shaken. The image of her father, his hunched body, his tired
face, spiraled through her mind. Sister put Azar's clothes down on
the bed. Azar inquired in a faint voice where her baby was.

"We'll get her on our way out," said Sister, and Azar realized
that the doctor's insistence had been in vain. Sister had won. It was
time to go.

Sister's foot hit the empty plate and made it rattle noisily on the
floor. She was standing directly in front of Azar, her eyes fixed on
her. "Have you seen Meysam?" she asked.

"Meysam?" Azar knew who Meysam was. He was the Brother
who told stories in the car, the recipient of Sister's prurient guffaws.
Azar had seen Sister, visibly older than he, frustrated yet unrelenting, following him around in the dark corridors of the prison and
the concrete-laden courtyard. She had heard the ring of that laughter across the hall. She had seen Sister bring him gifts: plates of food,

woolen gloves. She had seen her bribe the younger man, the young Brother, in a desperate hope to lay claim to his body.

"The tall Brother with the big brown eyes. The good-looking one." Sister's linear eyebrows pulled into an excited frown. "He was there with us earlier. Haven't you seen him?"

Azar stared back at Sister. It dawned on her that Sister's insistence on leaving the hospital today had nothing to do with security, with regulation, or with protocol. It had nothing to do with Azar's life or death. It was simply due to Sister's lust; she wanted to be with Meysam.

"No, I think he's gone," Azar lied. She could barely remember anything. She might have even seen him. But in that moment, as she looked at the spinster's face sprinkled with the irregular shadows of the sycamore leaves as she readied to lock the handcuffs again, disappointing her gave Azar a pleasant thrill.

Once they were out in the corridor, Sister left momentarily to retrieve the child. Barely able to stand, Azar lowered her shaky body onto one of the white plastic chairs that lined the empty hallway. Naked bulbs hung from the ceiling, giving off a feeble, hazy light. Her eyes burned.

From a few doors down, an elderly woman stepped out, closing a door carefully behind her. She stood looking at the posters on the wall in front of her, her hands folded on top of each other. She was wearing a knee-length navy blue manteau and a white headscarf and seemed to be waiting for something or someone. A child, a grandchild. She looked oddly neat and unperturbed in her grim surroundings.

She sat down and placed her brown leather bag with its worn-out strap on her knees. She stole a glance at Azar only to immediately avert her gaze. It hurt, how she looked away. There was fear in those gray-green eyes. And foreboding. Was there something in Azar's face that spoke of her destination? Was there something in her face that warned of iron doors and handcuffs and interrogation rooms? Life inside the prison walls was no different from existence beyond. Everyone carried fear, like a chain, carrying it in the streets, under the familiar shadow of the sad, glorious mountains. And in carrying it, they no longer spoke of it. The fear became intangible, unspeakable. And it ruled over them, invisible and omnipotent.

Azar looked at her own loose gray pants, at her black chador, half of it dragging, sweeping the floor. The prisoners were not as skilled with the chador as the Sisters. They fussed and fumbled with it, like children trying to put clothes on a doll for the first time—a broken doll with a hanging arm and dead legs. The chadors dragged on the ground half of the time.

Azar gathered her chador about her, pulled it over her face, and hid her handcuffed hands under it. Under the protection of the chador, she touched her bony cheeks, her small chin. She must be looking gaunt. An unwanted specter. An image emerged in her mind. Of herself, leaflets in hand, running down a deserted street, the roar of the Revolutionary Guards' patrol shaking the air behind her. She remembered how her heart raced, like it was no longer part of her body, like it had a life and a speed of its own, as she hid behind a car. She remembered the pothole in the asphalt, the candy wrapper that floated away in the drain next to her feet, a glimpse of the oilcloth covering on the table printed in yellow roses behind a window of a house, the smell of hot steel, the violent, explosive thumping in her temples.

It all felt like it was centuries ago. That day with its cloudless sky. Who was she then? What had happened to that Azar, with her determined voice and swift feet and the doubts about where all of this was going, which she never voiced, not even to Ismael.

At the sound of approaching footfalls, she lifted her head. The old woman was standing in front of her.

"Are you okay, *dokhtaram*?"

Azar looked at the woman, taken aback. She was tongue-tied. She had not expected the woman to approach her. The thought of speaking to someone outside the prison shook her.

"You look pale," the woman commented.

In the woman's manner of speaking, Azar immediately recognized the Tabrizi accent, just like her mother's, the same weight-less cadence, as if they were tiptoeing on the words when they spoke Farsi. She opened her mouth to reply, but her eyes brimmed over with tears.

"I'm waiting for my daughter," she said, her voice tangling up in her throat. The image of her mother washing her face with the cold water of the fountain, preparing for the Morning Prayer, rushed through her mind.

"Where is she? Is she in the babies' ward?"

Tears streamed down Azar's face. She didn't know when, how, where they had come from. It was as if a dam had broken inside her and tears were gushing down, engulfing everything. Her body shook at the force of sobs she was trying to hold back.

"Don't cry, *azizam*, why are you crying?" the woman repeated in a distressed, surprised voice. "Nothing to cry about. Your baby is out. *Inshallah*, she is healthy and beautiful, like you, although you should eat more. You're too thin. You have to feed two people now. In these times of war, we must stay strong. If we stay strong, not even Saddam can bring us to our knees." The woman spoke in a soft voice as she wiped away Azar's tears with the end of her white headscarf. Tears that seemed to have no end only flowed and flowed like waterfalls.

"Why don't you go and get your daughter?" The woman's eyes glittered with the apparent hope that the idea would distract Azar, put an end to her tears.

"Sister went to get her." Azar sniffled, bending her head low into her chador to wipe her face.

"Oh good, your sister is here," the woman said enthusiastically. "You're not alone. That's good."

"She is not my sister. We just call her Sister. She is—" Azar stopped.

The old woman waited for her to complete the sentence. Then it seemed as if something changed in the color of her eyes. A thought, fear, the unspeakable scuttled across them. Her thin wrinkled face fell. There was no longer that determination to bring a halt to Azar's tears, to speak to her of her daughter. She placed a hand on Azar's head.

"I see," she said finally. It looked like she wanted to say more; her gray-green eyes looked laden with words, with questions. But she did not. She kissed Azar on the forehead and quietly walked away as Sister appeared at the end of the corridor, holding a tight red bundle in her arms.

Forgetting the old woman, Azar rose to her feet. There was something excruciatingly wrong with the image before her. Her child in the arms of Sister, her wardress. Azar felt a rush of desperation so powerful that it left her weak. But no, she should not think about that. There was her child coming to her. She had been lucky. Her child was alive. Nothing else mattered at that moment.

She curled her fingers into a fist and watched Sister getting closer. Excitement battered through her. She could not get her eyes off the bundle in Sister's hands. Her frustration, her anger, was being swamped over by an acute sense of tenderness, of protection. She stretched her arms out toward her child, trembled with the prospect of holding her. But as Sister got closer, Azar saw more clearly what kind of blanket the child had been wrapped in. It was a rough prison blanket, and her child was naked. Azar winced at the sight of her child unprotected against the coarseness that clamped its teeth into the fragile newborn skin. She stood with her arms outstretched but could not speak. She knew if she opened her mouth, nothing would come out but a shrill, twisted wail.

"You're still too weak," Sister said as she strutted to the elevator. "You'll drop her."

Azar dropped her arms. She could not tear her eyes from the bundle. She imagined snatching it away and racing off down the corridor and into the streets and across the bridge, where, somewhere under the shadow of a tree, her father would be waiting for her.

Sister's face lit up when she looked at something or someone down the hallway. Azar followed her gaze. It was Meysam walking up to them, his slippers proudly slapping the tiled floor. His white polyester shirt hung loosely over his black pants. He walked slowly, his head held high, adhering fully to his role of the guardian of the revolution, omnipotent in his intentionally modest clothing. The beard he insisted on wearing was sparse. Not an adult beard yet. His gait was that of a boy who seemed to have just won a war. And at that moment, the thought flashed through Azar's mind that soon he and so many like him would be sent to that other war blazing along the borders of the country. It would be soon, for the country had nothing but bodies to defend itself with, and bodies were going to be sent, more and more every day. Bodies that might never return. Azar blinked, looking at Meysam, the thought filling her with despair.

Next to her, Sister snatched one of her hands away from underneath the child to tug a strand of hair inside her scarf. She lowered her gaze to the ground in a ghastly act of timidity. Azar looked apprehensively at Sister's uncontrolled arms. With every move Sister made, Azar's hands shot forward for her child, lest Sister, gripped by passion, dropped her.

"*Salaam Baraadar,*" Sister said, beaming. "I thought you'd already left."

"I'm still here. Are you ready to go?" Meysam asked, calling the elevator.

"Yes, with the help of God, it is all finished."

Along with Meysam, another man walked into the elevator. When his gaze met Azar's, his jaundiced eyes widened with recognition and astonishment. Azar hurled a glance at Sister, who, having forgotten her scripted coyness, had turned her body away from Azar while speaking animatedly to Meysam. Azar edged closer to the man, whose appearance had changed since the last time she had seen him. His face had hardened. His beard made him look old and severe. He had buttoned up his white polyester shirt all the way to his Adam's apple, as the dress code for the pious demanded. Just like Meysam, he wore plastic slippers.

As she slunk closer to him, Azar wondered if he still lived next to her parents' house on that dead-end street, if he still went over to their house for the evening tea, if he still informed her father of available government coupons for sugar and vegetable oil, which were becoming harder to find as the war continued. Or had becoming a man of the revolution, with his authoritative beard and plastic slippers and hardened face set him apart?

There was shock in his eyes as he looked at her. Obviously, her parents had not told him about her arrest. Azar was not surprised. They had been afraid. How could they not be? She shuddered at the thought of how her parents may have found out. She imagined the Revolutionary Guards swarming into their house, asking questions, threatening. And her parents in the corner, shaking as they slowly understood, while they watched the mayhem around them, why Azar had disappeared for so long.

Azar held the man's bewildered gaze with hers. "I'm fine. Tell them I'm fine."

Boggled, the man nodded. Another of Sister's guffaws dovetailed Azar's whisper. It spun through the closed elevator, bouncing off the walls and the neon lights.

Azar turned to Sister. "Let me hold her. I can handle it."

Sister hesitated before she placed the coarse bundle in Azar's arms. The child was sleeping. Tiny breaths hovered over the pink parting of her mouth. Azar wished to squeeze her to her heart, that small, soft body. She wanted to squeeze her so that the pressure would make it real. The mouth, the pink wrinkled skin, the black fuzz covering the forehead.

She was too weak. She only held the baby, feeling the tough skin of the blanket scratching her palms. It barely enclosed the child's body. Azar felt a rush of sorrow and guilt rise up the column of her body. What had she done by bringing a child into this world, where not the mother but the wardress first held her?

She hid her face inside the bundle and inhaled the sweet aroma of her child. She kissed her forehead and her shoulders and her chest. She kissed and inhaled deeply, glutting herself with the proximity of her body, asking for forgiveness. The child made a tiny move with her shoulder and opened her eyes.

Black as the night. The whites of her eyes looked almost blue. She opened and closed her mouth and looked around. Azar watched her with bewilderment, those large eyes that rolled around the elevator with a gaze so penetrating, it seemed she wanted to arrest someone. It was almost frightening. That gaze, that sharp look in her child's black-and-blue eyes—severe, unsparing, much like Sister's. Her heart almost skipped with fright. Azar lifted a tremulous hand and held it over her daughter's eyes.

There was an effusive buzz in the cell, with its walls that glistened because so many heads and backs had rubbed against them. The buzz that could happen only once—when life was about to change shape.

Seething with excitement, the women awaited the arrival of the newborn. They had cleaned everything, scrubbed the walls, washed the carpets. That day, no one had been allowed to exercise, lest they raise dust. One of the corners was decorated with all the windblown leaves found in the courtyard, gathered in an empty aluminum jar. The iron bars of the window cast thick linear shadows on the lemon-yellow headscarf that hung as a curtain.

The women had carried their excitement around with them all day. They were restless, barely able to stay put. Since daybreak, when Azar was first removed with her taut, throbbing belly, the women, unable to hide their glee, had grown nicer to one another. The hostile silence had burst open and words were spurting out, even between enemies who had despised each other's political parties and thus each other. They seemed to have put a pause on the wrathful rivalry and the usual sinking into ideological lagoons, suspending for at least a day their belief that the other was to blame for a revolution gone astray.

Good morning! they said to each other without reserve.

Their usually haggard, dismal faces were aglow with anticipation. It was not their shower day, but they preened nevertheless, braiding each other's hair, singing songs. They were all wearing their best clothes, as if it were the New Year. Packed away and unworn for months, the garments hung awkwardly over their bony shoulders and shrinking breasts. They constantly ran their hands over the fabric to unfold the creases.

That day, even Firoozeh could not contain her happiness. Her usual nervous ranting had come to a halt. Everyone in the cell knew Firoozeh had become a *tavaab*, a snitch, because she had been able to spend a night with her husband and had received a pillow softer than anyone else's. But that day, even Firoozeh seemed unwilling to betray the peaceful elation that had descended on them. She barely exchanged a word with the Sisters. Instead, she spoke to everyone of her own daughter, Donya. She spoke of how she had left Donya with her family when she was arrested. She spoke of the tears she shed night after night for not being able to see her. Once released, she would take Donya away with her and leave Iran. *Leave and never look back,* she said, frowning as if thinking of a bad dream.

At the sound of footsteps and the muffled cry of a child, they all ran to the door. They laughed, clapped, and patted one another excitedly on the shoulder. Joyful shouts erupted, like the happy cries bursting forth at weddings, when the door opened and Azar walked in with her bundle. Sister frowned, shouting at them to quiet down.

Azar laughed when she saw them, when she saw their best clothes, the scrubbed walls, the scarf curtain. Her body reverberated with their cries of joy. Surrounded by their happiness, she forgot about everything. She forgot the sharp gaze in her child's eyes. Forgot the pain, her torn insides, the fear, the guilt. She felt suddenly, unexpectedly, at home.

They clustered around her with glimmering eyes and expectant hands, their voices mingling, colliding, interlocking. They passed the child from one embrace to another, their bodies growing warm holding her, wishing to cradle her longer, reluctant to pass her on to where another pair of hands itched to hold her.

Hold on to her.

Clinging.

Then they saw her nakedness, the roughness of the blanket, and their hearts sank. But they said nothing. They unwrapped the blanket and swaddled her in a soft chador with tiny daisies.

They looked at the child and at Azar's eyes. If they concentrated enough, they could see the fear that still hung from her eyelashes, the disbelief that lay on her chapped lips: her child was alive, she was alive.

They brought the fresh bowl of water they had been keeping in the corner next to the stray leaves in the aluminum jar and washed her face.

"It's over," they said, and rubbed her hands. "You're safe now. You're with us."

They massaged her shoulders. They feared for her so much that they closed their eyes so as not to see how she had been torn inside.

"What's her name?" asked Marzieh, the youngest of them all, as she took the bundle cautiously from Firoozeh.

Azar took a deep breath. "Neda," she said, and involuntarily clasped her hands together.

She mouthed the name a few more times. Each time, the child grew more solid in her reality. Each time, the memory of that severe gaze faded further away. Each time she said the name, the child became more hers, entirely hers. There was a magical hand at work that reconciled her with the child, with her surroundings, with time, with herself. She felt no longer to blame. Instead, she was filled with a feeling so empowering, so unwavering, that it could only be called love.

They were sitting and watching the white handkerchief rise and fall to the rhythm of Neda's breathing. In the corner of the cell, Firoozeh was exercising, jumping up and down, parting her legs and arms like scissor blades, her face flushed. There was little air in the cell, so she panted heavily.

Azar had placed the handkerchief on top of the child's face to keep her from inhaling the dust raised by Firoozeh.

"I'm sure they'll organize a meeting with your husband before they send her out," Marzieh said in a dreamy voice, and lifted her green eyes to the child's few pieces of wash hanging on the rope above them.

A month had passed. The pinkness of the child's face was petering out. The wrinkles were unfurling. The unsteady gaze of her eyes had become more stable. And the milk, which was watery at first, had begun to thicken.

Azar basked in her newfound motherhood. She carried her swollen breasts around gloriously. Even in the interrogation room, she felt a thrill as her breasts swelled with milk. As if somehow they protected her, made her strong, invincible. The warm liquid oozed out of her nipples as the interrogator repeated the same questions in a different order, hoping to catch her at something, at what, he seemed not to know himself. She would barely listen to him. Instead, she would hand herself fully to the warm seeping of her body that craved the child, sweet and sticky like the nectar of a tree. *We all have a tree inside us.* She remembered Ismael's words. *Finding it is just a matter of time.*

For the others, Neda had become their main entertainment. They seemed not to get enough of the child. They would surround Azar and watch her with her baby and the child's pink lips. They watched the child's every move, every struggle for milk and air, every wail, every closing and opening of her tiny fist around their fingers. They admired her with their lonely eyes and mouths full of compliments. They gathered around her as if she were their shrine. They asked to hold her, to watch over her when she slept, to clean her mouth when she sneezed.

Life in the small cell had changed. It was no longer about following the crowlike Sisters to interrogation rooms or picking up the corpse of a fly from the floor and having to wait until bathroom time to throw it away. Nor was it about the loudspeakers that emitted the call to prayer five times a day. Or the screams of agony and breaking down coming from closed rooms that everyone heard yet no one spoke about.

Life was different now. It was about a child.

And the longer Neda stayed, the more brazen they all got. They made clothes for her from their own prayer chadors. *She'll be growing so fast in these months*, they said. They exempted Azar from washing dishes so that she could use the few minutes to wash diapers. They washed the child in a basin of warm water. They read letters for her. They played with her. They sang songs for her.

Everyone dreaded being transferred to another cell or prison. They did not wish to leave this cell, where a child's voice rang like a siren of life. Their world was now one with coming and going, breathing and eating, draining and suckling. A world that meant something, that was no longer a black hole.

They all knew it would not last. Every day could be the last day. They all knew it. Azar knew it. She had to be ready when the day came.

But how?

Hardly a month, and the child had already become the only thing on her mind. Everything else seemed to have lost importance. The child and her own passionate, protective tenderness. She had even begun to fret over the way some of the women held her. *Not the right way*, she would say, running to them, gathering all her strength not to shout at them to put her child down. They had to be careful. *The baby's neck is still so soft*. And she would take Neda from them, basking in the rush of emotion as she laid the child's tiny body against her chest, holding her neck and head gently in the palm of her hand. No one knew how to be good to the child, no one like her.

This was dangerous, she knew. She had to stop. She had to start learning how to let go. The child did not belong to her, could be taken away at any moment. She had to be ready. But how could she?

"Maybe they'll let you take the child to your parents yourself. You'll have a day to visit and leave her with them," said another as she fiddled with a loose button on her shirt.

Azar listened with a sad, skeptical smile. She could hear the slip-slap of slippers passing through the corridor, chadors sweeping past the door, chattering voices bouncing back and forth.

"None of this is going to happen," she said, trying to keep her voice as flat as possible. She lifted a hand to check if the clothes were dry. The rope was low. There was no need to get up. She pulled down the shirt with its tiny blue flowers and began folding it.

Of the clothes her parents—she did not how and when they had been informed about the birth—had sent Neda, only a few had reached her. Those and a bag of tea. Azar was sure they had sent more. She was not convinced by Sister's words that those were the only gifts her parents had been able to put together. Every time she went to the interrogation room, from underneath her blindfold, she could see a large bag abandoned by the bathroom door. Azar was sure that bag was hers. She was sure it was filled with toys and soap and diapers and clothes for her child. But no one gave her the bag. She waited for it every day, until one day it was no longer there.

"The day they decide I've had enough, they'll just open the door a little and take her away." She opened her hands slightly to show the narrowness of the opening.

Groans of disagreement gyrated round the room. *Azar and her fastidious pessimism.*

Under the handkerchief, Neda made a small noise and moved her head. All the women turned toward her. Neda had woken up.

She began letting out hungry wails as Azar removed the hand-kerchief and lifted her into her arms. She offered her heavy breasts proudly to the steady suckling of the pink mouth.

"But who says they're going to take her away?" said Parisa, who sat close to where Firoozeh was exercising. She was Firoozeh's only friend in the cell. They had known each other since high school, she had told the other prisoners. Like Firoozeh, Parisa had a child, a son, Omid, whom she had left with her parents and sister. She was pregnant with her second child when arrested. Even though Parisa knew of Firoozeh's having become a *tavaab,* she did not let the fact alter their friendship. Parisa never left Firoozeh's side. *I knew her before prison,* she once said when confronted by others. *I know she is good inside. She is only vulnerable, not strong enough for prison.*

Azar too knew Parisa. She had met her at the wedding celebration for Behrouz, Ismael's youngest brother. Parisa was the bride's sister. That was one of the last times Azar and Ismael had attended a family gathering.

What about Behrouz and his wife, Simin? Azar had asked Parisa on the first day, happy to see someone she knew, reassured. Both Simin and Behrouz had been arrested, Parisa informed her. She knew Simin was in another cell, but of Behrouz, she had no news. Behrouz with his lean hefty body, well-shaped eyebrows, and loud laughter. *What had become of him?*

"I heard of a woman who kept her child for a year, until she was released," Parisa continued, her large eyes glittering, perhaps with the hope of keeping her own child when it was born.

Everyone turned to look at her, wide-eyed. "Really?"

"That's what I've heard. Maybe you don't have to send her away if you don't want to."

Joyous voices filled the room as they discussed this possibility. Even Azar's eyes sparkled. The sad smile vanished from her lips. She felt a hopeful tugging at the pit of her stomach, and foreboding. She should not believe in these words. She must not fall into their trap.

"She kept her child for a year?"

"They went home together."

Azar looked at Neda. The tiny creature with the round head and beautiful black-and-blue eyes cuddled so comfortably, so trustingly, against her that it quelled any doubts in her about being right for the baby.

She clasped at the child to keep the tremor out of her voice. "I want to keep her as long as I can." She could not help it. She could at least hope, couldn't she? Hope was not forbidden. "Do you think they'll let me?"

Another week passed, and still nothing had been communicated to Azar about Neda. No one had called from Sister's office. Azar felt light, like she could do anything. Maybe they would not take the child away from her after all. Maybe there was no danger in hoping. She began sewing more clothes for Neda. She did embroidery for her, of a girl standing in the middle of a flower field. She began wearing her white shirt again, with its yellow and pink flowers, the colors so bright they glittered in the darkness of the night, and dancing *lezgi,* stamping on the ground, white and pink flowers bouncing up and down as the others clapped, singing for her. The flowers looked as if they had come to life, along with her flushed cheeks and shiny black eyes and thick wavy hair. Everyone told her how beautiful she was when she danced.

She even began giving haircuts to her cellmates, using the scissors that were given to them for an hour once every few weeks. Azar had wondered about these scissors. Weren't the Sisters afraid that the prisoners could use them to hurt themselves, kill themselves, even? *But, no, the Sisters are not afraid*, she thought. Or rather, they did not care. They probably preferred to have some of the prisoners hurt themselves, get rid of themselves for them. That made their job easier: fewer prisoners to worry about. The prisoners might have known this. That was why no one had ever used the scissors for harm. They were never going to do it; they were not going to give the Sisters that satisfaction.

The first to get a haircut from Azar was Marzieh, then another young girl who was soon transferred to another cell. Azar tried to bring back vague, unreliable memories of the way her hairdresser sister had held strands between straight fingers and led them to the blades of the scissors. There were no mirrors in prison. Her cellmates had come to trust her. Then Firoozeh asked for a haircut.

Azar did not wish to cut Firoozeh's hair. She knew Firoozeh had snitched on her when she was pregnant, told the Sisters that she had been dancing *lezgi* in the cell. Dancing was not permitted. They should have been praying, not kicking their legs around and jumping to a rhythm that was only in their heads. As punishment, Azar had been taken to the rooftop, where she had to stand under the rain for hours. The rain was supposed to wash the music out of her limbs, out of the limbs of her unborn child. The rain was supposed to make her understand that prison was no place to reenact childhood memories. There, Azar vowed never to have anything to do with Firoozeh again. And yet Firoozeh too had changed since the child's arrival, and prison was not a place to hold grudges, she thought.

That day, Firoozeh sat on a chair placed in the middle of the wet, dirty bathroom floor, Azar standing behind her with the scissors in her hand, looking at the thick, curvy braid that fell lusciously to the small of Firoozeh's back. Azar did not even have a comb.

After a long moment of quandary, she laid the open blades to where the braid started, somewhere close to the nape of Firoozeh's neck, and closed them. Little happened. Instead of the sharp snip she was expecting, all Azar heard was the painfully dull sound of the blades straining to penetrate the thick woven hair. She opened and closed the scissors again, but the hair was too strong. It only crumbled, cringing at the blades' timid touch. Azar tried again, kept on opening and closing the scissors, digging deeper into the braid. Firoozeh's hair started flying about in different shapes and lengths. Not one strand of hair matched another. Only then did Azar realize she should have unbraided the hair first. But she could not stop now. She hacked away until half of the braid, broken and rumpled, came away. Then she lifted her gaze. Her wrist ached.

Her cellmates looked on intently. Everyone except Firoozeh had realized what was happening. They looked on silently. The naked lightbulb above their heads cast a deathly pallor over their ashen faces.

Azar turned her gaze back to the braid, hanging from Firoozeh's head. She pulled the tufts of hair out of the scissors and began once again to snip away. She cut with desperate determination, as if trying to resurrect a child she knew was dead. Silence fell as they all watched the disjoined braid drop to the floor. Firoozeh's tousled, uneven hair struck out from every corner. Azar tried hard to fix it, cutting it here and there, but all she seemed to do was worsen the situation. At last, she stopped. *There are no mirrors here*, she thought, consoling herself.

"How does it look?" asked Firoozeh, looking around with dilated eyes, her irises tiny pinpoints.

"It's a modern haircut," Azar said, trying to lighten the situation. They were inside a prison, after all. *What importance could a haircut have?*

No one said anything. They looked from Azar to Firoozeh, from Firoozeh to Azar. That was when Marzieh, with Neda asleep in her arms, burst into laughter so loud it crashed against the ceiling and shattered over them like gunpowder. Everyone looked at her, stunned. But Marzieh laughed and laughed, and her laughter, like the flame to a long line of grenades, soon made everyone else break into earsplitting, breathless guffaws. A whirlwind of laughter sweeping them off the ground in wild, unleashed, dizzying effusion.

Firoozeh looked at them, startled. "Why are you laughing?" she asked, touching her hair.

"It's a bit messy," Azar said, tittering. Mirror or no mirror, she was probably better off telling the truth. "But it looks fashionable," she insisted.

"What?" Firoozeh turned abruptly to Azar. She sprang to her feet as if about to charge at her. The sides of her nose flared. Her dilated eyes looked larger than usual. "What did you do? What did you do?" she shouted. She grasped Azar's shoulders, shaking her.

Azar froze. She felt the heat rushing to her face. The laughter came abruptly to an end. The women looked on with apprehension palpitating in their eyes. Azar opened her mouth to say something, anything, to console Firoozeh, to make her let go.

That was when Parisa almost ran to them, laying a hand on Firoozeh's shoulder. "Calm down, Firoozi. It's nothing. Let her go."

Firoozeh glared at Azar without letting go. Azar could feel her fellow inmate's hot breath on her face.

"Let her go," Parisa repeated.

"It's just a bit uneven," Azar muttered, trying to take a step back. She kept a grasp on the scissors as if planning to cut her way out of those bathroom walls. "I should've unbraided your hair first. I'm sorry."

With a flushed face, still glaring, Firoozeh let go of Azar. There was something fanatic, unpredictable, in Firoozeh's eyes. Parisa slowly removed her hand but stood close by.

"I'm sorry," Azar repeated in a tight voice, the artery in her throat throbbing. She glanced at Parisa apologetically. "I didn't mean to mess it up."

"It's just hair," Parisa said quietly. "It'll grow back out."

Firoozeh touched her hair compulsively, as if she wanted to

smooth out the imperfections, without listening to them. She then stood still, no longer looking at Azar. Before walking out of the bathroom, she snatched the scissors out of Azar's hand.

Silence lengthened. The women in their gray clothes stared at Azar with their gaunt faces and anxious eyes. The sound of a leaking tap filled the air. Parisa glanced at all of them and smiled a sad smile before following Firoozeh out.

Azar woke with a start. Her thirst lay on her tongue like a chunk of clay. It was early morning. The silvery light of dawn flowed into the cubicle through the yellow chador covering the window, down the naked walls, and splashed over the irregular silhouettes curled up next to each other on the floor. It could barely reach the iron door, which was mercilessly, unwaveringly locked. Azar turned onto her side and placed a hand on Neda's warm body. Having made sure the child was sleeping and breathing normally, she sat up. She held her breath, listening carefully to the deep rhythmic breathing surrounding her. She squinted at the darkness and the mass of snoring shadows, looking for Firoozeh. What if Firoozeh decided to pay her back? What if she decided to kick Neda, to stomp on her head?

Azar had not slept for nights, not since the haircut, not since she had seen Firoozeh's angry, vengeful eyes constantly on her. Every night she remained awake until she was sure Firoozeh had fallen asleep. At times, Marzieh helped out, at times, Parisa, staying guard as Azar tried to have a few hours of sleep.

She spotted Firoozeh at the other end of the cell, by the locked iron door, lying on the ground like everyone else. She lay motionless, shriveled, under the blanket. Her body gave an impres-

sion of exhaustion; her arms lay lifeless around her, and her head
was thrown back on the pillow. She looked like an old woman
who needed to gather every gram of strength in order to stand
up. It was this exhaustion that frightened Azar, the exhaustion
of someone who no longer cared, who could as easily harm one
as well as let someone go. Unpredictable was the exhaustion of
the soul.

Azar propped the pillow behind her and leaned back. She
pulled the blanket up to cover the child. Soon Neda would wake
up and want to be fed. The minutes dragged by. Azar waited im-
patiently for Neda to rouse so she could offer her breasts, full of
milk, whose gush was already wetting her shirt. Every time the
child fell asleep, Azar almost counted the minutes for her to wake
up. There was nothing that made her feel so in control as the moment when she held Neda in her arms and the child's lips, after a
few moments of hungry, anxious searching and adjustments, fastened to her nipple and she began to suckle. That moment alone
was what Azar lived for.

She listened again to the sound of breathing thick in the air. She
looked back to where Firoozeh was sleeping. She had not moved.
Azar lay back and gathered her arms around Neda, tugging the
child's head carefully into the protective crook of her arm.

The day Azar was called to Sister's office was a cloudy one. It was
right after the afternoon prayer, and the patch of sky that could be
seen through Sister's office window was gray, overcast. The window of Sister's office did not have curtains. It was a room with a
desk, a chair, and a picture of the Supreme Leader with his long

white beard on the wall. Behind Sister were cabinets full of paper: documents, files, each with a life of its own.

Firoozeh has finally taken her revenge, Azar thought, half dazed, half demented, sitting there without being able to make the slightest movement. She heard the shrill scream of a crow in the distance. A fly buzzed at the windowsill. *Why are they going to take her away from me?* she asked herself over and over. *I still have milk.*

"You didn't think you could keep your daughter with you here forever, did you?" asked Sister, drumming her fingers on the table, her eyes sparkling.

Something twitched ferociously at the corner of Azar's left eye. A frost rose from the tiled floor into the soles of her feet and spread through her bones.

"What if she catches a disease here? This is no place to keep a child."

It was no place to keep the child, but it was a perfect place to keep them. To keep them small. Because one remained small when there was no sky to look at.

Sister paused, as if she wanted her words to sink in, to pierce. Time was endless, expanding around Azar, engulfing her, pulling her down. The chador felt heavy, oppressive, on her head. She felt she could hardly breathe, as if the walls of the room were closing on her. She shook her head slightly, trying to straighten her back.

Someone must have snitched on her, told Sister that Azar wished to keep her child for a long time, as long as possible. Sister could not accept that. If Azar wished to keep her child, it meant that she was happy. It meant Azar was so happy that she could not keep her happiness to herself, that she had to share it with everyone else. That she had to express herself. That was too much happiness in a tiny cell with a barred window.

This was not a place for happiness. This was Evin. A place for fear, brooding, boiling, steaming fear. If Azar wished to keep her child, it meant that she was no longer afraid; it was time to take the child away.

"We've already called your parents. The arrangements have been made." Sister lifted a finger slightly. "You can go now."

Azar stood up. On the other side of the door, the two Sisters waiting to take Azar back to the cell were speaking. Something about dinner, about buying bread, children's homework. Azar stretched her hand toward the doorknob. She felt dizzy. Something escaped through her mouth. She did not know if it was a whimper, a cough, drops of saliva. She heard thunder in the distance. She turned the knob.

After that day, they stopped giving her the basin of warm water to wash her child.

A tiny white butterfly entered the cell through the barred window. Azar watched it flit around for a while. The butterfly was coming from the mountains, which were so close. Azar watched until it settled on the yellow chador in front of the window.

The cell was empty. Everyone was in the courtyard for a few minutes of fresh air. *I'll stay in*, Azar had said without looking anyone in the eye. She wanted to use those few stolen moments of calm to feed Neda, which she did with more fervor than ever, as if she wanted to melt into her own milk and into the child's mouth. So that she could be with her forever, so that no one could separate them.

Four days had passed and still no news of when the child would be taken away. Azar bristled every time she heard the sweeping of the chador, the slip-slaps approaching the door, thinking that they were coming for her, coming for her baby. For a long while after the chador had swept past or the slippers had slapped away, she continued panting.

The anxiety had caused everything around her to slip away like sand. She felt she was beginning to lose her faculties. She could no longer see, no longer hear. Her milk had a strange, immaterial feel. Things had begun to lose their reality. She could no longer hold on to them. The only thing she held on to was every new day. She clung to each one as if it were the last day of her life. As if she were awaiting death with one arm around her child, the other wrapped around herself. She continued to breathe while her life was coming to an end.

Murmurs of conversation flowed into the cell from the barred window. Azar knew what the women were whispering about. Since the day at Sister's office, all conversations had turned into murmurs. It was like a weight had landed on the women, choking their voices out. They sat in rows along the low walls, their hair hanging lank against their lackluster, angular faces, lines of despondence etched in their foreheads. *When? When?* they kept asking Azar and one another. Something seemed to have flown out of their bodies, evaporating into the hard, stale air.

Azar stopped listening to the sorrowful susurrus coming from outside. She could not bear it. She gave all her attention to the sound of Neda's lips moving ferociously back and forth and watched the gentle glow of the day on her face, the dark eyelashes sitting in a neat, thick row across her lids. Anxiety rose in her like a tidal wave, the anxiety of separation, of once again falling deeper and deeper into the bottomless void when Neda was gone.

She had started to have nightmares of Neda crying in the basement of her mother's house. Alone, wet, hungry. And no one would come to her. Not even her mother. The basement was dark and cold, and Neda would continue to cry until Azar would wake up, her pillow wet with tears. Would her mother truly abandon Neda? Would she be so hurt by Azar's abandonment of them that she would find it impossible to love the child? How could Azar expect anything of her parents when she herself had let go of them so easily? Would they be able to forgive her for all those knocks on the door left unanswered? Her parents had not even known she was pregnant. That was what she had denied them: the anticipation, the joy, the pride of partaking in her life. What had her parents said when they received the phone call informing them of their granddaughter's birth? A granddaughter they did not know was growing in the womb of their daughter? Were they happy? Shocked? *At least this way they know I am alive*, Azar thought, though the thought did not calm her. Her guilt toward her parents gnawed away at her. The questions whirled through her mind, questions for which she had no answer. The nightmares returned night after night, and every morning, she placed her pillow in the corner to dry.

The sound of suckling stopped. Azar turned her gaze to Neda, who had fallen asleep, her lips slowly unfastening from her mother's breast. Azar watched and her eyes fogged over. Neda's face became blurry. Azar hid her eyes behind her hand. Something inside her had ripped into pieces, and she knew she would never be able to glue it back together. When she looked up, the butterfly was gone.

It was raining. Evening had not yet fallen. Somewhere in the courtyard, raindrops drummed incessantly on something hard, like a corrugated roof. Rolled bedding lined the walls of the cell on top of which the women were sitting, some exchanging memories in low voices, some writing letters to their loved ones, some reading for the umpteenth time a letter they'd received from their husband months ago, some staring at the wall in front of them with an absent gaze, humming old songs under their breath, someone's laughter at a funny memory rolling through the closed space. In a corner, plastic plates and spoons, washed and dried, were piled neatly. The feeble light of the naked bulb fell on the clothes folded and stacked next to each pallet.

The door opened slightly. Someone called Azar's name. The door was open enough for a child to go through.

Azar gave a start. Her eyes shot toward the door. At the sound of her name, everything seemed to come to a halt. The air in the room went still. No one moved. They all just gaped at Azar.

A few moments passed. Azar sat frozen on the ground. She could not move. She sat there panting, panting, as if her lungs had suddenly stopped pulling in oxygen.

Her name was called a second time.

Next to her, Neda was making tiny noises with her mouth, almost like she was singing. Azar picked her up. The child's body was soft in her grasp, a bit heavier than before; she had grown. Her feet flitted in the air. Azar thought she could get up but then faltered, as if something were pulling her down to the ground. A pair of hands shot toward her, held her from the shoulders, unfolded her, steadied her. Azar took a step, then another. The women gathered knees to chest as she hobbled past them, her face twisted in spasms of emotions impossible to describe, emotions that had gone beyond anything recognizable.

Trembling hands edged out through the opening. First they were holding a tiny body that carried life. Then the hands were empty. They were pushed away, back into the cell so the door could be closed.

Azar slid down the wall like a raindrop gliding down the window glass. Her head slanted and fell on her shoulder. Her heavy breasts swayed to the side. Her shirt was soaked with milk floating in a tide. Her arms were empty. The iron door next to her was firmly shut.

Silence held sway; silence of mourning. Marzieh and Parisa tried to hoist her up. Their faces flushed as they struggled to throw her lifeless arms around their shoulders. She was heavy like a corpse. Her milk streamed down to her stomach. The milk that was supposed to be her child's. It now belonged to no one. Orphaned milk. Warm, sticky, disgusting milk.

From the other side of the cell, Firoozeh walked up to Azar, a chador in her hand. She sat down next to her, her face twitching from pain or remorse or grief, Azar did not know. It was twitching like she was being beaten from inside. Azar wanted to get away from her, wanted to attack her, to dig her nails into her. She sat there, undone.

A voice rang out through the cell. A song, quavering, broken. The voice echoing of memories and of being uprooted, torn apart.

There were no more trees inside them.

Gently, Firoozeh lifted Azar's milk-sodden shirt and wrapped the chador tightly across her breasts to stop the flow.

1987

Tehran, the Islamic Republic of Iran

This was how Leila found Omid: wide-eyed, taut-limbed, and sucking ferociously on his fingers. He was sitting at the dining table, surrounded by a ravaged house. All of the doors were flung open; the cabinets and drawers had been gutted on the floor. There were books and papers and clothes everywhere, and envelopes and hairpins and pens and shoes. On some of Parisa's clothes, there were dusty boot prints.

Omid had been there when his parents were arrested. They were having lunch. The sky was blue, without a cloud, featureless. The air smelled of approaching heat; the season seemed about to turn on its hinges. Omid's father was mashing the meat and chickpeas and potato in a steel bowl, pestle in hand, fingers curled around the bowl, steam rising to his chin.

Omid dipped his finger into the bowl of yogurt that was

blended with crushed rose petals. Parisa frowned at him. "How many times have I told you to use a spoon?"

Omid didn't know what to do with his finger, with the wrong that had already been done, so it lingered in the bowl, where the yogurt felt cold and soft. He looked at his mother. At her beautiful eyes and luscious hair that cascaded over her shoulders. At the lovely purple blouse that enhanced the rosiness of her cheeks and fell over the growing bulge of her stomach. At the love that seemed to spill out of her eyes and submerge everything.

"It's okay," Parisa said. "Your finger's already in the bowl. But next time, use your spoon."

Omid lifted the finger to his mouth and tasted yogurt and roses.

That was when the landlady appeared at the door, flanked by two officers. She was pale, her eyes wide with terror. She spoke hurriedly, compulsively fixing her chador, and pleading, and saying words that had lost all sense in the face of her fear.

The guards came in and simply took his parents away. Omid was left at the table with the meal in front of him. Parisa had touched his face fleetingly, her fingers cold as ice. His father had placed a kiss on his forehead and told him not to be afraid, that they'd come right back. But his voice was so thin that something inside Omid made a quiet plop and vanished forever.

The guards had been looking for documents, letters, leaflets, poems, forbidden books. They left with their hands full. There were so many pieces of life that had to be carried away. Those papers were now going to decide who went and who stayed. His parents, with their love and their fight and their papery lives.

Were gone.

And Omid sat at the table. The chaos around him. He couldn't cry. He sat there shaking, saliva running down his fingers. The landlady ran after the guards who pulled his parents away, hand-cuffed and blindfolded. They were not pulling hard, because his parents were not resisting. They were not flailing their arms. They were not screaming.

It was all quiet, like a Sunday morning in a mosque. It was as though they had been waiting for it. His parents. For the guards. To come and make a shambles of their home and their life and the child who was left behind and the child who was yet to come. To ravage through it all and spew everything onto their faces.

Only later, when her voice died in her throat, her words lying life-less at the doorsteps, did the landlady run to the phone to call Agha-jaan and Maman Zinat. And Omid sat. Alone. With half-mashed stew and a bowl of yogurt in front of him that smelled of roses.

The shadows on the fake blue marble floor of the pharmacy were swept to the side as Leila, pushing Sara in a stroller and carrying Forugh in her arms, bustled out through the door and onto the street. Forugh, eighteen days older than Sara, was turning three in a few months. She was heavy and weighed on Leila, whose arms, wrapped protectively around the child, sagged. Omid, six years old, walked alongside her, holding her manteau tightly in his fist.

Leila was just about to adjust the weight of Forugh in her arms when a military jeep came to an abrupt stop in front of them, a rasping shriek squirming out from under the tires. A menacing cloud of dust and smoke blurred Leila's view. Immediately, al-most instinctively, she averted her face and, pretending to cover her mouth against the exhaust fumes, quickly wiped the lipstick off with the end of her headscarf.

Two men got out of the jeep. They wore military green Revolutionary Guard uniforms and matching green caps, with thick beards framing their faces. One of them was taller than the other, hobbling behind as if his feet hurt. He leaned against the hood of the jeep while the other jumped over the gutter separating the street from the sidewalk and stood in front of Leila. His eyes sank inside their deep sockets and seemed to be lost in the sagging folds of his skin. For a moment, all Leila could hear was the ferocious battering of her heart.

"Are these the right conditions to come out in public, Sister?" he said.

Since the revolution, they had all become brothers and sisters overnight. An entire country made of unrelated siblings, watching one another at times with fear, at times with defiance, and suspicion and show of force and contempt. *I am not your sister!* Leila would have liked to shout.

"Why? What's wrong?" She clutched Forugh's body to her chest and grabbed Omid's hand. Omid watched the smoke and the severe faces of the men with a mixture of fear and fascination. Behind his chunky lower lip, his tongue fiddled with his uneven front teeth.

"Are these your children?"

"No."

"Whose are they?"

"My sisters'."

"Why are they with you? Where are your sisters?"

Leila swallowed hard. She was tongue-tied. She fumbled with

worried. Was it because she did not have her parents around? Would it be different if her own mother were with her? Unanswered questions. They would just have to wait and see. As for Forugh, who pronounced words much better and was able to make full sentences, she barely spoke, which, in a way, worried Maman Zinat and Leila even more.

Sara tugged at Leila's headscarf as she burrowed into the back of the stroller for the pacifier. Leila drew her head back, pulling the end of her scarf delicately from between Sara's plump, curled fingers. Leila tried to quiet her down with the pacifier, which she refused to hold in her mouth. *No!* she shouted. Leila fastened it to her white overalls, with the shape of a red umbrella sewn to the chest.

"Omid *jaan*, keep an eye on Forugh while I speak to Agha Hossein." Leila unraveled Omid's fist from her manteau and placed his tiny hands on his cousin's warm, throbbing chest. "Put your hand here, and don't let her get off the chair."

Omid kept his hand and gaze fastened dutifully on Forugh while she looked around with wondering eyes. A tiny frown wrinkled her short forehead. Her hair stood on her head erect, as if currents of electricity were rushing through it. It had been like this ever since she arrived, standing on end, as if she had gone through a shock that her body could not overcome.

"How are your parents?" Agha Hossein watched the children with the sentimental smile of a grandchildless old man. He was short, with blemished skin and a large drooping nose that looked out of place on his baby face.

"They send their regards," Leila said slowly, lowering her gaze to the floor. She was angry with her parents for having sent her here alone. In fact, angrier with Maman Zinat, who was waiting for them at home. Maman Zinat, who never left the house, who waited and waited and cried and cried. With dry eyes. She cried for her daughters and for their three children. Maman Zinat, who had raised three children of her own and didn't blink once when, at the age of sixty-two, she was handed her three tiny, howling grandchildren to raise.

"Any news from their parents?" Agha Hossein indicated the children.

Behind them, the tiny, barely comprehensible words continued. A hiccup interrupted Sara's garbled song. Her laughter was an excited ear-piercing scream. Leila mumbled something about her sisters being fine. Whenever asked, she was supposed to say that her sisters had gone abroad for work. That was her father's decision. *No one is safe, no one can be trusted*, he had said.

Leila felt Omid's hand tugging at her manteau. Large dilated eyes looked up at her.

"Khaleh Leila, I have to go pee-pee."

"Oh, yes," Leila said apologetically. She had forgotten. She looked at Forugh, who was leaning back against the chair, fiddling with a loose string on one of her socks. Sara was struggling to climb out of the stroller, reaching for a pile of envelopes on a round glass table. Another hiccup escaped her mouth.

"Take him to the bathroom," said Agha Hossein, "I'll keep an eye on them."

"Thank you." Leila took Forugh's hands and helped her off the chair. She would be safer standing on the floor.

"Where's the bathroom?"

"In the back to the left."

Omid scuttled along with his thighs held tensely together, fists clutched in concentration. He had a slightly big head and rice-tray eyes that flashed back at his surroundings like those of a fawn on the run. He wore a red-and-black-checked shirt, neatly tucked into his brown velvet pants, that made him look like a miniature adult.

Leila opened the door of the boxlike bathroom, and a whiff of distilled air, smelling of rust and moisture, filled her nostrils. A fly buzzed fitfully on the windowpane. The window glass had bloated disks on it, like watery blisters, that made it impossible to look in or out. Leila rushed to help Omid with the buttons of his pants. He shook his legs and gathered his arms tightly over his stomach, straining to resist just a little longer. He stood on the outer edges of his feet, trying to avoid contact with the wet ribs of the porcelain platforms as much as possible. He was already turning into a male version of his grandmother, clean, obsessive, squeamish about anything unknown and wet. Leila turned on the tap and splashed cold water on her face.

"Is that man taking our picture?" Omid asked when he was done.

"Yes, he is." Leila dried her face with the pink-stained edge of her headscarf.

"Where's his camera?"

"You'll see it now." She looked down at his small fingers forcing the buttons of his pants into the respective openings. "Do you want me to help you?"

"I can do it myself."

She laughed. "You're my big little man."

"I'm a big man." He finished with the buttons and washed his hands. "Why did the man yell at you?" he said after a few moments, turning a serious gaze to his aunt.

"Which man?"

"The man with the car."

"He did, didn't he?" Leila murmured as she dried his hands with her damp headscarf.

"Why?"

"Because he knows he can."

"Why?"

Leila waved a dismissive hand, which she then let drop in a sad flap. "Because he has nothing better to do."

Omid looked at her like he was not convinced.

"Were you scared?" she asked, stooping a little over him, softening her voice.

Omid looked down at the floor. He continued to stand on the outer edges of his feet. Then he shrugged. An adult shrug.

"We listen to them when we have to," Leila said. "But deep down, at the bottom of our hearts, we're not scared of them. Isn't that true?"

Omid remained silent. He seemed not to have thought the concept of fear all the way through. As if it were a thought he had stowed away in the back of his mind and wished to bring up only when absolutely necessary.

"Most of all, I'm scared of cockroaches," Leila said, trying to distract him. "And lizards."

"But the lizards eat the cockroaches."

"Do they?"

"And the flies. And the mosquitoes."

"Then I shouldn't be afraid of them." She stretched her hand out to him.

"Not of the lizards," he said, grabbing her hand. They walked out of the bathroom. Omid's steps were exaggeratedly wide, as if he were light-headed.

They found Forugh with her shoes off and thrown under the chair, pulling at the green curtain behind the entrance door. Sara had succeeded in extracting one of the envelopes from the pile on the round glass table and was biting into it. Her saliva ran generously down its crest. Oblivious to what the children were doing, Agha Hossein was arranging an album of wedding photos.

"Shall we take the photo now?" he asked.

"Yes, we're ready."

Leila pulled the curtain out of Forugh's grasp and the envelope out of Sara's mouth and tried to smooth it out with her hand. The edge of the envelope wilted, hopelessly soggy, between her fingers. She hid the envelope under the crisp pile, grabbed the shoes from under the chair, wrapped her arms around the two children, and hoisted them up. Omid once again clutched at her manteau as they followed Agha Hossein down the two high concrete steps and into a dimly lit room.

"There's the camera." Leila pointed at the camera on an erect pole casting a linear shadow on the floor. Omid put his index and middle finger into his mouth and, looking at the camera, began sucking on them thoughtfully.

Agha Hossein hauled a green bench to the middle of the room. "As you see, Leila Khanoom, I'm not very busy these days. It seems like no one wants to take pictures in wartime. Who knows? Maybe they prefer not to keep records of themselves; maybe they want to forget. Or maybe they're afraid of remembering later. If that's the case, it means they're already looking ahead, thinking they're going to come out of this war alive. I don't know if I share their optimism, not with this damned crazy Saddam bombing us for seven years now. And there seems to be no end in sight."

Agha Hossein roamed about the studio, clicking things on, drawing curtains. His voice streamed into the studio in a soft, uninterrupted flow, as if he were speaking to himself and did not expect any replies. His movements were easy and unhurried, like his voice. It was perhaps this easiness that kept the children calm. They looked at him, seeming to listen.

"You can put the children on the bench here."

Leila lowered the children slowly. From the bench, the rice-tray eyes looked up at her. Wobbly teeth smiles. Tiny arms up, then down, flapping like the wings of a butterfly. Sara and Forugh had the same pacifiers fastened to the sides of their white overalls. They had the same tiny white shoes, the same milk bottles, underwear, toys. Maman Zinat's touch, that was, pedantically taking care of every detail, doling out her love in equal amounts, treating them as if they were twins, afraid of falling short. At night, Maman Zinat slept with Omid on her right, Forugh on her left, and Sara in a cot at the head of the bed. That was because Aghajaan had teased her once that putting Sara's bed next to Omid instead of next to her showed that Maman Zinat loved her other granddaughter less. Aghajaan had a strange way of amusing himself. And Maman Zinat fell for it every time. Maman Zinat had so much love to give. She had turned sensitive, persnickety. From that night, she put Sara's bed at the head of her own.

"Omid, you sit in the middle," said Leila.

Omid turned around, placed his hands on the edge of the bench, and pulled himself up between his sister and his cousin.

"Oh, wait a second." Leila picked up a small comb from the shelf. "Let me make you pretty for the photo." She knelt in front of Sara, lifting the comb to her fair hair. Sara shook her head and drew it back, trying to squirm out of Leila's grasp.

"Let Khaleh make you nice for the photo." She placed a hand behind Sara's head to keep it from moving and could feel the soft baby fat under her fingers. With the hair combed back, the dimples above her temples came into view. Leila kissed Sara's nose as she moved on to kneel in front of Forugh, who followed every move with her black liquid eyes. Leila arranged Forugh's sparse black hair as best she could, straining to comb it down. The thin hair stood tall, resisting.

Leila had found a handmade toy in Forugh's pants when she arrived. A stick figure made with broken sticks. It was Simin's gift, a sign telling them she was fine. Simin and Parisa had been separated inside the prison. Leila wondered if they ever saw each other, crossed in the corridor, exchanged glances during recreation time. What did they do when the sirens rang? Did they stay behind in their cells with nowhere to go, hoping a bomb would not fall on them? The solitude of her sisters made her feel numb all over. The solitude of the stick figure.

Sara had already begun to fidget, was trying to get down from the bench. Omid was preventing her with a hand on her chest. Leila had to hurry before Sara's patience ran out. She combed Omid's hair quickly and fixed his collar.

"They look very nice." Agha Hossein drew down a dark green screen behind them and arranged one of Omid's arms around Sara's shoulder, the other around Forugh's waist. "Keep your arms here."

Leila walked out of the camera's vision but stood close enough to jump forward if anything went wrong; if they needed her; if they felt afraid, not seeing her around.

Agha Hossein stood behind the camera. "Okay, now look over here." Screwing up the web of fine wrinkles around his eyes, he projected the light on the three little faces. The three turned still, staring at the light, like squirrels caught by approaching headlights.

Click.

The tip of Forugh's tongue was slightly visible between her lips. A drop of saliva glinted over Omid's front teeth. Sara's mouth was open in an expression of astonishment, her gaze fixed on the light. Leila imagined them going through life in the same way they sat here, with their brittle arms wrapped around one another's shoulders, waists, knees. Their destinies as intertwined as their arms. She could not see them as brother and sister or as cousins. She could see them only as three reflections of one body. Three in one, like the branches of a tree, the jacaranda tree in their courtyard. One could never tell where the tree ended and the branches started. That was what they were, the three children: the tree and its branches.

Click.

Three tiny faces stared blankly at the camera.

Afternoon light was petering out, slowly taking its leave from the narrow courtyard. The air felt impregnated with summer seeds. The jacaranda flowers glided to the ground in a resigned gentle somersault. The space between the cobblestones seemed to have been colored in, purple and pink and sometimes green. A crow swooshed across the courtyard, looking for something glittery to steal.

Leila entered the room holding a large basket of clothes in her arms. Her wild hair, at last free from the headscarf, flowed down her shoulders like thick slippery wires. She let the basket drop to the floor with a low thud, which made the clothes inside it tremble. She sat down and began folding the tiny shirts and pants and aprons and socks.

She was tired. In her mouth, she could still taste the dust that came up from the endless streets, with the hot asphalt and flashing windows and screaming children and history reduced to pompous slogans on grimy walls. Particles of grit crunched between her teeth. Her legs ached from walking to and from the photographer's studio. She walked because she had not been able to catch a taxi. Not with the three kids who held on to her like a life jacket and whom she vehemently kept away from the chaos. People had jumped into the taxis and disappeared before she had time to open her mouth. She seemed to have lost her efficiency in this rasping, humming, cluttering city. There were times when the city felt immense, expanding without a moment of rest, winding around her like an enormous husk. She wanted to shout sometimes just to see if her voice could overcome the relentless din.

Only three years ago, everything had been different. Nothing could touch her, block her way, bring her to an unwanted stop. She would jump in and out of taxis and buses with the agility of an experienced city girl, efficiently weaving her way through the traffic to the clothing factory where she had a job packaging hospital gowns and blankets in plastic bags to be sent to the makeshift hospitals at the front lines of the war, where she had heard there was barely room for all the injured. Although it was menial work, Leila had never been happier. She had never felt so liberated as when she punched the time clock after arriving every morning, the click of the puncher sweet to her ears. It was the click of independence, of security, of finding a foothold in a country that was crumbling, hammered down by war and the soured ecstasies of a revolution. It was punching into shape a life that had felt like molten lava.

Her colleagues were women her age or older, with husbands at war, who found themselves from one day to the next as the heads of the family, the breadwinners. Women with linear yellow faces and blazing eyes. Thin women in wide brown manteaus, like scarecrows. Full of virtue and suffering. Some brought their newborns with them, placing them in cradles at their feet under the table. They kept one eye on the child and another on the sewing machine, pricking away at the dull-colored fabric. At lunch breaks, the women continued to sit at the tables, embracing their children, watching the tiny mouths clamp on to the giving, swollen, blue-veined breasts. The sewing machines had fallen silent.

Leila had to quit her job when Sara arrived, just like Forugh, wearing clothes made of prayer chadors and buttons that were date stones. She could not leave Maman Zinat to raise three children on her own. Not at her age, not with her obsessions, not with the nightly anguish that gnawed at Maman Zinat's nerves like termites.

The day she left the factory, her colleagues surrounded her. She was leaving so soon, they said. They wished they could leave too. Leave this prison with its sewing machines and transparent plastic bags and smell of war. They lifted a hand and waved it in the air. A hand sweeping across the stale air that smelled of warm milk, sweat, and uncertain dreams. Leila wished she could stay, folding her hospital gowns, punching her time clock, measuring her life. But she was afraid to say so. The women thought her lucky, and she didn't want to disappoint them. She shook their hands one by one. Their dry, tired hands. Yearning eyes. Outside, on the other side of the tall brick walls of the factory, the afternoon sunlight was hazy with dust.

"When will the picture be ready?" Maman Zinat's slightly raised voice intruded into Leila's thoughts. She was sitting in the adjacent room, on the other side of the glass doors, in front of a hill of fresh herbs clumped in bunches by wet green rubber bands. Light splashed through the French windows, which opened to the courtyard, on her long salt-and-pepper braid that embraced the curve of her neck, ran along her waist, almost grazing the tight knots of the rug. The sleeves of her black dress were folded up to her elbows so as not to get them dirty. The black dress made her look old, in mourning, which she was not. She was only sad. If she could, she would have replaced her daughters in prison. She would have been happier that way, more at ease with herself.

"In about a week," Leila said. "He said he'll give us a call."

"They'll be so happy when they receive the picture. My poor girls."

Maman Zinat chopped off the mud-clinging ends of the stems without untying the rubber bands, nipping off the leaves, dropping them into separate basins. Her fingers were soiled, brown, muddy, but the rest of her almost glimmered with cleanliness, making the brown fingers look out of place.

"Leila *jaan*, pour a cup of tea for your father," she said.

Leila's knees made a loud cracking sound as she got to her feet and walked up to the electric samovar thrumming in the corner like a disgruntled grandmother telling the stories of a happier past. She rinsed a narrow-waist glass cup in the bowl of water next to the samovar, dried it with the towel wrapped around the kettle, and poured the red tea into it. Spirals of steam rose, settling on the samovar's tap as she added the boiling water. The room breathed a minty, nose-itching green-onion breath.

"We're running out of rice," Maman Zinat said, tossing her head back the way she always did when remembering something.

Aghajaan made a little dry grunt as he made himself comfortable on the floor, leaning against the cushions with flying sparrows and a deer with disproportionately short legs embroidered on them, his back to the fresco on the wall of white swans swimming down a blue river. He took the cup of tea from Leila.

"Already? I got some just last week," he said.

"You did. But there isn't much left. Also sugar."

"We'll have to wait for coupons. Maybe tomorrow or the day after."

The gold chain around Maman Zinat's white neck swayed to the side as she leaned forward to drop a handful of parsley leaves into a plastic basin. She flung the stripped stems onto the frayed floral blanket protecting the rug, covering her knees. "I'll get some potatoes. The neighbors say Jamal Agha has brought some."

Aghajaan's eyebrows drew close in a frown as he lifted his gaze to his wife. The curly ends of his eyebrows looped up toward his forehead. "How many times do I have to tell you not to buy from that thief? Charging everything ten times more. He's sucking our blood. That's what he's doing. Sucking the blood of people like you who go and buy his expensive potatoes."

"If there's no rice, then I'll have to buy potatoes," Maman Zinat said without looking up. "We can't starve the children, can we?"

"No one's telling you to starve the children. Just don't buy from that Jamal. He thinks war is the time to make money, not to help his people. At the end of the war, he'll be a millionaire, and my daughters will probably have to go work for him when they come out of prison."

Maman Zinat did not respond. She seemed too upset to speak. Aghajaan too fell silent, drinking his tea in one angry gulp. Leila turned her gaze away from her mother and father and let it glide on the large chunky wardrobe that no longer contained any clothes, only blankets and covers for the three children. She had never understood why her sisters had kept on fighting even though the revolution was over, a war had taken its place, and everyone was first struggling to make a new beginning and later to ward off death. But Simin and Parisa fought on, along with their husbands. They threw leaflets over walls, held secret meetings at home, read outlawed books, watched the news and jotted down how many times the name of the Supreme Leader was mentioned and how his name was taking over everything, growing louder, omnipresent, and how their own political presence—along with all the others not part of the regime—was being scratched out, their existence denied, stifled, washed clean, like a stain on a table-cloth. They sat there in front of the television screen, pens in hand, putting into numbers how they were slowly vanishing, purged from the collective memory of the country, buried alive. They were now the enemy, the anti-revolutionaries. That was shortly before their arrest, when the process of being undone came to its last strike.

"I'll take the photo there," Aghajaan said, picking up the radio from the shelf. "I'll make sure I put it in their hands myself."

Leila looked at him, at his thick curly gray hair that used to be always perfectly oiled and combed back and now just fell on his forehead in careless disarray. He now always wore his pajamas at home, which revealed the almost orange sunburned skin of his forearms and face and neck that seemed to have grown so old, so quickly. For the past year, Aghajaan had been going to the prison every week, but most of the time, he was turned back, empty-handed, the desperation of the closed doors chiseled deeper and deeper into the lines of his face, into the deep of his hazel eyes. But he did not give up. Week after week, month after month, he waited in front of the prison door, asking to see his daughters.

Aghajaan switched on the radio. It coughed in his hands and lapsed into silence. "What happened to this radio?"

Maman Zinat looked up from the green onions, her eyes glimmering red. "It stopped working a few days ago. Didn't I tell you?"

Before Aghajaan had time to answer, the phone rang, loud and jarring. Leila dropped the clothes in her hand and ran to the telephone, her heart racing expectantly.

"Hello?"

An unknown female voice issued from the earpiece. "Is this Mr. Jalili's home?"

Leila felt a twinge of disappointment in her chest. "Yes?"

"I'm a friend of Parisa's. Are you her sister?"

Leila paused, her hand smoothing out the folds of her dress.

"Yes, I am," she mumbled hesitantly. She knew she should not be answering.

Aghajaan's voice came from the other room. "Leila, who is it?"

Leila felt her back growing tense.

"Do you have any news about her?" the woman asked. "And Simin?"

Leila turned around, drawing the mouthpiece away from her mouth. "It's a friend of Parisa's," she said, and involuntarily looked at Omid sitting on the tiled step at the foot of the French windows. He hurled a glance at her. His eyes, wide, alert, as if he were listening with them. Listening, watching, slipping, clutching at the name of his mother that lingered in the air.

"Hang up the phone," Aghajaan ordered.

Leila looked at him, the phone still in her hand.

"We're all very worried for them. You see, we haven't—" the woman continued.

"I said hang up!"

"I'm sorry. We don't know anything." Leila put the receiver down.

Silence fell. No one spoke. The roar of a passing airplane shook the house. Leila turned around and walked back to the disheveled pile of clothes.

She felt sorry, furiously sorry, for her sisters, for their friends, for Aghajaan, for the size of his fear that was bigger than he was. She knew that deep down, Aghajaan was happy when people asked about his daughters, when their friends called. There was a twinkle in his eyes, hearing their names pronounced. It seemed to console him, as if the mere utterance of their names somehow confirmed their being alive. And yet his fear prevailed all the same.

The more time passed and the less he knew of his daughters, the more afraid he grew to ask, the more afraid to speak, the more afraid to let anyone know of their seething, blazing, devastating world of the unknown, of the unspoken. It was as if the silence were burying him alive, burying them all alive.

A few moments passed before his voice broke the tense silence that had encroached upon the room. "Who knows who's listening in on our conversations," he said, not looking anyone in the face. "Watching the comings and goings to our house, following us around, writing down the names of our acquaintances. Better not to raise suspicion; better to avoid contact."

No one said anything. Leila began refolding the clothes that she had thrown down in her rush to answer the phone. She saw Maman Zinat lift her gaze to Omid. Everything about her face was soft except the tension crinkling around her mouth. "Omid *jaanam*, can you get me the plastic bag by the door?" Maman Zinat said.

Omid got up slowly. His eyes looked too large for his body, the confused pain in them too heavy. He almost staggered through the French windows to the courtyard. He *pishhhhhhhhed* angrily at a cat eyeing the goldfish swimming back and forth in the blue of the fountain before grabbing the bag and slipping into the room the same way he left.

"Like a little thief." Maman Zinat forced out a laugh. "Climbing in and out of the window. What are you, a gypsy? Or a cat, maybe?"

Omid handed her the bag and sat down next to her, watching her hold a dill stem from the top and tug her other hand down the stem, across the soft delicate leaves, with one resolute jerk. Maman Zinat began singing quietly, almost exclusively for him.

Leila squeezed the last pieces of clothes inside the bureau. Her face was set in a tight frown as if something had hardened under her pale skin. The drawers made a loud rasping sound as she pushed them shut one by one.

In the corner of the room, Sara and Forugh were asleep. Leila slipped out a blanket from the wardrobe and spread it over them. That was when she caught sight of Sara's bottle on the pillow. It was half-full of milk. Maman Zinat insisted on giving milk to the children even though, according to Leila and Aghajaan, they were too old for bottles. Maman Zinat wouldn't hear of it. *They haven't had their mother's milk*, she would say. *Powdered milk is not the same. They should have it for longer, to compensate.*

Leila picked up the bottle and looked at Maman Zinat. Maman Zinat was not looking at her. She was observing the green hill in front of her, her back stooped over it as if she were looking down a well. Leila walked quickly toward the door. On her way out, her gaze met Aghajaan's. He took a look at the bottle in her hand, then at Maman Zinat, and nodded approvingly to Leila. She hurried out the door and down the corridor toward the fridge. Leila knew and Aghajaan knew that Maman Zinat should not, under any circumstances, see the bottle. If she saw it, she would not hesitate to throw the milk away. *The milk could be rotten*, she would say, even if it had stayed out of the fridge for a mere half hour. She would pay no heed to Aghajaan's angry tirade about having had to haggle in the black market for hours for one container of powdered milk.

The haggling had begun a few years ago and worsened as the war continued guzzling up the country, growing fatter, greedier, more ravenous every day. Everything had been rationed. Lines formed around supermarkets, where empty shelves glared back, around bakeries, around fruit vendors. Chicken feet and heads returned to the windows of butcheries as thighs and breasts disappeared. Cow bones were bought when the price of meat was so high that no one could afford it. In every cabinet of the kitchen, there were coupons for sugar, oil, rice, eggs. At every street corner, men with shriveled bodies and toothless mouths sold these coupons that expired as quickly as they were sold. They were precious, the coupons, and Aghajaan listened to the radio, read the newspapers every day, to find out when the government would issue new coupons. He could not bring himself to throw the old ones out. *What if they extend the expiration date?* But the coupons were not enough. The black market was booming. And that was when the haggling would start. *There is so little milk*, Aghajaan would say to Maman Zinat, berating her, pleading with her, *and there are so many babies*. The children of the revolution, they were, the generation of powdered milk. Didn't Maman Zinat understand? But Maman Zinat's ears were deaf to all of this, and the milk would stream away down the drain.

The shriek of the telephone once again rang through the house.

"In the end, they'll wake the kids up." With brown muddy hands, Maman Zinat looked through the last of the dill.

"If it's the friend again, hang up immediately," Aghajaan warned as he watched Leila scuttle back to the room and toward the phone.

"Hello?"

Silence crackled on the other end of the line.

"Hello?"

"Leila?"

Her mouth opened into a wide smile, to the extent of her happiness. *At last!* She turned her back to her parents, her voice trembling gleefully. *"Salaam."*

He laughed. "For a second, I thought it was your mother answering. You two sound too much alike!"

"Who is it?" Aghajaan called out.

Leila put her hand over the mouthpiece. "It's Nasrin," she lied. "How are you?"

"I'm fine."

"I want to see you," Ahmad said. "Can you come to the park?" *Yes! Yes!*

She lowered her voice. "My parents are here."

"I have to talk to you, Leila." He hesitated. "I've got the visa."

Leila paused, winding the phone's curly wire tighter and tighter around her finger. She lacked the strength to speak. She wished to block the words from seeping out of his mouth, to keep them lying quietly on his tongue. To keep them there, quiet, unspoken. She knew that the words hanging on the edges of his mouth had the power to crush her. But it was too late. The words had rolled out and up and away from him, locking their fingers gently on her throat, until she could no longer breathe.

"I'll be there," she muttered.

"I'll wait for you."

Leila stood for a long time, her heart pounding, with her hand on the receiver.

"I'm going to Nasrin's for a little while." She walked back to the room, chewing nervously on her lower lip.

Maman Zinat was cleaning up, gathering the naked stems of the herbs in the plastic bag. "Now? It'll start getting dark soon."

"I'll be back in an hour." She struggled to smooth out her voice where it hit the lump in her throat.

Aghajaan looked at his watch. The soundless radio was at his feet. "Make sure you're back before nightfall."

Leila saw him sitting on their usual bench in a remote part of the park. Dusty shrubs hid him partly out of view. His dark brown eyes flashed back at her, and his mouth, with the neatly trimmed mustache above it, curled into a smile.

"I thought you'd never make it." His gentle voice failed to quell the shaking inside her. She sat down next to him, full of fear and grief.

"I always come," she said, and turned her face so that he would not see the trembling of her chin.

"Yes, you do."

The first time they spoke to each other, he was waiting for her outside her high school on the opposite side of the street. He did that every day, but when she came out, he pretended not to have seen her, shifting on his feet, crimson-cheeked, doe-eyed like a child. She was seventeen. He was eighteen and too timid to make his presence known. He had come all the way to her high school but did not have the courage to take one more step. She had no choice but to walk away. She didn't want to get into trouble with the school's Morality Sisters. There were eyes always watching.

Then one day, she decided to cross the street and put an end to whatever it was he was so afraid of beginning. He stood motionless, watching her walk up to him with wide gleaming eyes. He lacked the courage to greet her. Instead, he gave her a book of poetry. The poems of Ahmad Shamlou.

She forgot about ends and beginnings. She felt light-headed, airborne. She let him accompany her home. He accompanied her home every day from then on. And he accompanied her when she graduated from high school and began working at the clothing factory. Then the children arrived, she left work, and they rarely saw each other.

They sat quietly, watching the breeze graze the untidy head of the shrubs. Their nostrils filled with a whiff of wet earth and freshly cut grass. The intermittent hubbub of the city wafted through the air and lay entangled in the leaves of the sycamore trees.

Ahmad took her hand in his. "Look at me, Leila," he said.

Leila lifted her eyes to his, all the tight coldness of her body clenching in her stomach. The skin of his recently shaved face was smooth and glossy. She had to repress the urge to reach out and run her fingers over the strong curve of his jaw. Her other hand was hidden in her pocket. She clasped her fist so tightly that her nails dug into her palm.

"When will you leave?" she asked.

"In twelve days."

She nodded. She could feel the blood draining from her face as her cheeks turned pale and her lips gray. She closed her eyes and waited, waited for that crushing sensation of the end.

"Aren't you going to say anything?"

Leila let go of his hand and sat with her icy hands clasped between her knees, swaying from side to side. There were so many things she imagined, hoped, would happen to her. At times, she felt so stifled that she wished to leave just so she could get away from herself, from what she was in that house with its old fears, new fears, from the inertia she felt doing all the things she had to do day after day, which made her fall into an exhausted, dreamless sleep at night. It was the greatness of her sacrifices, the certainty of them, and the ease with which she made them, quitting her job, staying home, that made her shrink away from herself, from what she was and what she had to become, from the happiness he was offering her. She postponed it all, her decisions, her plans, for that unclear future when her sisters would be released. Postponing, giving up, giving in. First painfully, then sweetly, like falling back asleep at the crack of dawn, eyes tingling, body going limp, cozy warmth spreading over the limbs. There, fear and foreboding ceased to exist. There were only the children's cries, whose reassuring urgency could not be mistaken for anything else.

"We can still save things, Leila. We can get married and go away together. I just need one word from you."

"I can't leave the children," she said in a trailing voice. If there was anything she ever wished for, it was for him to stay, but sacrifices were not something she asked of others. "I've told you."

"I know you've told me. But, Leila, this is about our life. My life and yours. The children will grow up with or without you. But we . . ." He averted his face, his voice receding, running back and up his throat, dissolving behind the sad flicker in his eyes.

Leila felt her limbs going numb. She knew she sounded like she was pleading, and her own voice made her shiver. She wished he would stop. "They need me here, Ahmad. I can't leave."

"I need you," he groaned. He kept rubbing a finger across his palm, rubbing until it turned red. "You see everyone else's needs except mine. You make sure of everyone else's happiness and trample mine."

She placed a shaking hand on his arm.

"What you're doing is not right, Leila. You're destroying everything. You're turning your back on happiness."

Leila got to her feet and went up to the hedge. Guilt caught in her throat, metallic, gigantic, blocking her lungs. She plucked one of the ashen leaves, then another, then another. Ahmad came and stood next to her.

"Are your parents at home?" Leila asked after some time.

He shook his head. "They went to *shomal* this morning. It's not safe to stay in Tehran."

"Why didn't you go with them?"

From the extreme corner of her eyes, she saw him look at her.

"I wanted to speak to you."

Leila kept her gaze fastened on the bush and the tiny leaves that she was nipping one after another. "I want to go to your house," she said. She was astonished at herself, at what she was saying. She didn't know where her words would take them, where she wanted her words to take them.

He looked at her, surprised. He seemed to hesitate. "To my house?"

She turned and looked straight at him. She looked at his long chin, at the imposing length of his nose, at the almond form of his mouth. He was pallid; only his eyes glowed.

"I want to go back home with you."

"Yes." He paused. "Yes, okay."

The walk back to his house was silent. Neither spoke. They listened to the city, to the lilting din of kids returning from school. Tiny girls in heavy blue uniforms, the ends of their white headscarves carrying the speck and stain of bread crumbs, memorized poems, chalk powder, and the lives of prophets. The boys in their own heavy uniforms and big shoes, with their closely shaved heads, like small soldiers. Their leaden backpacks looked to be pulling them to the ground. Their eyes were full of poetry and slogans and verses of the Koran. In the fall, this was going to be Omid's look, the same heavy backpack, the same shaved head. And in time, Sara and Forugh would have to wear the same white headscarves. Leila's mouth flickered into a smile as she pictured them. *Will they really grow so fast?* she thought. *I will make the clothes for them.*

A taxi passed by, trailing a confused noise of singing. Along the gutters, the rusty garbage cans stank sourly. Everything crinkled dusty and black, cluttered with policemen and Revolutionary Guards and Morality Guards and religious guides and food shortages and blackouts and the menaces of a war, at times far, at times near. A man who seemed to have fallen off his motorcycle hobbled back to it, lifted it up, lugged himself over it, and rode away. At the turn of the street, a church with its blue gate and wide treeless courtyard heaped into view. The air smelled of gasoline and asphalt and mulberry trees and turmeric powder and sweat and burning coal and bread.

Leila walked next to Ahmad, feeling like her knees were going to give way at any moment. Where was she going with him? What did she want from him, from herself? Her body was in commotion, inebriated with the seething energy of fear and guilt and despair, of plummeting down a precipice, of an urge to undo herself. Ahmad was all she had, the last person who was hers. What would remain of her after he was gone? What did she have to keep with her? Her hands were empty. She had no keepsake. He would simply be gone, and she would be left with nothing. Nothing to give, to look forward to, nothing but a quicksand of loneliness that would pull her in and in. And she couldn't do anything to stop it. She was trampling upon all their dreams.

Was this the right way? Everything blurred when she pictured herself in his house that she had never seen, that just a few days ago, she never would have allowed herself to go to. She knew that she had not thought it all the way through when she told him she wanted to go home with him. It had been an impulse, a desperate impulse. She was so afraid of losing him. But was she doing the right thing? What was going to happen to her once they arrived? She did not know. All she knew was that she could not stop walking, that she could not stop taking step after step after step, that she wanted nothing more than being near him.

They soon reached his house. Ahmad pushed the key into the lock and opened the door to a courtyard filled with geraniums. The trailing sunlight placed its last kisses on the soft leaves of an apple tree whose branches were being tested by swallows, first one branch and then another, all the while making such commotion, like children in a candy store. The hard little apples were not yet ripe. The swallows noisily ignored them.

Leila paused at the doorway, Ahmad next to her. She could feel his eyes on her, the heat emanating from his body. A prickly sensation ran up her neck at his proximity, at his scent, which she could almost taste in the air. She could no longer change their destiny, but she still had this moment, didn't she? She was here now. She was here with him.

She entered the courtyard, holding her heart in her hands, like glass.

They walked through a corridor that led to a room furnished

with red armchairs, a pink-and-green rug, and miniature paintings on the walls. Leila lowered herself onto one of the armchairs, gathering her wide manteau around her, watching as Ahmad flitted nervously around the room, putting books back on the shelves, cushions back on the armchairs.

It was hot in the room. Leila was sweating under her manteau. But the mere thought of taking it off was enough to send timidity stealing into her like cold air seeping through the crack under a door. He had never seen her in anything other than her long brown manteau, even though she wore a pretty dress under it every time she went out with him. He never saw these dresses, was not the least aware of their presence under the manteau, but she insisted on wearing them. It was important to her to know that she could choose those dresses, that this choice, although hidden from view, was still made, was still hers. And now even the thought of taking off her manteau, to at last let him see her in one of the dresses, made her so shy, she felt like she would be taking off her very clothes. It was absurd. She was being absurd. She was not going to give in to it. She straightened her back and lifted a hand to the buttons of her manteau. A liquid tingling began at her fingertips and ran up her arms into a hazy whirling eruption in her body as she undid them. She pulled off the sleeves and let her manteau fall back on the sofa.

"Ahmad," she called out to him, her voice barely audible. Her hands ran over her dress, smoothing out the gray and pink polka dots.

Ahmad turned around and stood staring at her from where he was, next to the bookshelves. The ticking of the clock trotted resolutely through the room. "You're beautiful," he said, his gaze so full of emotion that her heart skipped a beat. He walked over and sat down next to her.

They watched each other through the opaque darkness. Their eyes burned, their tongues, dry and tense, lay flat in their mouths, tasting like sawdust. Neither moved a muscle or batted an eyelid. Outside, the wind blew through the leaves of the apple tree. A siren howled in the distance.

Leila opened her mouth to say something. A sigh skipped through her lips. So close. He was so close to her. His face assumed all the space in her vision, becoming the only thing that existed. For a moment, this closeness, the novelty of it, the overwhelming intimacy of it, made the heavy cloud of guilt and fear and sorrow rise and dissipate into the air. Leila edged her hand forward and touched his with the tips of her fingers. He looked at her but didn't make the slightest movement. He seemed to have frozen in place, in a daze.

Leila lifted his hand and placed it hesitantly on her face. What was she doing? What would become of her? Was she ready to lose everything along with him? If it happened, if this was what it all meant, was she ready to live her life afterward without him, as a woman without a man? The questions continued to hammer in her head, bouncing off one side of her head then the other.

"Leila," Ahmad whispered. A blush ran all over his face, to the roots of his thick black hair.

Something inside her squirmed. Once this was over, there was no turning back. She knew that. This was all madness. She was going to lose everything. And yet something inside her continued to roar like an insatiable lioness, cruel, thoughtless, and pure. She could not silence it. She could not chain it down. She could not lose him so simply.

Ahmad's hand was hot on her face. His mouth parted in an expression of pain and joy and fear. He seemed on the verge of breaking down. His fingers edged hesitantly to her neck and touched it as though he were picking a cactus fig, careful not to touch the thorns. Then he ran his fingers along her spine, vertebra by vertebra, all the way down to the arch of her back, pressing her closer to him. The way his fingers grazed past snapped something open inside her. Every molecule of her body responded to this touch that she had never felt, that she had not even imagined could one day be running along the line of her neck. It evoked such sensations that it astonished her. Something hard, a blow in her stomach. That was what it felt like.

What will I take away with me? The thought of having his child flashed before her eyes. It made her gasp, the fear of it, the joy of it, the sheer audacity of it. Her heart raced so loudly that she thought even the birds in the courtyard might hear it. And yet he would not be there, and she would be alone. What would become of her then, with a child?

But I will have him. A part of him that no one will be able to take away from me. Even if he is not there.

She pressed her body against him, finding herself choking not only with desire but with the shock of life itself, with an unexpected sense of weightlessness, of conviction, of liberation hitherto unknown. There seemed to be an alien force at work inside her, stripping her of her inhibitions and imbuing her with a new will, even if tentative, even if uncertain, to take possession for one last time of that which from tomorrow would no longer be hers.

"Leila, are you sure?" Ahmad whispered one last time, with

red, flashing eyes. He watched her with the absorbed penetrating gaze that she could not withstand and yet did not wish him to stop.

She lifted her arms and wrapped them around his neck. Slowly, she was letting go of everything, of time and place and herself, and the sudden nothingness of everything else, and the sudden everything of being alive. This was who she was now, and she clasped this moment, this blossoming of life, no longer frightened or apologetic, that was going to be hers, that no war, no prison, no revolution, no children—her heart ached with love at the thought of her nephew and nieces—could take away from her.

From her lower back, his hand once again climbed and then pressed on the zipper of her dress. Leila closed her eyes and arched her back to ease the unzipping. She listened carefully to the zip rustling down her dress, uncovering her back, as if uncovering a secret. She then opened her eyes and watched as the dress slipped off and spread around her feet. She stood with a battering heart, claiming herself. In the waning light, she slid the stockings off her legs.

She stood in her bare body and realized with astonishment that she still had her headscarf on; it burst with the force of her squirming hair. Ahmad stood falteringly to his feet, lifted a hand, and untied the knot under her chin. The headscarf glided down her shoulders and down onto the floor. It was the first time he had ever seen her hair.

The shrill cries of the siren thrashed about in the courtyard like an enraged lion. It was an hour past curfew. Leila's hands shook as she tied her scarf under her chin. Her entire body was abuzz, mysterious sensations running against her skin. She could barely stand. She felt drained. Her arms, her legs, her spinal cord all felt as if they had turned into powder. Ahmad stood next to her, watching her, immobile, helpless, like a statue cracking from inside.

"I have to go." She heard her voice coming from the distance. "The sirens. It's so late." But she didn't take one single step; she couldn't. Instead, she shook her head and covered her face with her hands. Overwhelmed with grief, she couldn't bring herself to say anything else and so just looked at him.

Ahmad was silent. His chapped lips drew apart in a desperate smile. The wild sorrow on his face unsettled her. She couldn't endure his falling apart. She looked away from him, from the ache in his eyes. The sirens seemed to grow louder and louder. The curtains fluttered. The swallows had flown away long ago.

Ahmad made a sudden move; thrusting his arms out, he pulled Leila to him. She gave herself up to his last desperate grasp. Her eyes welling up, she threw her arms around him. A cool breeze wafted into the room from the open door. The yelps of the sirens crashed against the closed windows, the echo bobbing, wiggling, then coming to a standstill. Golden twilight seeped through the window and splashed on their bodies.

She knew she had to go. But moments passed before she could summon all her strength to pull away from him, inhaling for the last time the smoky aroma emanating from his mouth, from behind his ears, through his hair. She knew she was leaving a part of herself behind, that right here in this room, her skin still tingling with the last residues of longing and satiation, she was watching a part of her die an inexorable, irreversible death. *The forest*, she thought as she walked away with blurry eyes, as if a mist were descending, turning everything into indefinable silhouettes. *He was like the forest*. She waved at him, and he could do nothing but watch her slipping out the door, her heart as heavy as the sky.

Outside, the copper red of the setting sun sprinkled over the stiff-limbed deserted streets. There was barely anyone around. The emptiness of the city frightened Leila as she hurried down the street. Everything around her seemed to have grown hard and enameled and silent, except the siren that rampaged through the streets, roaring, shaking everything. She jumped over the gutter, a smell of wet leaves and dead birds rising to her nostrils. She stumbled on the uneven asphalt as she crossed the street. The last of the cars whirred past her, leaving behind a puff of gasoline-blue air.

She rushed past the windows reflecting the cringing form of the city. She knew there were people behind those black windows, sitting in the dark, watching the dwindling light outside, waiting, holding their breath. Those with houses or relatives in the countryside had already left the city. Those with cars but no houses took refuge in the countryside every time the sirens rang. And those with no houses or cars stayed behind their closed windows, hoping a bomb would not fall on them. Leila could almost hear their gasps, their frightened murmurs, and wished they could all come with her, that there could be enough room in a car to take the entire city.

Simin and Parisa too were left behind. The thought of her sisters cringing in the darkness of their cell made her almost dizzy with despair.

She quickened her steps; she should have been home an hour ago so they could leave the city on time before the sirens began. Now Aghajaan and Maman Zinat had to wait for her, simmering with worry, the warning wails of bombardment and death shattering in their ears. She could not forgive herself for being so late, for putting them in danger, and she began to run.

She turned onto an empty side street as sweat ran down her back. A cat shrieked while jumping over a heap of rubble. She ran past the gray shutters of closed shops, past a man slouched on the steps of a mosque, his head on his knees, past a soiled blue shirt on the edge of the curb, past bolted doors behind which mothers clutched at children, lovers sought each other, fathers listened with their heads between their hands. Blue darkness splashed over the trees, dousing the buildings. The jarring shrieks of the siren trailed behind.

Where was Ahmad now? Was there a safe place he could go, a basement where he could hide? Leila breathed hard, trying to choke back the lump forming in her throat, tight and unrelenting. She didn't know; she hadn't even asked him. Her eyes tingled with unshed tears. She felt alone, tired, scared. She just wanted to turn around, run back the way she had come, curl up in Ahmad's arms wherever he was, and go to sleep. How safe she had felt with him, how untouchable. Now, in these deserted streets, with the shrieks of the sirens closing in on her, her loneliness felt so great that she doubted she would ever again have the strength, the ability, to squirm out of its grasp.

But she kept on running. She had no choice. She stepped on a crushed cigarette pack, a blown-away piece of newspaper, and kept on running, past shattered glass on the ground, past a half-written graffito on the wall. The bundle of toilet paper she had piled up in her underwear against the blood that had at last stopped flowing rubbed against her thighs as she ran. Her hands and cheeks were cold. She clutched at her headscarf, quickening her steps, the shrieks of the siren chasing her.

At last, she saw the door of her house come into view, and her body, almost of its own accord, came to a stop. A single violent sob tore through her throat. It was as if the view of that house, her house, was the sign that it was all over, definitely, irrevocably, that she would never see Ahmad again; that once she was through that door, Ahmad's face already would be a memory of the past.

She paused outside of the house. She closed her eyes and leaned against the wall. She needed a moment to gather her bearings, to prepare herself for the new and yet same life that awaited her on the other side. A few moments passed before she drew enough strength to push the key into the lock.

Omid seemed to be waiting for her inside the courtyard, his bloodshot eyes riveted on her. He too had been crying.

"What are you doing here?" She slipped through the door, grasping his hand. "Come on! Let's go inside."

The house was drenched in silky darkness. The children were screaming inside. Aghajaan stalked toward her, pale, hollow-cheeked, clenched fists. He was no longer in his pajamas but in a blue-and-white-checked shirt and black pants. Ready to leave.

"Where were you?" he shouted, biting the words. He lifted a hand, ready to strike. Leila cringed, bringing a trembling hand to her face. Aghajaan looked at her for a long while, his eyes seething, and let his hand drop. Leila clasped Omid's narrow shoulders and pressed him to her. She bit her tongue hard to keep her lips from twitching. Maman Zinat sprinted out of the room, pulling on her chador. Forugh wailed in her arms; the siren had frightened her.

"Hold her." Maman Zinat passed the child to Leila. She ran back to the room, picked Sara up, and scurried back into the corridor.

They rushed out into the liquid of the night. Their shadows

tense, cringing, as if whipped by the sirens, shuffling feet on the cobblestone courtyard. Darkness slithered through the leaves of the trees and hung above them. The crescent of the moon appeared from behind the frayed tufts of clouds.

Aghajaan's old yellow Peykan made a grunt as he turned the engine and eased the car away from the curb. Maman Zinat sat in front, Sara in her arms. The words of prayer spouted out of her mouth in a long, uninterrupted, anxious susurrus, calling on the Prophet and the imams and their sons and daughters to come to their aid. With the siren raging, her prayer was barely audible.

They drove through whitewashed streets, past tall shapeless trees and chunks of fitful blocks and three-story buildings and giant billboards and a million black windows. Aghajaan was leaning forward, the muscles in his back taut, gripping the wheel, staring down the narrow street.

Occasionally, a taxi rattled past, crammed with the family of the taxi driver, trying to make an escape. Bodies squeezed together, ten in a car, leaving the city behind.

Leila shifted Forugh in her arms. The child continued to whimper, frightened tears streaming down her cheeks.

"She's afraid of the bombs." Omid grabbed Forugh's hand and lifted it up and down playfully. She was inconsolable, and another of her high-pitched screams sprinted through the car.

"Shhh, baby, shhhh." Leila kissed Forugh's forehead. Her nerves were sharp steel, rasping wires cutting through her. "It's okay. It's okay," she whispered, almost pleading with her to stop. Forugh raised her head, and her hot tears wet Leila's lips.

"Are the bombs going to reach us?" Omid was now covering his ears with his hands.

"No, they're not." Leila clutched his chin between her fingers. "We're almost out of the city."

The windows were fogging up. Aghajaan rolled down the window; cool air hissed through the opening. Maman Zinat covered Sara's head with her chador. Leila erased the steam off the window with the back of her finger. The mural of a young war martyr surrounded with a wreath of tulips flashed past them. *Tulips have blossomed from the blood of the youth of our land*, it said underneath in red.

"Khaleh, where were you?" Omid suddenly asked.

Leila turned to look at him, somewhat taken aback. "I was at Nasrin's house. Remember Nasrin? I took you there once."

Omid gazed at her without speaking. Was that blame in his eyes?

Shaken by Omid's stare, Leila changed the subject. "When you see the mountains, that means we're safe," she said, pointing at the blurry outlines of the Alborz Mountains nestled against the sagging sky. The buildings on the streets had grown sparser, and beyond them were bits and pieces of the barren fields, glazed in black. The sound of the siren had grown muffled and was gradually dying down.

"Can you see them?" Leila asked.

Omid nodded, dropping his hands, his two fingers safe and wet in his mouth. Forugh had gone limp in Leila's arms, exhausted. The intermittent light of the few remaining lampposts cast fleeting shadows on her tearstained face. Leila put the pacifier in her mouth. Dwindling in the distance, the city looked like a giant sprawling pyramid flattened by the night. A sense of peace slowly began settling in the car.

"Did you take the lanterns?" Maman Zinat unclasped her hands, loosening her grasp on Sara. Aghajaan nodded, drawing his shoulders back to relieve the strain.

"I forgot to check the oil in them," Maman Zinat added.

"I'm sure there's enough."

Sara tried to wiggle out of Maman Zinat's grasp and stand.

"Where are you going?" Maman Zinat said gently. She pointed at the taillights of the car in front, darting through the mist-laden space. "Look at the lights going so fast."

For a moment, Sara watched the lights flashing in the distance along with her grandmother. But soon, having grown bored, she started fidgeting again. Maman Zinat shifted her weight to the right and tried to rock the girl in her arms.

Omid rested his head on Leila's arm, silently watching the night and the expanding black fields. Forugh had fallen asleep. Once in a while, her mouth puckered around the pacifier and then lapsed back to a pink stillness.

With the city behind them, Leila felt her nerves slowly untangling. She leaned her head against the seat and watched the powdered starlight that sifted through the mist and down on the vast quiet fields. The wheels of the car rumbled, whirring in her head. She still carried the bittersweet scent of Ahmad under her skin, could still feel the texture of his skin on her palms. She took a deep breath. Her hand crawled down to her legs, in between, and clasped hard, as if to keep the memory of his body from slipping out of her and disappearing into the night.

Forugh made a small movement with her head. Leila watched her lips scrunch up around the pacifier. The white of her eyes peeked through the half-closed lids.

At last, the car came to a stop on a dusty road, straddled between long rows of parked cars. A few oil lanterns flickered, bringing to light the haggard faces of those who, like them, had escaped the bombs and yet seemed to have nothing to show for it. Fugitives seeking shelter in the vastness of the fields, under an empty sky. Fugitives who were finished with the myths of courage and martyrdom, of virgins and paradise, with which those in power had called their sons and brothers and husbands to the minefields. Fugitives who were left with nothing but an endless war, a million dead and wounded, and a country burning, crumbling.

Aghajaan opened the trunk and brought out the sleeping bags, the kilim, the covers that were always ready and packed in the car for a quick escape. He spread the kilim on the damp ground between their car and another. Maman Zinat swathed the children carefully against the cold streaming down from the far invisible mountains.

All around, there was movement. Fathers carrying sleeping bags. Mothers running after children who, excited by the nocturnal outing, fluttered around lanterns. The elderly sat on folding seats as if at a picnic. A mist had descended, soft-fingered and luscious, like an old smiling silver-haired bride. Omid leaned against Leila, half awake, watching Aghajaan light the oil lantern with a match. The newborn flame a bobbing glimmering reflection in the hazel of his eyes.

The dark, stretching bodies of the plains surrounded them. The sparse shadows of trees stood alone on low hills like armless men. The night thrummed with voices and whispers. Maman Zinat, flanked by the bundled-up bodies of Forugh and Sara, unfolded a spread abloom with flowers, unpacking the bread and the containers of cutlets and sliced tomatoes. She flattened a cutlet with her thumbs on a piece of bread, added two slices of tomato, rolled up the bread, and handed it to Omid. He took the sandwich from her and bit into it sleepily. Maman Zinat stroked his cheek, smiling. "Poor baby's sleepy."

She then made sandwiches for Aghajaan and Leila and herself.

In a circle they sat, nibbling, each welded to his or her own little planet of thoughts and fears and hopes. The lamp on the ground threw blurred, bobbing shadows over their faces and the tired tension around their mouths.

"It's getting cold again," Maman Zinat said as she placed a slice of tomato in her bread.

Aghajaan nodded to Omid. "You want another sandwich?"

Omid shook his head and snuggled deeper in the crook of Leila's arm.

"What does this cursed Saddam want from us?" Maman Zinat said, her voice trembling. "Our land? Our oil? Seven years aren't enough? When will it end?" She paused, sprinkling salt on the tomato with an automatic gesture. Her tear-filled eyes glittered in the light of the lamp. "Where is my Parisa now? Where is my Simin?"

No one answered. They were too exhausted to speak of the war. They just wanted to close their eyes and forget about it all.

A damp hush was gradually falling, flawed by the muffled voices of mothers whispering lullabies into their children's ears, their murmurs whirling, dancing, and mingling with the mist. One by one, family by family, the crowd thinned out, slipping under the covers, their eyes to the open sky, with its few blinking stars, and the clouds moving away into the distance with the grace of sleepy mermaids.

The children counted the stars until they fell asleep. The adults watched the clouds gliding above, holding hands. No one knew if, upon returning to the city the next day, they would find their houses still standing. Or rubble, shattered, leveled, unrecognizable.

The night breathed around them, giving away nothing.

1983-1988

Komiteh Moshtarak Detention Center
Evin Prison, Tehran

He sat blindfolded in the corridor outside the bathroom doorway. A dirty shapeless blob on the wet cement floor. His beard grew longer by the day, and his body smelled as if it were decomposing. The pajama-like uniform hung loose on his sharp bones. A thin man—a thinning man—wearing a fat man's uniform. The ends of the sleeves dropped down to the middle of his fingers. The shoulders sagged, and the bottom of the pants folded underneath his feet, soiled.

Inside the fat-man uniform, Amir was falling into pieces, little by little, like old paint sloughing off a wall.

It was hard to breathe. There were no windows, and the air was laden with moisture. Every day, the guards dragged in new prisoners who staggered down the corridor, leaving behind scattered traces of blood in the shape of deformed footprints. The thick black water spilling out of the gutter gagged with torn pieces of clothes, hair, and bread crumbles; despair blended with the blood, further deforming it. The bodies were then dumped next to one another like damp bags of flour. The sounds of groaning, weeping, a leaking tap, and labored breathing lingered in the air.

Forty-five days had passed.

In forty-five days, Amir had been made to know the smell of rotting meat. Day after day, filth upon filth, interrogation after interrogation in which the same accusations, questions, and threats were repeated like a nightmare without a beginning and an end, he was being taught to feel like an animal. A wretched, smelly, blind animal with nothing to look forward to except the hours to pass, being given some food, and being taken to the bathroom to relieve himself.

Gradually, he found himself losing grasp of the outside world: of Maryam, of the blurry Damavand mountain peak seen from their living room window, of the busy Tehran streets at twilight. It all felt like a dream, a sweet irreplaceable dream. Maryam's laughter had slowly lapsed into a hazy echo in the alleys of his mind. Her laughter, her declamatory voice when reading poetry aloud, sitting on the carpet, leaning against the foot of the sofa.

Amir could not remember any of those poems. His mind had been wiped clean by attentive, capable hands, and instead of poems, it was now filled with screams, howls, and bones breaking.

Even Maryam's face was slowly disappearing from his memory. In his dreams, she was always headless.

She would come near him and put her hands on his cheeks,

but from her shoulders up, there was nothing. Emptiness; she had been beheaded. Amir would wake from the sound of his own stifled cries, soaked in cold sweat. Maryam would vanish, and the only thing that remained was the sound of the leaking tap echoing in his ears.

A young man called Behrouz was sitting next to him, murmuring a folk song. His legs were stretched out in front of him, and from underneath his gray pants, a scar could be seen close to his ankle.

"What happened to your ankle?" asked Amir. All he knew about Behrouz were his scar and his songs.

Behrouz stopped murmuring. "I fell from my bike when I was a kid. I kept fiddling with the wound to make sure it left a scar."

"Why did you want a scar?"

A moment passed in silence, during which Amir imagined Behrouz shrugging.

"As a memory."

From underneath the blindfold, Amir saw Behrouz's dirty fingers creeping down to his memory.

Wound. Pain. Memory.

Amir knew that soon he would be so sick with memories that even taking the smallest step would be an impossible task. Memories were like snake poison, encroaching on the body, paralyzing one limb at a time.

One of his memories, still smelling of fresh blood and acidic breath, was being called an anti-revolutionary. His interrogators seemed to take special pleasure in calling him an anti-revolutionary or a spy. Different threats were accompanied by different nicknames, as if only through labeling him were the interrogators able to trust their own existence. By blindfolding the prisoners, they had reduced themselves to invisible beings, neither men nor shadows, merely voices with hands that needed victims and prey to survive.

Behrouz started singing again. His voice mingled with the sound of a cough from the other side of the corridor. Amir gave a nervous laugh, pressing his hands on top of his knees. A drop of sweat glided down his back.

Then one day, just when he thought they would let him be to contemplate his animal instincts, they took the lesson of humiliation a step further. They decided to show him off, their work of art, their installation of agony, to eyes that were not supposed to see.

They decided to break him.

The door screeched open, and from the end of the corridor came the indifferent slip-slap of disembodied feet in slippers. They stopped in front of Amir.

Amir could see the thick black hair on the toes sticking out from where the gray plastic slippers opened their maws. No words were uttered. One of the disembodied feet was lifted and landed against Amir's leg.

"Get up," commanded the voice belonging to the slippers and the hairy toes.

Grabbing the head of a pen that the guard told him was in front of his chest, Amir was led through a series of labyrinthine corridors. Next, he heard a door opening. They walked in. The air smelled different. It was still a bit musty, but nothing compared to the stench of the gutter Amir was getting used to. He felt the hands of the guard behind his dirty hair. And at last, for the first time in forty-five days, the blindfold came off.

A naked bulb hanging from a long wire coughed out white light around the room. Amir covered his eyes and tried to look through his dirty fingers at the liquid images and shadows around him. He felt light-headed, and his eyes took a few moments to adjust to the light. Slowly, the shadows began to take shape as if pushing through a cloud of smoke, and there emerged Maryam, pale like the day moon, gaping at him through the hole of her black scarf.

Amir stood rooted to the ground. He could feel the thick layer of filth coming to life on his body, his long itchy beard, his pajama-like uniform. He felt it crawling all over him, claiming him, leaving him no escape. He didn't want Maryam to see him like this, nibbled away by his own damp, growing dirtiness. He took a few steps back, bringing his hands to his face as if in pain. In Maryam's eyes, he could see the reflection of the humiliated animal standing before her.

Maryam took a step forward, her arms wide open, a quivering smile on her lips, new wrinkles around the corners of her eyes. *What have they done to you?* The unuttered question tossed and turned in her eyes.

"Where are you going?" the guard yelled out at Maryam as he pushed Amir into a chair. "Sit down!" As the words spurted out of his mouth, his gaze paused with unexpected slowness on Maryam's protruding stomach. In his eyes was the curious twinkle of someone who had never seen a pregnant woman. Maryam covered her stomach with a protective hand. The guard immediately turned his gaze away. He walked to the corner of the room and stood as the imposing shadow of authority.

The room breathed around them. One hand of the clock touched upon a passed minute.

Maryam straightened her neck the way she did, like a swan, when she was afraid and didn't want to show it, when she wanted to be strong for him. Her face was hard, almost stern, save for the red-rimmed, slightly puffy black eyes. Amir longed to wrap his arms around her; he longed for his hands to fly to her, over her, in the quiet of the room, under the blue twilight seeping in through the window. He looked at the blue veins bulging from the once spotless skin of her hands. He would have given anything to touch them, to lay his lips on them and kiss away the shadow of suffering from their every pore. But in that semi-lit room, with its pale tiles, its damp walls, and its neon light buzzing interminably like a fly, touches were prohibited. And when touches were absent, words had to fill their emptiness.

"How's my beautiful *banoo*?" Amir finally managed to say. He tried to smile, to sound unperturbed, for her sake, for his own. But he was terribly bad at it, and his voice cracked.

Maryam nodded; her eyes flashed at him. Anxiety throbbed in her eyes, haggard yet strong, unbending, as if in all her anxiety, she refused to accept the universe of this prison as her husband's only option. *You are going to be free*, her eyes seemed to tell him.

"How's your back?" she asked.

Amir looked at her. For a moment, he couldn't say anything. The question had catapulted him back to their house and the smell of roses in the garden and the yellow walls of their room and the photo of a drawing by Victor Hugo on the wall and a brand-new air conditioner that sat at the bottom of the stairs waiting to be taken up to the bedroom. He had hurt his back carrying the air conditioner by himself. He'd refused Maryam's suggestion to hire some men to do the job. He could do it himself. It would save them money and time. The pain had begun to subside the day he was arrested and had disappeared after a few days.

Amir smiled. He wanted to crawl into Maryam's arms and cry until he melted into her embrace. He realized he had never been able to tell her that his pain had indeed ceased. Everything had been interrupted, slashed right in half, as if each of them had been hurled into a different time zone. His had turned overnight into a nightmare of handcuffs and blindfolds, whereas hers still hung from those last fraying threads of air conditioners and sunlight, where pain could be caused by carrying something heavy and for no other reason, a time zone of innocence when they could still argue over who would carry the air conditioner, when he could still hear her chiding him while pressing hot towels on his back where it hurt. It was a reality from which he had been cut off so abruptly, so violently, that he could not believe it was once so simply his life.

He glanced at his wife. Maryam was looking straight into his eyes, almost challenging him, and not only him but the guard and the prison and God itself.

He opened his arms wide and then closed them, embracing himself. A weak smile rippled over her lips, and he knew. He held his breath, shuddering with gratitude. With this simple question, Maryam had been able to resuscitate his former self, which had begun to fade in his memory. She had come to him, ripping apart the last forty-five days of his life and throwing him back into that other life of heartening triviality, of beautiful quotidian worries, of the liberty to make unwise choices. Maryam had reminded him that he was still a man; that the old life was not over; that she would be there in a room cool with the air conditioner, waiting for him to come home. Maryam had been able to tell him that this agony was only a stopover; that sooner or later, it would finish. And so he knew that as long as he had her, he would survive.

"I'm fine. It's okay. The pain's gone," he said, feeling the defiance trickle through her fingertips, into the cheap, austere table, and spread through his bones. "How's the baby?"

"It's growing," she said. The mention of the child made her smile again, made them both smile. Her mouth parted with an unsustainable energy. Her cheeks flushed. The outlines of her face seemed to have taken on a certain softness. Her skin was smooth, impeccable. "It's incredible."

Then her eyes swayed involuntarily toward the guard, and the glow died immediately in her cheeks. Her face closed like a stormy sky. "Forty-five days." The words stumbled out of her mouth in a low voice, which, though it never rose, seemed to become heavier and heavier as it rolled away, unleashing her suffering. "Forty-five days they've kept you in here and I didn't know where you were. I didn't know whether you were alive. They wouldn't tell me. I went everywhere." Her voice faltered. She bit her lips hard as if trying to punish them for their quivering betrayal. Her earlier defiance seemed to vanish as she remembered her fear of having lost him, the fear that was still visibly raw, gashing away at her.

She was sitting on the edge of her chair, her breathing uneven, her hands tremulous, folded like toppled nests on the table. She seemed not to know what to do with her hands, or her eyes, or the sob knotted in the back of her throat. Amir tried to say something.

He couldn't. His throat too felt clogged by the devastation that came forward to engulf him. He took a deep breath.

"I couldn't see your face when I was dreaming," he said, leaning as close as he could to her. It was his turn to be strong, for her sake, for his own sake. *They cannot break me. They cannot break us.* "It was just empty space, like a halo. But now that you're here, I know I won't be alone anymore."

With a beautiful little shiver of her head, Maryam looked up at him. Her eyes flickered like fireflies at night. "You're never alone. I'm always with you."

"And the baby?" His heart swelled with joy and hope just from the thought of his child, their child, on the way. He wanted to ask Maryam to get up so he could take another look at her belly, but he was afraid the guard's gaze would turn too. He didn't want the guard to look at her, to intrude upon, with his gaze of impurity, what was theirs alone. "Does it move?"

Maryam's face once again spread into a smile. How he loved to see her smile; how he longed to smell the breath hovering over her lips.

"At night, it kicks and kicks, like it's dancing," she said.

"Like its mother."

"Yes."

"You like to dance."

"Yes."

Outside, a key turned inside the keyhole. The guard made a move toward them. Maryam and Amir looked at each other. Their eyes snatched at each other, tugged at each other, as if they wanted to carry a piece of the other in that safest, most intimate place that was their eyes.

"Sheida," Maryam said urgently. "If it's a girl, shall we call her Sheida?"

The guard pushed Amir away. The ten minutes were over.

Back in the hall, Amir's knees almost gave way.

They were forty in a tiny cell with strips of paint hanging from its walls. The prisoners were squeezed together like bees in a hive, at times sidestepping, at times crawling on top of one another. The situation got worse at night, when each body sought to claim its sleeping space. There were times when arguments broke out, and times when mouths twitched in nervous restrain. Finally, to put an end to the tensions, they decided to draw lines on the thin, foul-smelling carpet to indicate the boundaries for each body. They slept head to foot, without moving a muscle, huddled together like children frightened by thunder.

It was a little before dawn break when Amir opened his eyes. In the past year, he had made it a matter of principle to wake up every day before the sound of the *azan* spouted into the cell, calling the prisoners to prayer. He wanted at least the act of waking to be his choice. He wanted his days to begin when he and only he decided to open his eyes.

Praying was part of their education in the new prison. They had been transferred here to be formed into God-fearing men. But in that world of violence and madness, God was not what Amir feared most.

Behrouz, now his right-side sleeping mate, snored softly. Amir remained motionless, looking at Behrouz's scar and the toenails that tipped upward at the end.

After a few moments, the cry of the *azan*, which Amir used to find beautiful as a free man and now found smothering as a man in a cage, shook the cell out of its slumber. The signs of awakening were slow. The sounds of a cough, a yawn, a foot gliding down rough blankets came from the other side, where the cell ended in the door. Amir curled up and wrapped his arms around his bent knees.

Forty disheveled men rolled up their bedding and piled it against the wall. One by one, they were taken to the bathroom and brought back, shuffling. One by one, they stood next to each other in straight lines, ready to speak to God. Surrounded by divine words, Amir bent and genuflected automatically, like a despairing puppet. Heavy whispers bounced off the walls.

When they finished, they sat on top of their piled bedding rolls and waited for breakfast: a cup of tea, two sugar cubes, a piece of bread, and some feta cheese. Today, the holy Friday, they were also given a spoonful of powdered milk, another of jam, a few figs and dates. The sugar cubes were denied when jam or dates were given.

Amir was sipping his tea when the heavy door of the cell squeaked open and a guard with a barely noticeable shadow of hair above his upper lip appeared at the doorway.

"Amir Ramezanzadeh," he called out, trying in vain to control the hormonal slipperiness of his voice.

Amir heard his name roll out of the boy's mouth and then crack open at the "za" of the "zadeh." He felt his heart sink. Whenever anyone's name was called, it meant long hours of disappearance and then the exhausted, crushed body returning from the interrogation room, where not even God mattered as much as the body did, where no confession, no denial, no apology was worth anything. The interrogators were not interested in words. It was only the body that mattered in those hot, dark, airless rooms. The body, the broken ribs, and the endless, incomprehensible shouting in the ears.

Amir had thought his interrogations were over, but he was obviously mistaken. He walked toward the guard, who kept the door open to the feeble light of the corridor. He stood still as the guard covered his eyes with the black blindfold.

There, once again, darkness and vulnerability; once again, realizing how out of his control his life had become. Amir was not living his life anymore. He was living someone else's life: blindfolded, led from the cell to the interrogation room, holding on to a pen.

This time, Amir was taken not to the interrogation room but to the "courtyard," a room that had been stripped of the roof and left with glaring naked iron bars in its place, and where once a week, the prisoners milled about for ten minutes, filling their lungs with fresh air. The prison was close to the mountains. The same mountains whose peak Amir was once able to see from his living room window.

"Sit down," the guard ordered as he untied the blindfold and left the courtyard.

Amir squatted on the ground. It was raining. The smell of rain blended with the bitter smell of asphalt reminded him of his childhood and the first day of school. Lost, his cheeks wet with hot tears and cool raindrops, he had run from one street to another, looking for the big iron door of his school. That was one of his most vivid childhood memories: the first day of school and not being at school.

A few moments passed with no sign of the guard. It started

raining harder. Amir looked around. The more time passed, the more nervous he grew. Why had they brought him here? Why was he alone? Was this the end of the line? Was he living the last moments of his life without knowing it? Sitting on the wet ground, in a roofless room, waiting for a teenager in a guard's uniform who held Amir's life in his hands like a crumpled packet of cigarettes.

Amir took a deep breath and then another. Taking deep breaths could keep one alive.

At last, the guard reappeared, holding something wrapped in blankets. He walked slowly up to Amir while trying hard to not meet his eyes. He bent slightly forward and placed the thing on Amir's lap. "Here's your kid," he said.

Never in his life had Amir felt so conscious of his own heartbeats and the rush of blood in his veins as when he pulled aside the blanket and saw two big brown eyes looking at him, the soft black hair grazing her forehead. A few drops of rain fell on her face and she blinked quickly, opening her mouth. Amir stared at her, dumbfounded. He held her without making the slightest movement, as if suddenly paralyzed.

Three minutes later, the guard came and pulled her out of his embrace. Amir was led back to the cell, trembling.

Amir's first trial took about five minutes. Two years had passed. A guard took him to a small room where a mullah and a young man were waiting for him. Amir was to say his name. He was not allowed a lawyer. The issue had not come up. Amir had never thought of asking for one, knowing it would be impossible. He had not even thought there would be a trial.

All the charges against him seemed to be known and clear to the mullah reading them. All Amir could do was listen to them and accept the sentence given to him. The mullah started reading the charges: "Founding a Marxist group, participating in a Marxist group, planning a coup, planning the overthrow of the Islamic Republic of Iran, atheism . . ."

He read on and on. Amir was charged with so many crimes that he thought he would be on the execution list. He felt a dizzying tightness in his chest. His palms grew sweaty, and he thought of Maryam and Sheida and the life that would never come. The mullah finally stopped reading. Amir knew the penalty for atheism was capital punishment. That was the only thing he was certain of. In those few seconds allowed him, he said, "I'm a Muslim."

It took a few more minutes for the young man to read out his sentence. Amir was sentenced to six years of imprisonment. He looked at the mullah and the young man. He inhaled so deeply that the air scratched his throat. He had survived. The relief was so powerful, it almost knocked him down. He had to hold on to the wall not to fall. Now he had something concrete to tell Maryam. Now they both knew how long they had to wait. Six years, and they would be all together again. Six years, and all this would be over.

He was moved to another cell and told this was where he would spend the next six years.

Amir stood, his feet planted on the two blackened white platforms on either side of the hole in the ground with dead cockroaches floating in it. His back was to the door with a broken lock; the locks on all the bathroom doors were broken. It was to make it easier for the guards to break in when necessary: someone fainting, another breaking down, another killing himself. The locks were broken so that no *breaking in* would be needed. They could just walk in, the guards, and put an end to whatever it was they needed to put an end to.

Amir stood, straddled, and urinated when he was supposed to urinate.

He turned to leave, nauseated by the thick smell of old urine, when he saw a small wooden box on the ground. It was unusual to see a box there. Nothing from the outside world ever found its way into the prison, not even abandoned wooden boxes. Amir picked it up and began examining it like a precious antique. His fingers grazed the rough wooden texture and felt the head of a protruding nail. With his fingertips, he twisted it. The nail was looser than it seemed and came off easily. He put the nail in his pocket and left the bathroom.

Starting from the weekly ten-minute-fresh-mountain-air time, Amir began eliminating the head of the nail by rubbing it against the cement floor. He sat there, unshakable in his pursuit, as though he could rub away the whole prison if he were persistent enough. He could clearly see it, the bracelet of date stones, on his daughter's tiny wrist. Or maybe she would have to wait. Maybe Maryam would have to wear it first and then pass it on to their daughter once she was old enough. There were so many possibilities. His heart seethed with excitement, his body warming up as a few timid autumnal sunbeams reached the crown of his head through the iron bars of the naked roof.

On Friday, he went around the cell, holding an empty jar of

powdered milk in his hand. "Don't throw away your date stones. Put them in here."

Hands reached out, fingers let go, date stones clapped down into the jar. When the jar was half full, Amir filled it with water and left the stones to soften.

Days passed. Amir watched the stones, and as he waited, day after day, anxiety began to replace his earlier excitement. What if he ran out of time? What if they called his name again and this time it was not to see his daughter? What if those who had to decide what to do with his life changed their minds before he had time to finish? Before he was able to leave something for his daughter other than an evaporating memory?

His head was throbbing. For the umpteenth time that day, he went over to the jar to test the stones' softness. He knew it was useless; the stones still needed several days. But he couldn't help it. He couldn't sit still. He prowled around the room, barely able to stand the sound of slip-slap that came and went out in the corridor. Every time, he thought they were coming for him; that his time was up.

He decided not to lose time. While waiting for the stones to soften, he began making a screwdriver by sticking the headless nail into the semi-melted handle of his toothbrush. He gripped the nail tightly in his fingers. If he gripped it tightly enough, he thought, his hand would stop shaking.

Another day went by, another day of uncertainty, of gathering every force in him not to run around the cell, holding his head in his hands, of constantly keeping an ear to the door and snatching everything into his pocket when the sound of slip-slap approached the cell.

He spent the next day making a string by unraveling brown threads from his own socks and those of Behrouz, who had offered his.

"My daughter's being brought up by her grandparents," Behrouz said, holding the socks in his hands. "Along with two of her cousins. The children of my wife's sisters, who are also in prison. Do you think maybe one day they'll be able to bring my daughter to me so that I can see her?" His eyes glistened with something like a plea, as if Amir had all the answers.

"They will, of course they will," Amir said, looking at Behrouz's worried face, thinking how fortunate Sheida was to be with her own mother.

Amir spun the threads around a toothpaste tube filled with hardened dough, which he used like a spindle to weave the threads. His forehead wrinkled with concentration, his lips pressed together tightly, his chin went up and down with every left and right movement of the spindle. He tried not to think. He had to distract himself and focus on the bracelet. If only he could finish the bracelet and be able to give it to his daughter, he would finally not be afraid of anything anymore. Then he could relax, thinking that there was something of him out there, from the inside to the other side, to freedom, to where his daughter would grow, knowing her father never gave up; that life never gives up.

Night fell. Amir went to sleep, keeping the nail and the string in his pocket. Feeling them close reassured him; half of the job, at least, was done.

The first thing he did when he woke up the next day was to

wind his way through the sleeping bodies toward his jar. *Let them be ready*, he murmured under his breath. Dawn had not yet broken, and the room was filled with a stifling, lucid darkness. He couldn't see the stones well; all he could see were small black lumps in the jar. He dipped his finger into the cool, slightly slimy water and picked one of them up. A warm breath slipped out through his half-open lips. It was time.

Soon after the Morning Prayer, he began drilling tiny holes into the thick sides of the stones using his screwdriver. As he drilled, he felt the fingers of the cramped cell begin to loosen around his neck, the nerves on his forehead to unwind, the tight muscles of his shoulders to relax. In every date stone he held between his fingers, he felt the haunting sense of vertigo begin to diminish. In every date stone, he felt one step away from the edge of the world, the precipice, where the earth came undone under his feet. Perhaps time was indeed on his side. Perhaps he would not lose everything after all.

When all the stones were ready, he began stringing them. Evening had fallen. The naked lamp had come on, suffusing the cell with what seemed for the first time like a gentle glow to Amir's eyes. A hum of conversation surrounded him. From the corner of the cell, he could hear Behrouz and some of the other prisoners playing a poetry game, picking up the last letter of a line of poetry to start a new line.

Amir smiled as he picked up another stone. Every stone danced a little dance as it glided down the string. The last stone slipped down with a slight tremble. Amir shivered with excitement, like a marathon runner who could see the finish line for the first time.

It was almost dinnertime when he tied a finishing knot at either end of the string. Outside, the wind groaned as it blew between the naked bars of the courtyard. Amir laid the bracelet of date stones carefully on the carpet. He had injected his entire urge for life into it, and now he felt he had no strength left. He heard the doors of adjacent cells opening; the guards were getting closer. He quickly picked up the bracelet and hid it in his pocket.

The door of the cell squeaked open. A bucket of rice went from hand to hand until it reached Amir. He was in charge of dividing dinner that night.

Amir had to wait weeks before he could pass the bracelet to his daughter, weeks of impatience, solitude, and despair. Weeks when he carried the bracelet hidden in his pocket, like a cherished memory on which his entire being depended, a cherished memory that the guards were sure to tear into pieces if they discovered it.

At last, on a gloomy afternoon, he was granted a visit. This time, the visiting room was a long, narrow hall with glass screens marking the frontier where one life stopped and another began.

Maryam sat in front of him, behind the glass, holding Sheida on her lap. Sheida had grown. She bore little resemblance to the child Amir had held in his arms on that rainy afternoon. Even the color of her eyes had changed. They were darker, almost black. Her gaze fluttered around the hall, then settled on Amir's face for a few moments. As soon as Amir warmed up to the idea of his daughter recognizing him, her eyes started to flit again, all around the hall, the hospital-green walls, and the glass screen.

Smiling, Maryam picked Sheida up and headed toward the door that led to the prisoners on the other side of the glass screens.

Standing by the door was the guard whom they had seen during the first visit with Amir. The smile vanished from her face. Her steps took on a certain heaviness, as if she had forgotten how to walk.

The guard looked at her with a blank stare as she told him Amir's name and number, tightening her arms around Sheida. He nodded and grabbed the girl. His hands looked surprisingly old. Maryam waved to her daughter as she disappeared behind the door in the arms of the guard.

On the other side of the glass screen, Amir was waiting with his hands strong but unsteady in the air. The bulging vein on his forehead throbbed violently. And Sheida came to his arms, crossing the frontier between life and death, time and purgatory, her baby feet dangling in the air, her eyes dancing like butterflies. Amir held her so tightly that she let out a scream. Maryam laughed and wiped a tear hanging from her new wrinkle. Sheida struggled to get up. Amir looked around him and hid the bracelet inside Sheida's sweater.

The guard reappeared. He took Sheida, with her secret bracelet of date stones warm against her heartbeats, back to where life awaited her.

Amir's second trial was also just a few minutes. Three years had passed since the first, during which Behrouz had seen his daughter once. On that day, Amir taught him how to make a bracelet, as a way of celebration.

This time, when Amir was called, he did not give the trial much thought. It did not worry him as a guard took him to a small room, where this time a mullah and two men in black suits with austere faces were waiting for him. *I have already been sentenced*, he told himself, *I have only three more years to go.* No one, he thought, could take that away from him.

"Do you pray?" The mullah raised his small, glaring eyes from a folder open in front of him. He looked tired, in a bad mood.

"Yes," Amir said, having an inkling that this must be the right answer.

"Does your father pray?"

"Yes."

"Do you fast during Ramadan?"

"Yes."

The questions stopped. One of the men in a black suit wrote something down. No one said anything. They looked at Amir and called for the guard to return him to his cell.

A week later, sometime before dawn, Amir woke to the sound of rapid footfalls echoing in the corridor. He opened his eyes, listening to the noises outside, wondering what was going on. The door shrieked open, and Amir was seized before he had time to fully get up, along with a few others, Behrouz among them. They barely had time to speak to each other, even to exchange a glance. The blindfold once again covered shocked, confused, sleepy eyes. Handcuffs were fastened. He was dragged out, pushed left and right down the corridor. A door was unlocked; cold predawn air pierced the skin. Hurried incomprehensible murmurs were heard all around. Amir's heart hammered violently, beating, beating, galloping. His blindfolded head constantly turned and twisted as he tried to look around. His mouth was dry. Darkness was inescapable.

"What are you doing?" he heard Behrouz shout. "Where are you taking us?"

No one answered him. His voice was drowned out by the shouting of others.

Amir was pushed violently forward by a pair of hands from behind. Then he felt the rough texture of the rope around his neck. He wanted to shout but couldn't. And that was the last thing. Next, for just a moment, time froze, and then, as sudden as an avalanche, it was over.

2008
Tehran, the Islamic Republic of Iran

Two days before Maman Zinat died, she and Forugh ate a pomegranate together. Forugh cleaned it as Maman Zinat watched, sitting on a wide armchair wrapped hermetically in a floral slipcover. Her knees protruded from the pistachio-green blanket like two soft, round lumps. There was a fresco on the wall behind her, of white swans swimming down a blue river, surrounded by green trees and a clear sky with white bushy clouds.

Forugh held the pomegranate from the top, dug the knife right underneath its crown, and cut it in half. Scarlet-colored juice spilled onto the white tray, and there was a soft sigh as it sliced opened.

The television was on. A satellite channel run by Iranian expats in America was broadcasting a Persian music video.

"I like Mansour." Maman Zinat turned up the volume. "He's polite; not like the rest of them, jumping around the stage and screaming. He obviously comes from a good family."

Translucent arils, like rubies. Forugh's hands danced clumsily around them, her fingers soaked in the sticky scarlet juice. She looked up from where she was sitting on the red flowers of the handwoven carpet and glanced happily at Maman Zinat, at her smooth skin, the long silver hair fastened into a labyrinthine loop at the back of her head, the fold of pink skin falling over her eyes and giving her a sleepy look, at her hands, white and dry, folded on top of her blanket, their only luxury a quiet gold wedding ring.

Forugh had not seen her grandmother in over twelve years. And so she watched her with admiration, with love, with a mixed feeling of joy and curiosity. She was amazed by how little Maman Zinat had changed. The years had not taken their toll on her skin, on the palpitating youth in her eyes, on the composedness of her movements.

The pomegranate seeds burst under the pressure of Forugh's fingers, and the juice splashed on her blouse. Her gaze caught Maman Zinat's hand swiftly snatching the blanket away from the damage. Forugh laughed.

"I hope I have your genes, Maman Zinat." She tried to clean the red spots on her blouse with the back of her unblemished hand.

"Why?" Maman Zinat asked with the smile of a woman who knew exactly why her granddaughter would want her genes. A woman who knew she was still beautiful.

"Your skin has fewer wrinkles than mine."

"You don't need my genes. You're beautiful like a flower; like those flowers on the jacaranda tree."

Morning light scatters across the horizon and trickles down on the narrow horizontal patio, shattering into the blue water of the porcelain fountain, spreading like moisture underneath Forugh's skin. She stands underneath the jacaranda tree, looking up at the purple-pink panicles. She clasps her hands and draws her shoulders in. As she hangs her head, her tears drop on her yellow silk shirt, leaving salty stains. She crumples next to the fountain, where gold-fish flutter restlessly before sleep. Half of her body on mud, half on the cobblestones reaching the edge of the flower bed. She weeps.

She feels a hand on her shoulder and lifts her red-rimmed eyes.

"Maman Zinat loved this tree," Khaleh Leila says as she stretches her hand out to the leaves, caressing them.

"I should've come earlier. I came when it was too late."

"You were with her during her last days. I'm sure she died happy. That's all that matters."

The last image Forugh has of Maman Zinat is of her cold body laid out on the bed, covered by a white sheet. Maman Zinat's heart had stopped beating at dawn. Forugh removed the sheet to look at her. Maman Zinat was clinging to her chest as if she wanted to extract her heart and hurl it through the window. The back of her other hand lay motionless on her forehead, her mouth twisted in pain, her fixed gaze terrorized, incredulous, as if she could not believe death could be at hand so easily.

Forugh did not see happiness in Maman Zinat's face, nor peace.

She saw only pain. The pain of clutching at the heart when it suddenly ceases beating. The pain of having to face death before sunrise. Alone.

Dante places the trays of dates and halvah on the cement ground and rings the bell. The mild breeze is heavy with the smell of dust and cement that rises from the construction work in the house at the end of the alley. As he waits, he watches the door of the adjacent house open and a woman with a black chador appear in the doorway. A little boy almost pushes her aside and springs out of the house. He is clutching some money in his hand. He runs past Dante, toward the street. His mother calls after him, saying she'll be right there, watching out for him. As he runs, one of his slippers slips off his foot. For a second, it seems like he doesn't understand what has just happened, what has stopped him from running. He sees the plastic slipper behind him, close to the halfway stream. He slides his foot back into it and begins running again. He stops and turns to his mother. "Just soda, right?"

She nods, and he runs out of the alley and into the street.

The little boy and the way he runs remind Dante of himself as a child. He used to run like that every time Maman Zinat or Khaleh Leila sent him to buy something from the grocery store up the street. He'd run all the way to the store, get whatever he had to buy, and run back. He never walked. Little boys never walk. They run all the time, as if currents of time are after them, swirling and swishing about. His gaze trails behind the little boy until he goes into the shop.

The boy's mother looks at Dante, who nods and says hello.

"My condolences," she says quietly, tightening the chador over her face.

Dante thanks her as she skulks back into the house, disappearing from view. Although he can no longer see her, he knows that the mother is still there, behind the door, waiting for her son. That she is the first person her son will find when he comes running back to the house.

Dante returns his gaze to the blue door and rings the bell again. He doesn't want to be here. He doesn't like funerals. He's here only because of the two women with their gray hair and smell of the past. The two women who raised him, passing him from one warm embrace to the other, telling him love stories of Persian princesses and their poor beautiful lovers. The two women for whom he shed bitter tears when his mother, released from Khomeini's prison, wanted to take him home with her.

Now one of these women is dead, but Dante can't cry. He's furious with the glorious sun in the white-blue sky. He does not understand why tragedies always happen on beautiful sunny days.

From the other side of the blue door comes the sound of high heeled shoes rapidly striking the cobblestones. Dante cocks his ears. These can't be Khaleh Leila's footsteps. Not the high heels. Not the rapidity. The approach of the battering alien echo unnerves him.

A woman opens the door. A heart-shaped face; audaciously long eyelashes framing brown eyes; curly black hair cascading over her shoulders. She tosses the hair back with a small hand and smiles. There is something about the light of her smile, the cut of her dress, the uninhibited flow of her hair that makes her look foreign.

Then he remembers. *Forugh!*

Dante stammers as he introduces himself while quickly picking up the trays from the ground. Forugh seems not to have caught his name. She looks distracted. Her eyes are disturbingly sensual with sorrow. She takes one of the trays from him but doesn't introduce herself.

Dante follows her in, lowering his head in order to pass through the door. The house is silent. He wonders where Khaleh Leila is. He looks up at the house, his gaze involuntarily drawn to Maman Zinat's room. He sees the closed windows, the drawn curtains, and a sharp pang goes through him.

Forugh walks in front of him. She is wearing a black dress that falls slightly below her caramel-colored knees. Her hair bobs on her shoulders as she walks across the patio like a proprietor, confident and at ease. It makes him nervous, the way she walks. He feels like she is going to dispossess him of something, though of what he can't tell. The heels of her shoes tap on the ground like heartbeats.

In the house, whose old walls and low blue door make it look out of place among the newly constructed apartment complexes surrounding it, Leila and Maman Zinat lived together through Leila's divorce and Aghajaan's death, year after year, among shadows and murmurs. They were the last guardians of the past. This house was their territory, the relic of their youth. No one had been able to lure them out. No promise of comfort in a smaller apartment, no promise of money for a journey—to Mecca, maybe, or Germany to visit Forugh and her mother—could convince them. As long as the house stood and they were in it, they were mistresses of their own destiny.

On the day after Forugh's arrival, Leila, holding a bright yellow silk scarf in her hand, asked Forugh to blindfold her.

Maman Zinat laughed softly. There was an amused glitter in her eyes.

Blindfolded, Leila walked with short confident strides from one room to another, her fingers grazing the uneven surface of the walls, like a blind woman reading. She stopped accurately in front of every room and told its story. Where someone was born. Where someone had died. Where someone had spent his or her wedding night.

"Here," she told Forugh, pointing to a door, turning her blindfolded head toward it, "your mother was born."

She could not see Forugh's face; could only hear her breath quickening. At the end of the tour, she took off the blindfold, smiling triumphantly. Maman Zinat applauded. Forugh laughed, perhaps thinking both of them mad. That was only a few days ago, before Maman Zinat's heartbeats disappeared as lightly as a pebble in the fountain.

Leila lets out a sigh. She has grown so old, so fast. She sits slumped on the floor with her back to the window. Her eyes, tingling and burning, are closed. She is overcome by such languidness, such dejection, that she can barely move. She thinks she has heard the door opening but is not sure. Could it already be Omid and Sara? She called them this morning at their hotel in Shiraz to give them the news. She had not heard Omid sob so loudly since he was a child. How had Sara reacted? Leila had not spoken to her. Parisa was there with them. She was in shock. She could not speak. *So much for a family vacation.* Leila presses her eyes shut. *Poor things.* They told her that they would be on the first plane back to Tehran. She told them about Forugh, about her return. They seemed not to hear. Their ears were full of death.

Leila shifts her body around. She would like to know if some-

one has arrived. But she doesn't have the strength to call out to
Forugh and ask. Instead, she droops farther down, listening to the
birds chirping outside.

Forugh did not listen to Dante as he introduced himself. He
seemed too young, too nervous, too impatient to present himself, so she immediately lost interest. She took him as some sort
of a housekeeper, here to give them a hand with the afternoon
ceremony. Now, apprehensive, she watches him move about the
house, tall and wiry, with the liberty and certainty of someone who
knows every nook and cranny. Without consulting her, he goes
down to the basement and carries the silver samovar, the golden-
rimmed glass cups, the fragrant tea from Lahijan, the trays, and
the sugar cubes up to the kitchen. He moves swiftly in and out of
the kitchen, in and out of the guest room, in and out of the basement. He does not seem like a housekeeper but a man coming
back to his childhood home. It unsettles her, his intimacy with the
house. He moves about as if it is *his* childhood home, as if it is *he*
who listened to the two women's love stories about Persian princesses and their poor beautiful lovers at night, as if it is *he* who was
raised among the women's breathing and memories.

Dante climbs up the stairs, carrying a table. The lean muscles
of his arms and chest protrude under its weight. Soft black hair
bounces on his forehead as he climbs one step after another.

Forugh does not know what to do with herself. She would like
to help, to seem in control, to ask him again who he is. Obviously,
he is not a housekeeper. But she is embarrassed to admit that she
didn't listen the first time. She follows him around the house, fid-

dling with things she knows very little about. Things she has not seen in years. Things he seems to know well. His apparent belonging to the house intimidates her, enrages her. She feels useless, extra, covetous. She runs to give him a hand with the table, but he declines politely. He smiles. She finds his smile patronizing.

He is treating me like a guest, Forugh thinks, and tries to compose the angry speed of her heels thudding down the carpeted stairs as she runs up to Khaleh Leila's room. She doesn't know why she is heading up there. She feels like a child who is going to complain to her mother about the boy who does not let her play with him and feels slightly ashamed of herself because of it.

Khaleh Leila is lying on the floor, her head on a big white cushion, her pressed eyelids hidden underneath a layer of cucumber skin. Forugh knows she has been crying all morning.

"The guy is here." Forugh is out of breath. She ran too quickly up the stairs.

Khaleh Leila removes the green skins from her eyes. She is a scrawny woman with long black eyes and a thin, severe mouth. Her head of thick curly hair is just like Forugh's. She looks older than her age. "I thought I heard the door." Her voice is weak, faltering. Without lifting her head, she fumbles for a small plate where a thin cucumber lies vulnerably naked. She picks up fresh skins and replaces the old ones on her eyes. "He's Marzieh's son. Remember Marzieh?"

Forugh has a flash of a little boy running around the patio, kicking a ball. The boy with gray eyes and fleshy cheeks. That was when Forugh and her mother came to visit. Although they were more or less the same age, the boy looked much younger than Forugh. She was not interested in getting to know him.

"How come his name is Dante?"

"For the same reason your name is Forugh. His father was a big fan of the Italian poet. Just like your mother loved Forugh and her poetry and named you after her."

"And they let his parents name him Dante?"

"Of course not. The name on his birth certificate is Hossein." The breeze lifts the curtains, lets them drop. "Tell him to get the stuff for the tea. He knows where it is. "

"He's already taken everything."

Khaleh Leila lightly lifts her cucumber-folded head and smiles.

There is a sense of intimacy in that smile. Forugh wonders if Maman Zinat ever smiled like that at the thought of Dante. She closes the door petulantly but makes sure it does not slam.

They stand in front of each other, holding the corners of the white tablecloth, waving and flapping it in the air. The cloth fluffs up, then flattens like the sandy end of a wave.

"When did you arrive?" Dante asks as he watches Forugh squint, check the two corners of the tablecloth, and pull one of the sides slightly down. Dante smiles at her precision. She sees the smile but doesn't smile back.

"On Tuesday."

"Just a few days before, and you would've been here for the New Year."

"I know."

"And your cousins? Do you know when they will get here?"

"Probably this evening."

Dante hoists the samovar up from the ground and places it on the table. His gaze falls on her delicate hands straightening out the wrinkles, brushing against the tablecloth in short jerky movements as if she wants to wipe out an invisible stain. She has a European way of gesturing. Feeling frustration mounting in him, Dante plunges straight in with who is at the core of his hurt, their hurt. "Last time I saw Maman Zinat was about a week ago."

Glass cups clink against the saucers as Forugh arranges them on the silver tray.

"They were at our house for dinner. She was laughing at something Khaleh Leila had done. That's the last thing I remember of her. The way she was laughing." Dante pauses. He takes a deep breath and tries to swallow the unexpected knot that has taken shape in his throat. "She seemed just fine. I don't understand what happened."

On the breeze drifting through the opening of the window come faint sounds: the creaking of a door, the whipping of a rug, the distant pounding of a hammer.

"It was a heart attack." Forugh lifts her eyes to him, her hands now immobile on top of the golden-edged cups. "Early in the morning. The doctor said it was immediate."

Dante looks away from her and out the window at the flowers basking in the warmth of the late-morning sun. He wishes he could be somewhere else; on top of the Darband Mountains, perhaps, looking over the city, far away, unreachable. He stands there, listening to Forugh pour the sugar cubes into the container, pierced by an unsettling and benumbing grief. He wishes Forugh would smile at him.

For years, after Forugh left Iran for Germany with her mother and Naser, her mother's second husband, Dante read Forugh's letters aloud to Maman Zinat. Letters that didn't go beyond giving news and yet were full of sadness. Letters written in an uncluttered, cautious handwriting that did not change shape, did not mature, neither improved nor deteriorated over the years. A handwriting standing witness to the halt of time in that hidden corner of the mind where memories lingered.

At times, snuggled in the heart of a letter, there was a drawing of a river and its swimming swans. Similar to the fresco in the yellow room, yet different. It was like a drawing of what Forugh remembered of the fresco. Other times, there were photos of Forugh promenading through life in still images: birthdays, graduations, New Year's. Dante came to know Forugh through the frozen illusion of her smile in a surrounding as alien and awe-inspiring to him as anything that Forugh herself presented in her heart-shaped face and brown eyes.

Now standing before her, he realizes that this part of his life, the part connected like an umbilical cord to the house and the women inside it, has been lived under the hovering shadow of the images, words, and memories of this woman. And now she does not spare him even a glance. He would like to tell her about the letters, about the drawings.

"Let's arrange the fruit here," she says, or rather orders. With long elegant strides, she moves toward the door.

"Everything's in the fridge upstairs," he calls after her. "That's where they usually keep the fruit."

Forugh turns around, her gaze as cold as crushed ice. Suddenly, he feels like a child before her, as if she can sweep him away with a glance, with a whisper, with a smile. "I know," she says. "I lived here for years, you know."

"I know you did," Dante says, startled. His mouth feels dry. "I just told you where the fruit is, because there are two fridges."

"That's fine. Shall we get it, then?" She looks impatient to flee his gaze.

"Okay, let's get it."

His gaze follows as she disappears down the corridor. He was not expecting this hostility. He straightens his back and waves a hand as if trying to clear the air. He wants nothing to do with whatever it is gnawing at her nerves. Not here and not today. He caresses the edge of one of the saucers that have been neatly arranged on the tray and waits a moment before following her out to the kitchen.

Leila traipses down the corridor, descends the steps into the kitchen, walks past the wall that Maman Zinat always wanted to knock down and never did, and stops at the tiny window looking out to the reflections of light in the blue fountain.

She sees them working, their backs turned to each other. Forugh is washing the baby cucumbers in the sink; Dante is trundling a bag of golden grapes down into a basin of water.

Here they are, her children, the children she never had, under the same glow of light. The children who were once without mothers and fathers and they were hers and they were Maman Zinat's. Then the mothers came and took them away. They were mothered and everything fell apart. They were mothered and solitude crept in, the echo of their laughter disappearing through the blue door. Her heart squeezes with the thought of Omid and Sara. She cannot wait for them to arrive. *What is taking them so long?*

Leila never had her own children. After the afternoon with Ahmad that became a memory without leaving any trace, she no longer desired any. She refused to have children with her husband in the three-year marriage that followed. That was perhaps what broke up her marriage. She did not care. At that point, it no longer mattered.

What is life, she thinks, *except a long lullaby of separation?*

Dante is the first to see her. He comes to her with his arms spread, and she sinks into his embrace. *How he has grown,* she thinks, as she does every time in his embrace, and tears flow down her face. He places a kiss on her head. She stays locked in his arms until she calms down. She unravels herself and looks at them.

"*Elahi bemiram khasteh shodid.*" *I hope I die before I see you tired.*

They smile, and their eyes are sad. "*Khoda nakone!*" *God forbid!*

Leila opens the fridge and takes out a crystal pitcher. "Come and have some cherry sherbet." *To rid your body of fatigue.*

Forugh takes the pitcher and pours the ruby liquid into three glasses. Dante comes forward, water dripping from his fingers. She hands him a glass. Their eyes lock. The sparrows' chirrup carols through the window. Their eyes unlock.

Leila pulls up a chair and slides the tray of dates in front of her. She hums a sad song as she opens a date with her thumbs, extracts the pit, and inserts a piece of walnut inside the sweet stomach. She closes the date and lays it on the tray. Gradually, a sense of peace comes to the kitchen, like that inside a mosque once everyone has left after the prayers.

Forugh and Dante work together. When one washes, the other dries. When one cleans, the other polishes. When one takes out the china plates from the cabinet, the other places them on the table. When one's hand runs over the table, the other watches. When one breathes, the other listens.

"How Maman Zinat liked dates," Leila says in a faraway, melancholic voice. "She would buy boxes of them. And with her diabetes!

She had such a sweet tooth. Once she bought fifteen melons all at once. The fruit seller was passing by here. As soon as she heard him shouting, she told me to call him. It was after she had broken her knee. She bought fifteen of them. I kept saying, 'But it's just the two of us, how are we going to eat all these melons?' She wouldn't listen to me. The house was full of melons, in the fridge, on top of the fridge, behind the fridge, under the fridge. When she realized they were going bad, she started eating two melons a day. She finished them all in a week." Leila chuckles. Forugh comes and takes her hand. Dante stops working and stands in front of them.

"How many of the melons did *you* eat, Khaleh Leila?" he says teasingly, giving her a smile.

She throws the date stone to the side, her eyes glistening. "Oh, maybe one or two."

Forugh smiles and caresses Khaleh Leila's salt-and-pepper hair.

"I always tried to hide the sweet things from her," Leila continues, "but she would find them anyway. There was not a corner of this house that was safe."

"She had me buy dates once or twice for her," Dante says. "She'd tell me to hide them in my bag so you wouldn't see them, and she'd take them straight to her room."

"Oh, and you did that! Shame on you!"

"What did you want me to do? Maman Zinat always got what she wanted. I couldn't say no."

They both laugh. Forugh stops caressing Khaleh Leila's hair. Leila feels the tense heaviness of the immobile hand on her head.

"Our Forugh ate a few of them herself. Do you still like eating melons, as you used to?"

"Oh, yes." Forugh gives a short, forced laugh. "I could finish fifteen of them right now."

Khaleh Leila pats Forugh's hand. "When you're done here, you two should look through the album for a nice photo of Maman Zinat to put on the table at the entrance."

"I can do it myself," Forugh says, not looking at Dante. "Where are the albums?"

"There's just one album. It's in the wardrobe in my room. I think you can find an empty frame there too."

"You go ahead," Dante says. "I'll finish up here."

Forugh walks out of the kitchen. Leila looks up at Dante, who turns away from her.

Forugh sits on Maman Zinat's armchair, the album on her lap. She sifts through the photos carefully, one by one, her fingers crawling on the wrinkled, yellowed glassine covers protecting the photos. She still can't bring herself to believe that Maman Zinat is no longer there. It feels unreal, impossible, absurd, the absence. Her fingertips trace Maman Zinat's face, her half-closed eyes in one photo, her smiling mouth in another, her hand holding a plate of grapes. Forugh's eyes fog over. The coverings rustle as she pries open the pages that have glued together over the years.

Her memories of Maman Zinat are mostly of her at home, sitting in front of the fresco. When she was a child, Forugh always combed Maman Zinat's hair after she came out of the shower, the steam trailing behind her. They would sit on the floor of Maman Zinat's room with the windows open, facing the geraniums in the courtyard. Maman Zinat sat with one leg crossed and the other stretched out in front of her. Forugh would sit behind her, peering at Maman Zinat's naked legs, the plump knees. Forugh was told that she had Maman Zinat's knees, the roundness and the soft edges. Forugh would look at her own knees and ask Maman Zinat if it was indeed true that they had the same kind of knees.

Maman Zinat would shuffle her body, making herself comfortable on the white towel underneath her. One under her, another wrapped around her robust shoulders, barely covering her prosperous breasts.

"Of course we do," she would say. "Knees and a lot more."

The long wet hair dripped on her shoulders, the drops sliding down to the small of her back. Forugh would run the comb through the thick body of that hair, all the way down, the water splashing on her face.

Now the breeze lifts a few strands of hair and lets them fall on her cheek. She brushes the hair aside and looks up over to the window and onto the patio. It is much smaller than she remembers. The walls are lower, even surmounted with the fence. She remembers how, during summer nights, while trying to escape the heat, they would all sleep in the courtyard: Forugh, her mother, Simin, Khaleh Parisa, Sara, Omid, Maman Zinat, and Khaleh Leila. Only Aghajaan would sleep inside. He did not like sleeping in open air. She can't imagine how they could have all fit there. Where did they all sleep?

When she told her mother about how small she found the patio, her mother said, laughing, "What about the garden?"

On the left side of the patio, there is only the persimmon tree, its branches naked, old, and dismal. It is not the persimmon tree she remembers, its branches lopsided with leaves and fruit. But again, it is not the season. She should have come earlier. In the same flower bed, there is a raspberry bush. In her memories, the bush looks more like a tree, with Omid on top, perched on a branch, picking berries. His white shirt stained, purple stains, raspberry stains. All this could not possibly have happened. Raspberries do not grow on trees.

She also remembers a swing here that hung idly above small rocks. Once, Simin let Naser, a friend of her father's who, a few years later, became Forugh's stepfather, push Forugh on this swing. She probably thought it would make Forugh happy to be on the swing, or perhaps she thought the swing would bring Forugh and Naser closer.

Forugh remembers going very high on the swing. Naser kept pushing her higher and higher. Forugh was afraid, so afraid that she couldn't even close her eyes. Her mother was inside the house. She was lying with the back of her wrist over her eyes. Forugh was too afraid and too shy to call her mother. Instead, she bit her tongue, then her lips, then the insides of her cheeks. It all tasted like blood.

She remembers the raw anger she felt at her mother for letting Naser push her so high. She remembers being terrified and wanting to cry. Her mother probably thought that Forugh would love the swing, that she would like to fly. But all Forugh felt was fear and the absence of someone to call out to.

Dante's footfalls at the doorway interrupt the chain of her thoughts. He is carrying an enormous bowl of fruit. Forugh's eyes snap away from the courtyard and dart back to the album.

"Have you found the right photo?" he asks as he places the bowl on the table.

Forugh hesitates. "Not yet." From the corner of her eye, she can see Dante standing next to the table, watching her. She finds herself enjoying being watched by him and feels the heat rushing to her cheeks. She raises her chin without looking up.

"There is a photo of Maman Zinat that I like very much," he says. Forugh allows a moment to pass before asking, "Which one?"

"She is standing out here in the courtyard, in front of the persimmon tree. It's fall, so the tree is full of persimmons, not like now. She's looking away from the camera and laughing."

"Is it here?"

"No," he says, smiling. "I keep it in my wallet." Dante slides his hand into his back pocket to extract a wallet. After a few moments rummaging through it, he pulls out a photo. "Here." He walks over, his hand extended with the photo. Forugh does not meet his eyes, which are gentle, or look closely at his smile, which is sad and fills her with a sense of guilt that she doesn't wish to recognize. She takes the photo from him, half curious, half angry with herself for not carrying Maman Zinat's photo in her own wallet. It is indeed beautiful. Perhaps the most beautiful image of Maman Zinat she has ever seen. Maman Zinat as she remembers her, as she wishes to remember her, with her loud, clear voice and her silent laughter and her unease in front of the camera.

They look at the photo in silence. Forugh places her hand on the album to keep it from trembling. The thin glassine cover is warm against her skin.

"Khaleh Leila washed the body," she says without taking her eyes off the photo. "She didn't let anyone into the bathroom, neither I nor the lady who had come to do it. We waited outside the door in case she needed us. She never did. She called only when she was finished. She had dressed Maman Zinat in a white dress and a headscarf. The lady had to take the shroud back."

Dante leans lightly against the armchair. "Maman Zinat always said she would never want to be wrapped in a shroud."

"She was afraid of shrouds."

"And of being alone."

And she was always worried. She was worried when I was tired. She was worried when I was sad.

She was worried when I wouldn't eat. She was worried when I wouldn't sleep.

She was worried when I wouldn't leave with my mother.

She was worried when I left with my mother.

A bush of white clouds wheels across the sun, leaving a momentary shadow on the fountain and half of the persimmon tree. Then it glides past, and the sun holds sway.

"Tell me about the last day you saw her," Forugh says. "She was laughing?"

"She was." He looks surprised by her sudden openness. She doesn't understand it herself, does not wish to ponder it. She just wants to hear him speak. She wants him to tell her of Maman Zinat. "She was laughing at Khaleh Leila."

"What had Khaleh Leila done to make her laugh?"

"She was arguing with my mom over the recipe for a dish, and Maman Zinat was just laughing at Khaleh Leila, who was getting very excited, her face all red."

Dante sits down next to her on the rug, folding his arms over his knees, his eyes twinkling. Forugh feels her body growing tense at the proximity of his body, there at her feet.

"She was so happy you were coming," he says. "She talked about it constantly."

"I had been away for a long time," she says, and she thinks of the wide Berlin avenues, the colorful buildings of Kreuzberg that looked so striking, so conspicuous, against the darkening early-afternoon skies, of the first day at school when, surrounded by children, their blue eyes palpitating with curiosity, she was asked what her name was and, not understanding, fearful to the point of dizziness, Forugh had said, *I don't know.*

"Yes, you had," he mutters pensively. "Maman Zinat talked about all the things she wanted to do with you, all the dishes she wanted to cook for you. It had been a long time since I'd seen her so excited."

Forugh shifts the album on her lap and tosses the long tassels of hair over her shoulder. "The day after I arrived, she took me to the market, asking what fruit I wanted. She bought everything there was in the market, like she thought I'd never eaten fruit before."

Dante pulls his legs closer to his chest. The skin of his forearms is smooth, the color of gold. "She knew how much you liked pomegranates. She kept them in the freezer for you."

She laughs. "That was the first thing she gave me. On the day I arrived."

The geranium petals flutter in the breeze like butterflies. A crow calls out as it flies over the patio. Forugh hands the photo back to Dante.

"You can use this one if you want," he says.

"I think I'll choose another one." Forugh turns the page, feeling suddenly nervous, threatened. "This one's too small."

A few moments pass. Dante rises to his feet and leaves without saying a word.

It was Leila who found the body prostrate on the floor. The last breath evaporated through the pink-green knots of the rug.

Leila clutched at her stomach and howled on the patio. She howled and staggered through the geraniums. Soon the neighbors appeared on terraces, on rooftops, on balconies that led from one house to another. Children, sleepy-faced, climbed over the walls. Husbands first sent their wives, and then they came themselves, for Leila could not stop howling. Forugh stood by the window, pale as moonlight, gasping. A few of the women took Leila by the shoulders, calling out to someone to bring some water and sugar. One of the women took off her golden ring and dropped it into the glass, stirred it with a spoon, and cajoled Leila to drink it, the golden ring settled at the bottom like a lost treasure.

In their arms, Leila at last collapsed. They laid her against the wall on a wooden bench, holding her head up, rubbing her shoulders. She took a few sips of the sugary water, her lips trembling. She had nothing left in her throat. She closed her eyes, the first gentle light of the day shining from her tears.

Later, when everyone was gone, she closed herself in the room that already reeked of the poisonous stench of loneliness and did what she had not done in years, not since that day with Ahmad: she cried.

Black curtains, long, elegant. Dante brings them in, draped over his outstretched arms so they won't wrinkle. Khaleh Leila spent at least an hour ironing them. Forugh is inserting a photo in the frame. She closes it from the back, turns it around, and inspects it. She sees him come in but does not ask his opinion. He doesn't know which picture she has chosen. He lays the curtains on the floor.

"What are those?" Forugh asks, standing up, holding the frame to her chest.

"Curtains."

"Curtains?" She takes a step forward. "But they're black."

"Khaleh Leila wants to substitute the white curtains with these."

The white lace sweeps over the window as Dante loosens the tiebacks. The impeccable white. Maman Zinat's curtains. Like her. Dante remembers Maman Zinat's smell, that smell of clean. It is still in her room. He can smell it every time he passes, lingering without a body, like a spirit that cannot turn away.

"Remember Maman Zinat's smell?" he says, filled with nostalgia that he cannot contain. "She always smelled so clean."

Forugh looks at him. The sunlight sieving through the lace douses her eyes. Her brown eyes are golden in the light. She raises her eyebrows, widens her eyes, which flicker, just slightly, with a mocking smile, as if she can't believe he could possibly know how Maman Zinat smelled.

She is mocking me, Dante thinks, overtaken by exhaustion and irritation. He feels the tide of anger rising through his body; he's had enough. He no longer wants anything to do with her convoluted urge for belonging. He wishes to be left in peace, to leave her in peace. He feels suddenly tired.

"She did," Forugh says, then brushes her hand against the black curtains, changes the subject. "I'm not sure black curtains are a good idea. They'll make the room dark."

With her other hand, she is clutching the frame to her chest. Dante wonders if she is clasping it like that because she doesn't wish him to see it. He finds himself bristling against that clasp, the ownership it exudes, against that smile, against her flat refusal of his attentions.

"I know Maman Zinat wouldn't want these curtains," Forugh avers.

"But if Khaleh Leila wants these, then I'll go ahead and hang them," Dante says in a huff, unleashing his anger. He knows his words will provoke her, hurt her. He feels the far echo of shame. But he presses on. He is tired of commiserating with her loss while she flippantly dismisses his. He is tired of being refused. As if it is his fault that she was gone and not here. *She cannot return after so many years and demand to claim the present, to make it her own. Life is not unpracticed handwriting, always on pause.*

"They won't make the room too dark; they're lace, after all," he continues as he lifts himself on tiptoes to pull the curtain off the pole. If he sounds patronizing, he doesn't care. She is a grown woman. She can take it. "Besides, black curtains are more appropriate for funerals. Maman Zinat would want what is appropriate. You should know that."

Forugh takes a step back. He thinks he has heard her gasp, but he refuses to look at her. The memory of that derisive smile, of Forugh's nervous hostility, rankles.

After a few moments, Forugh comes closer, takes the sides of the white curtain as he lowers it to the ground. The sunlight glares through the window as Dante moves to take off the other curtain. The curtain rustles in Forugh's hands as she folds it. She places it on the table, takes the other from him.

Having stacked the curtains on the table, she folds her hands momentarily as if she doesn't know what to do next. Dante saunters over to where the black drapes lie on the floor, like an indolent woman in bed. Having been vacated of his anger, he feels even more exhausted. He would like to lie down on the curtains and sleep. *Who am I to decide what is whose to claim?* he thinks.

Forugh helps him, holding the black curtain as he runs the pole through the top. He steals a glance at her. She has bent her head low over the fabric. He can't see beyond the sadness peeping through the ring of her eyelashes. As he carefully arranges the pole on the bronze metal brackets, Dante wishes he could find a foothold in the welter of emotions that he feels for this beautiful, proud, imperious woman, her hands gliding down the sides of the curtain, letting go.

Through the black lace, the pink-purple panicles of the jacaranda tree can be seen like love bites.

The guests have arrived. They are all women. The few men who came earlier left after a ceremonious half an hour. For this is not a place for men. This house is a women's realm. Since Aghajaan's death, women have reigned in this house without anyone or anything standing in their way. As years passed, neighboring women began to take shelter there. Women who had nowhere to go. They all ended up in this house: young women who fled husbands, girls who fled home, women who didn't know where to leave their children. The house was their refuge, where no one could come after them.

Women with staring, smiling eyes that are dripping with tears take off their black chadors, revealing gray hair, supple curves, and worn hands. They sit on red velvet cushions on the ground, encircling Khaleh Leila. Their wails reverberate through the house.

Dante places plates of halvah and dates on the rug in front of their crossed legs. Forugh goes into the yellow room for the tea, but there, disaster awaits. She finds the electric samovar huffing and puffing, blowing out forceful clouds of steam. She has forgotten to turn down its temperature. She scurries across the room and lifts the steel lid. A violent onslaught of steam clamps its teeth into her wrist. She jerks her hand back, throwing the lid on the table with a loud bang. The soft skin has turned a painful pink. She blows on the stinging. All the water in the samovar has evaporated, leaving nothing but angry, blustering rushes of steam.

In the kitchen, she turns on the tap and holds her burning wrist under the rush of cold water while tears threaten. She picks up a plastic pitcher from the shelf and watches the water stream down into it as a tide of anxiety rises up the column of her body. It takes two full pitchers to fill the samovar again.

Back in the yellow room, she rearranges the cups on the silver tray. The pink scald on her wrist has turned scarlet, and her hands are trembling. Through the narrow door with stained-glass windows that leads to the guest room, deformed lumps of shadow can be seen huddled against the wall. Forugh listens to the muffled hum of tears. She can distinguish Khaleh Leila's sobs. By now, she has come to know the harsh sound of suffocation in them, as if strong hands are constantly squeezing at her neck, pressing her sobs back into her throat.

Forugh thinks of Maman Zinat's silent laughter and the way her shoulders bobbed up and down. She thinks of her own mother lying on a hospital bed at this moment, waiting for her kidney stones to be removed, alone, without her daughter. *And now without a mother.*

Simin had howled so loudly on the phone when Forugh told her of Maman Zinat's death that it felt as if the phone were going to burst in her ear. On the hospital bed, she couldn't move, but Simin's voice was strong as ever, as strong as her mother's. Thinking about her, Forugh is gripped with infinite grief and loneliness.

The door opens and Marzieh, Dante's mother, comes in. She has staring, smiling eyes that are wet with tears. She blows her nose into a pink Kleenex and gives Forugh a dismal smile. She looks like someone who can never stop smiling, not even when death beckons. Looking at her, Forugh feels a squeeze in her chest. Her gaze flits around Marzieh's face, jumping from one corner to the other. In the wet eyelashes glued together, the rumpled eyebrows, the soft mouth, the sharp strong jaw, the gentle green eyes, Forugh finds herself looking for Dante's reflection. She does not understand herself. She cannot help herself. She looks at the mother and searches for the image of the son. And she feels somewhere, through Dante's image taking shape in her mind's eye, when she least expected it, in the most inner layer of her body, the hesitant ripples of desire.

The samovar soon begins blowing out white steam once again. This time, Forugh turns it down. She pours the tea from the kettle into the cups and slides one of the cups underneath the samovar's pipe and turns the tap on. Boiling water squirts into the cup, working up red-golden froth.

"This is like Dante's second home," Marzieh says, waving a hand in the room. A hand that covers everything: the stained-glass door, the shelf with the porcelain-framed mirror, the fresco, the samovar, the rug underneath their feet. "He lived here when I was in prison with your aunt Parisa. When Parisa was released, she told me to send Dante here. She knew I had no one to leave him with. At the time, your grandpa was alive too. They took him in as if he were their own grandchild. Just like you and your cousins." Tears rise in Marzieh's eyes again. Her voice quavers. The pink Kleenex dances around her face. "I'll never forget this kindness."

Forugh gazes at her. She now remembers the little boy, an elderly couple bringing him to the house. Simin had mentioned him a few times. How could she have forgotten? "I forgot Dante lived here," she mutters. She feels her face heat up.

Marzieh nods as she blows her nose. "It was a few months after you left for Germany. I first sent him to my parents, but they couldn't take care of him. My mother was sick with cancer. And my in-laws had disowned my husband for his political activities. They didn't want to have anything to do with him. Leila and your grandparents saved my life. They took him in like he was their own son. He lived here for two years." Then she cries out, wringing her hands at the samovar. "Watch out!"

Forugh turns. The boiling water is spilling out of the cup and into the tray. She quickly turns the tap off.

Dante walks toward the stained-glass door. He has already served the dates and halvah twice while everyone waited for the tea. At last, his mother sent him to give Forugh a hand.

"She is not used to this sort of thing," his mother whispers into his ear. "She was spilling tea all over the table. Go and help her a bit."

He finds Forugh busy drying the cups on a towel. He closes the door and stands in front of it.

"Do you need help with that?" he says. He keeps his voice even, distant, determined to no longer give in to her.

She looks up at him. For just a fleeting instant, her eyes soften. She looks vulnerable, brittle to the touch. He feels the urge to embrace her tiny body, hold her fragile hands, hide her from the world. He almost starts to make a move, to stretch out his hand. Then he sees a flicker, just before she snaps her gaze away. A hint of hardening. It happens so quickly that Dante is not sure if it was not merely a trick of his imagination. His hand shoots back immediately.

"No, that's okay," she says. "Thank you."

"It's just that everyone's been waiting for the tea for a long time. I served the dates and halvah twice. It's time to take the tea out."

Forugh presses her lips. Her jaw is set, slightly bulging. He can see he is making her angry. Her anger suddenly frightens him. Her lower lip is pushed lightly forward. Its smooth, fleshy curve disturbs him. He tries not to look at her mouth or the enormous eyes flashing back at him. He leans his back against the wall and folds his arms over his racing heart.

There is something about Forugh's expression that makes Dante's hair stand on end. It catapults him back to a night long ago, when he first learned what it meant to live with a lonely mother. It was a week before Nowruz. The entire city was abuzz with the last preparations for the New Year. Goldfish flitted inside bowls of water, the wheat and lentil sprouts in colorful ceramic dishes with red and pink ribbons wrapped around them, the fragrance of hyacinth flowers in oval crystal vases, mothers tugging tired children behind, doing last-minute shopping. There were light decorations everywhere. Street to street, shop to shop, everything shone with blinking lights embracing the night like colorful dew.

Marzieh had just bought a car, an old creamy-colored Peykan. Another year was about to come to an end with Dante's father still in prison. The night was cold, the sky clear. Dante was sitting at the dining table, doing his homework, when his mother entered the room and flapped a newspaper on the table. "Let's go see the lights," she said, pressing her small hand on the table.

"But I've got homework."

"Come on. It won't take long. We'll just drive around here."

"I have to finish. I still have a lot to do."

Dante saw a new shade of anger explode in his mother's eyes, anger dark in its despair, a wandering despair, leaving now and then but always returning, darker and more destructive than before.

"What have you been doing all day, then? This is not the time for doing homework. It is the time to spend with your mother."

Dante looked back down at the open notebook, the claws of his mother's solitude squeezing her throat. "We drive past the lights every day," he protested in a low, uncertain voice, lifting his gaze. He still missed Maman Zinat and Khaleh Leila and cried every night in his sleep.

Marzieh clamped shut. A nerve fluttered underneath her eye. Her eyes glittered under the yellow light in the room. There was an avalanche in them, ready to hurtle down and bury them. Her hurt silence chilled the air. "I won't ever ask you for anything again." She turned around and dashed out of the room, leaving behind a huff of sad perfume.

Dante remained sitting for a few moments. A strong sense of

guilt flapped its enormous wings inside him. He slowly got up, closed his books, and piled them at the corner of the table. Outside, he could see his mother's shadow in the car, hands gripping the wheel. Dante went out, opened the car door, and got in. His mother would not look at him. She was staring straight ahead at an unknown point amid the shadows and the wind. It was very quiet. After a few moments, she turned the car on, and the silent journey through Nowruz lights began.

"We might not have anything in this city"—Marzieh's voice shattered the moist, stifling silence—"but we can at least look at its lights."

Tiny lights glided past them. The heater buzzed dolefully. Dante looked at his mother but not at her eyes. He was afraid of what they would reveal, of their clutching need for help. He watched his mother's mouth instead and the perspiration glistening on her upper lip under the cheerful lights. All around them, the refulgent solitude roared silently.

And as he looks at Forugh now, this is the gaze he sees: one at once proud and broken.

The door opens, and Dante sees his mother's head peeking through. "Forugh *jaan*, we're still waiting for the tea. Is it going to take long? Shall I come and do it?"

Forugh opens her mouth. It seems that she is going to say something. But she closes it again and lapses into a tense, hostile silence. Dante sees her chin tremble. She continues staring at the tray without moving a muscle, without uttering a single word. Her chest heaves up and down. Her hand moves toward the cup of tea she has just filled. Dante and his mother watch her clamp her fingers around the cup and pick it up. She does not look at any of them. She lifts her arm and smashes the cup against the fresco, splintering it into pieces.

The red tea drops splash across the blue lake. The swans look as if they are bleeding.

Her eyes wild, her mouth twisted as if she's gasping for air, Forugh makes a sound, a yelp, a wail, a strangled sob. It's hard to tell. She runs out of the room.

Dante rushes after her.

Glass barrels of garlic pickles basting in vinegar, cauliflowers, white and glossy in salt water, long-necked brown bottles of lemon juice, olives marinated in crushed walnut and pomegranate juice.

The smell of vinegar stings Forugh's nostrils as she descends the giant steps to the basement. A small naked bulb above the staircase spits out hazy yellow light. The air in the basement is cool, sour, and moist. All the barrels and containers have been arranged neatly, either against the gray wall or on top of the two shelves curved inside it. Since her return, Forugh has not been down here. And yet this used to be her sanctum. Where she came to think, or play, or hide whenever there was a stranger in the house: a neighbor, a friend, the electrician. She saunters across the long narrow basement, inhaling the vinegary smell of her childhood.

She walks past the bottles and glass barrels and plastic containers, sacks of rice, pink plastic bags of potatoes and onions, jars of jam, unused pots and pans piled where the light cannot reach, and everything is soaked in darkness. And as she walks, the old peaceful, protected feeling gradually comes to reclaim her. She sits down on a tile-covered shelf and wraps her arms around her knees. The wall feels cool against her shoulders. She sits in the dark, a lonely woman looking back at the gray-white wall of her childhood.

She remembers the day when she saw her mother for the first time. She was five years old. Omid and Sara had already left. Forugh knew that soon it would be her turn; soon the day would come when she too would have to leave.

Forugh did not want to spend the night with her mother. She clutched at the skirts of Maman Zinat and Khaleh Leila. She howled. She bellowed. She kicked. She was afraid of the woman they told her to call Mother. A gaunt, forlorn woman with liquid eyes that blazed with reproach, with unspeakable agony, and an alien crackling sound in her voice, like a fire dying out.

After spending hours in vain to coax Forugh to her arms with smiles and caresses and kisses, in the end, Simin pinched Forugh on the thigh, her face distorted with pain and rage and despair. "Come to my arms," she demanded. She begged. Forugh wailed some more. Simin pinched her again, her own tears racing with those of her daughter.

That night, Simin slept without her daughter. Forugh spent her last night snuggled in the protective heat of Maman Zinat and Khaleh Leila's bodies.

The next morning, Aghajaan had a long talk with Forugh about how she must love her mother and be happy because now her mother would always be with her, and Maman Zinat would be there too and so would he and Khaleh Leila and Omid and Sara, and Forugh would never be alone, because there were so many people who loved her. Forugh realized she had no choice. She was silent in the unknown, estranged embrace of her mother, who held her softly on her knees, trying not to cling to her too tightly, not to frighten her. She told Forugh that she had come back, that they would have a lot of fun together, that they would go to the park and have some ice cream.

"Would you like that?" her mother asked, her voice tiny like a child's. "We can have chocolate or strawberry or any other flavor you want." As they passed the purple-pink flowers and left through the blue door, Forugh turned to look at her two beloved women. They lifted their arms slowly and waved at her.

Forugh picks up one of the small jam jars and opens it. Orange blossoms coated in saffron-colored sugar. She dips her fingers in; the jam is sticky and soft.

She misses the heat of her mother's hands.

The way her mother held her and sang lullabies to her every night even after she started school. The way she cut fruit in pieces for her and washed her hair without letting the shampoo burn her eyes. The way she taught Forugh how to swim in the small pool near their house, and when the pool was closed, they lay on their stomachs on the floor and practiced the strokes, laughing their hearts out. The way she clasped and unclasped her thin fingers when, a year later, she told Forugh of her father's death.

Forugh misses her, misses the sound of her footsteps in the house.

The door on top of the staircase squeaks gently open. Forugh lifts her head and listens. One step after another disappears beyond the flat echo of tentative footfalls. She thinks of getting up but doesn't. She puts the jam back on the shelf, leans against the wall, and closes her eyes. She breathes deeply, feels the cool air on her skin, the goose bumps on her legs.

And there, surrounded by all her memories of love and fear, Forugh finds herself hoping, from the depth of the tender layer of her heart, for it to be Dante's footfalls approaching. Her heart hammers in her chest.

Dante finds Forugh huddled against the wall in the translucent darkness. The cool air is swollen with moisture. He runs a hand over the dust sitting on the vinegar bottles and the jam jars. He knows the bottles and the jars one by one. He helped fill many of them. The evenings when he came to visit the two women, who kept making pickles and jams as if they were supposed to feed the entire neighborhood, Maman Zinat would send him down to the basement to fetch a jar of jam as she cut the hot bread into slices. The three of them would sit on the wooden bench on the patio next to the fountain. There was butter and jam and tea in the golden-rimmed cups. The scent of wet soil emanated from the flower beds that Khaleh Leila had just watered.

Forugh looks at him. Silence in the basement swoops down and tightens around them. But it is a different kind of silence, one fresh, weightless, smelling of vinegar and expectation and longing. Present.

"I remember hiding here once." He points at the pots and pans. "There used to be a tall wardrobe there. I hid inside it."

Forugh smiles. "Just once? I used to hide in it all the time."

There are two perfectly curved lines next to her mouth that deepen as she smiles, lines that stay long after she stops smiling. The velvet of her eyes shines even more brilliantly in the transparent darkness. "And what made you hide here?" she asks.

"My mother had been released from prison and came to take me home with her."

Forugh gazes at him with fervor. "Didn't you want to go with her?" The voice issuing from her throat is nothing but an entangled murmur.

Dante smiles sadly. "I didn't know her. She was a stranger to me."

"And your father? Where was he?"

"He was released much later."

Forugh holds his eyes with her inflamed penetrating gaze. "It's a strange feeling, when they tell you someone's your mother and all you feel is fear because you see a mere stranger. Only later do you realize she is all that you have."

The basement breathes around them, over them, through them. Its breathing seals up the distance between them.

"I've heard your mother's in the hospital," Dante says. His tongue feels dry and flat in his mouth. "I'm really sorry."

"She had to have a kidney stone removed. It's a very painful process." A sorrowful smile quivers on her mouth. "But she'll be okay. She'll be released soon. She was happy that I was here and got to see Maman Zinat before it was too late. She's coming too, as soon as she feels better."

"It must've been very hard for you." He feels contrite for the way he spoke to her earlier.

Forugh gets up and walks toward him. "Let me show you something." She grabs his sweaty hand. Her hand is small and delicate in his grasp, fragile like lace.

Next to the biggest barrel of pickled garlic, she kneels, never letting go of his hand, and sticks her other hand behind the barrel. She gropes through darkness and dust. Finally, she pulls something out. It is a small flat box with a clear lid, varnished in a thick layer of grime. She straightens her back and lets go of his hand to open the lid, smiling triumphantly. Inside, there is a tiny dragonfly pinned to a yellowed piece of paper.

"I had to hide it here because Khaleh Leila never would've let me keep it. You know how she is with insects. She would've thought it was a cockroach or something."

Dante laughs. He laughs because he does know how Khaleh Leila is with insects. He laughs because of Forugh's intimate voice. He laughs because Forugh smiles at him.

He touches the back of the dragonfly with the tip of his finger. It feels dry, like a piece of wood. Forugh closes the lid. Dante takes the box from her hand and hides it back behind the pickle barrel.

"I miss Maman Zinat," Forugh whispers. Tears lurk underneath her long eyelashes. She lays her thin length against his body.

"I miss her too." Dante digs his head into the heaviness of her hair and holds her.

Daylight is petering out when Leila goes out to the patio. She turns on the tap and drags the hose toward the flower beds. She watches the earth drink.

The house is immersed in silence. Marzieh is the last guest to leave. She tells Leila of what happened in the yellow room, of the glass splinters and the bleeding swans, of the wild look in Forugh's eyes, of Dante's rush after her.

Leila does not say anything as she walks Marzieh to the door. She does not call out to the children; nor does she look for them. She suddenly feels the need to protect them from the outside world, as if they are a secret yearning. She leaves them to care for each other's wounds.

She watches a flight of swallows soar up through the orange-and-yellow sky. Returning to the house, she takes off her slippers. She sits on one of the red velvet cushions arranged by the wall and waits for the children, for her children, Maman Zinat's children.

Soon two shadows appear at the doorway. They smile timidly, as if they are going willingly to face their punishment. Forugh and Dante come forward with fresh, flushed cheeks. They sit down. Leila is flanked between their bodies by that smell of the mysterious ripples of love and pain, of breaking and blossoming, of past and future.

"The swallows have begun migrating," she says.

The two bodies stretch out and put their heads on Leila's lap, one on either side. She reaches her hands out to the youth of their hair, caressing. They give in to her touch like thirsty trees to water. Her voice issues slowly from her throat and expands into the room, telling them the love story of Persian princesses and their poor beautiful lovers.

Dusk falls on the branches of the jacaranda tree.

1983–2009
Tehran–Turin

Tehran, 1988

When she answered the phone and heard his voice, her heart sank. He didn't introduce himself, only said where he was calling from. But she knew before he said a word. There were faraway screams stifled in the hardness of his voice. He told her to come to the prison and collect her husband's belongings. She quietly hung up the phone and then wailed so loudly, the windows rattled.

She had not seen her husband in months. All the visits had suddenly been canceled. No one knew anything, and everyone was dreading the worst. Later, she heard of families who went to visit someone in prison and instead were handed belongings. They were told the person was no longer there.

He was no longer anywhere.

There was a piece of paper on the desk. First the piece of paper was silent. Later, it spoke. Of death, although silently.

They were told to write as their hands trembled:

My husband is no longer anywhere.

My wife is no longer anywhere.

My son, my daughter, is no longer anywhere.

That was how death was handed to a family. On a piece of paper with a bag half full of splinters of life, asking for their signature.

She was told that she'd been lucky. Not everyone had received a phone call. She'd been lucky to know that he was dead, to have been warned in advance.

She didn't feel lucky. She felt empty, like a cave.

That day, she kept death to herself. She sat among his clothes spread on the bed. She couldn't move; it was as if her body had gone to sleep. At night, she lay down on his clothes. She smelled his shirt, smelled it and bawled, smelled it and cursed them, smelled it and screamed his name, and cursed him too. She was angry with him, so angry that, had he been there, she would have attacked him with her bare hands.

In the middle of the night, she heard the sound of crying coming from the next room. It was like an alarm. She opened her eyes. His shirt under her skin was damp with tears, as if her face had shrunk and melted into the fabric. She used her hands to heave her body up and drag herself to the other room, where her child sobbed desperately. She embraced her, whispering "Shhhh" under her breath, patting the child softly on the back. In reality, she was trying to calm herself down, to buck herself up. The lightness of the child's body intimidated her, as did the child's vulnerability and the inconsolableness of her whimpers.

Then and there, she decided she would never tell her child about her father's death; about how he died. Even if it were the last thing she did, she would never let her daughter know this suffering. She didn't care what lies she had to tell, what secrets she had to keep. All she knew was that she had to keep history at bay, to keep her child safe, sheltered behind iron walls where the blood could not seep through. She stretched the tiny length of her daughter on her legs and gently rocked her until they both fell asleep.

It must have been the desolation in her eyes that cast a spell over everyone. No one dared to contradict her, to try to change her mind, except his mother. With her, it was not easy. His mother fiercely refused, called it a monstrosity. She insisted that the child must know. *Like this, you are letting them kill him twice.* His soul would never rest, she warned; his body would tremble in the grave.

"You owe it to him," his mother said. "You owe it to his memory."

She should have been more tactful, but in those days, being tactful was not her strongest point. That was anger.

"I don't owe him anything!" she shouted, her voice quavering with rage. "It's he who owes me everything! He owes me the happiness he promised me. He made me believe in it, and he failed. He failed me. He failed his daughter. I won't let him take her away. He destroyed everything!"

His mother cried. She had lost a son, her only son.

She should have been less cruel.

His mother never ceased to make her request, asking for her sealed lips to break open. When his mother died, she wrote a confessional letter to her daughter and hid it in the dead woman's shroud. The letter was buried along with the old woman.

Turin, 2009

There is barely anyone at the airport. The line at the security check is short and moves quickly. Maryam is about to turn around and look beyond the glass screen when the security guard pushes a blue container forward. She places her purse, jacket, and boarding pass inside the box and lifts her gaze to him. He has a bulging forehead and lentil eyes.

"*Le scarpe,*" he says, pointing at her shoes.

Even the shoes! She bends down, her face already crimson with embarrassment and awkwardness. She unties her shoelaces and places her unprotected feet very cautiously on the ground, as if she's stepping on a minefield. She steps through the metal detector; the floor is cold and glossy underneath her feet. The metal detector beeps frantically. She stretches her arms out for a red-haired girl who, not having discovered anything dangerous or suspicious with another beeping hoop, finally lets her go.

Maryam turns around, scanning the crowd on the other side of the glass border, and sees Sheida raise a hand. Sheida looks so young in that white dress, with her delicate face and all its singing vulnerability. Maryam swallows the knot of stunted sounds and tears in her throat and waves back. She thinks she has seen glittering tears, but Sheida is far, and Maryam cannot be sure whether they are tears or merely the reflection of lights flickering in the black of her daughter's eyes.

She walks away from the metal detector and its repeated screeches of alarm; from the glass wall; from her daughter on the other side. She saunters past a series of clothing, souvenirs, and duty-free shops where the sales assistants loiter about, not knowing what to do with themselves in a half-empty airport. She reaches the designated gate and lets out a deep sigh as she sinks into one of the yellow seats. She's tired and her back aches. She drops everything on the seat next to her and folds her hands like a woman waiting for a benediction, enclosed in a sad glow.

As a child, Sheida used to cry as soon as Maryam was not in sight anymore. Now Sheida rarely cries, not even when they part ways across two continents. Maryam wishes Sheida had cried. She wishes she had been sure about the tears. They would have comforted her. She has nothing else to hold on to. And yet the image of those tears is more slippery than the tears themselves.

She takes out a tissue from her bag to wipe the sweat off her upper lip. There is something about their relationship that no longer convinces her. She feels like it has become distant, their intimacy replaced with some sort of friendly affection. She has a feeling that Sheida does not tell her everything. She tends to laugh off questions and shake off concern like a tree shaking off its dead leaves. But what did Maryam expect? She could not possibly hope for the same closeness they had in Iran, while Sheida now lives in another country. That would be naive of her, mere wishful thinking. Sheida is a grown woman, not a child anymore. After all, it was Maryam herself who took Sheida to Italy.

It had not been easy. Maryam had been waiting for a visa for years. They had been rejected once already because Maryam's sister, who lived in Italy and was applying for them, had problems with her bank accounts. Maryam did not let that hinder her. She plowed on, pressuring her sister at every turn, putting money aside, until, when Sheida was almost seventeen years old, their visa finally arrived.

All those years of waiting, Maryam firmly believed that if they just went over the border, they would both be safe, that taking her daughter so far away would be the ultimate step in safeguarding her against the past, the death, the blood. That far away from Iran, they could live peacefully, Sheida's happiness would be guaranteed, and somehow everything would be easier. But Maryam suffered from her own impulsiveness. Her wishes always got tangled up. Her decisions backfired. Once, when Sheida was fifteen, Maryam threatened to kill her daughter if Sheida ever left her. That was before leaving Iran, before she went and dropped her daughter off in another country. She had not thought his death would chase them, chase her, so far. Soon she realized memories were heavier than her will to move on. A part of her was still there, right in that cemetery, rotting along with Amir's lifeless body. Every night in her little apartment in Turin, facing the square with its beautiful eighteenth-century fresco of Mary and her child, Maryam dreamed about the cemetery she had never visited that had become a nightly haunting vision. Such nightmares had never happened, not even in the beginning. Maryam was suffering away from that prison, away from that cemetery. She needed to be close to him. She couldn't leave him alone in that hostile land; she had to go back to him.

But didn't this mean she was choosing him over her child? Widowhood over motherhood? The questions harrowed her night after night. And yet she had no answer for them. Maryam had lost shape on the day she heard the news of Amir's death. She had become a caricature of the woman she used to be. Something inside her vanished, and she got fettered to that land and cemetery forever. No matter how hard she tried, how many times she stood up determined not to fall, how she struggled to be the strong mother her daughter needed her to be, she stumbled again and again. And she was tired. The world had beaten her long ago. She had been doing nothing but floundering about. And she could no longer fight it. The only way she could survive was to be close to him, to her past. Without them, she would crumble to the ground. She had no choice; she had to save her world.

Four years after their migration to Italy, when Maryam was sure that Sheida's job at the bookstore was stable and she could take care of herself, she decided to go back to Iran. Sheida stayed. She didn't want to go back, she said. Maryam left Sheida in that cold, enigmatic city at the foot of the Alps, thinking, hoping, the glue between them would never dissolve. Now she sees Sheida distracted and feels like she has grown behind her back, that the glue has gradually come off. But Sheida is not to blame. She did as her mother had planned for her to do. She obeyed her mother's wishes. It had been Maryam who left.

She unfolds her hands and stands up. In the bathroom, she washes her hands with precision, just like her own mother used to do. Lathering them twice, covering every corner. She holds each hand three times under the water. Hold it and pull it back, hold it and pull it back, hold it and pull it back, then the other. It is like an ablution.

An anonymous voice announces the initiation of boarding. Maryam quickly gathers her things, dries her hands on the way, and runs out of the bathroom.

Sheida lingers behind the glass screen, looking at the metal detector. Maryam is gone, but Sheida hasn't been able to detach herself. Her body feels like a separate entity, struck motionless, like when her legs would fall asleep from sitting cross-legged on the floor of her grandmother's house, counting the fish in the blue-and-silver pattern of the rug. Her body refuses to move. She doesn't know what to do with it.

It is a hot, cloudy afternoon. The parking lot in front of the airport is blanketed in a heaving layer of humidity. It encroaches upon Sheida as soon as she steps out of the air-conditioned hall, curling around her arms, her legs, her white dress, up around her shoulders and neck, swaddling her like a heavy wet towel.

The bus heading back to Turin is half full with the haggard, dusty faces of travelers. Sheida drops into a seat at the far end, by the window. The bus driver closes the door. It makes a huff as it slides to the side and presses shut, blowing the air out. The bus slowly moves off.

Today is her day off work. Usually, Sheida has many things planned for this day, from doing chores to seeing friends, but today she does not feel like doing anything. Her mother's departure has left her with a sense of emptiness. She would like to find a way out of this day, out of having to go through it, having to live it. *How nice it would be if we could just press a forward button and skip a day!* she thinks. She would like to go home, put her head under a pillow, and wake up when the day is over.

It will be night by the time Maryam arrives at Tehran's bustling airport. The thought—by now the eroded image—of the airport makes Sheida jittery. It's been years since her last visit to Iran. She has stopped going without really knowing why. She's been busy with life.

The road cuts across green plains stretching to the foot of the Alps, blurring into the wet, mournful sky. The gray clouds hover

over the plains, so low she almost feels like she can raise a hand
and pull the thick, fluffy tufts apart.

The image of her mother kneeling, untying her shoelaces,
flashes in her mind. She looked so tiny, almost like a child. And
that is what she becomes every time she comes to visit: a child.
Just like she was in those first four years when they lived together
in Italy. It was as if her solidity gave way. She lost the old vigor,
the old authority, always waiting for Sheida to make decisions on
where to go, what to do, what to eat. She turned into a different person, almost infantilized. So many years and Sheida hasn't
grown used to this new unglamorous version of her mother.

The bus noses its way into the chessboard-shaped city. The pale
pink and yellow baroque buildings stand tall against the sagging
clouds. She gets off near the Po River, which loops its way through
the center of Turin, closing off the hills. Standing at the top of the
bridge, Sheida looks down at the river moving gently underneath
her feet. Pink and purple violets have been planted in the clay pots
held up in green scaffolding on top of the banister. She takes a
deep breath, filling her lungs with the moisture and the smell of
green water and the damp summer leaves sitting on branches of
old trees running along the riverbed.

At home, the first thing Sheida does is to turn on the radio. The
music streams into the tiny living room, with its cream walls and
white curtains and unframed film posters. She takes off her shoes,
throws her bag on the sofa, and opens the window. In the sink is
a cup half full of tea with her mother's lip print on its edge. The
scent of her is still there, warm, inside the half emptiness.

The neighbor in the opposite building is mercilessly screaming
at her children. Her screeches swell in the patio and break open in

the room. Sheida turns up the radio to drown out the hysterical, piercing cries.

Maryam never screamed at her. Maryam never raised her voice.

In the middle of the room, listening to the song, her body hurting within and unruffled without, Sheida begins to dance. Her body moves side to side lightly, steadily, as if she's trying to find her balance. The song picks up pace, and Sheida moves more quickly. She springs off the floor and stamps her feet on the rug. Her arms are outflung in the space that throbs with music and screams and the jasmine scent of her mother that lingers in the air. Her heavy breasts bounce, pulling her dress along. She dances recklessly, swinging her arms and legs about like a woman struggling to squirm out of a straitjacket. Her cheeks begin to burn with the rush of blood and the tears that roll quietly down. The higher she jumps, the faster the tears roll. Her sobs tumble into the song, undoing the words into a jumble of incomprehensible, gurgled sounds.

Her mother is not happy. She's never been happy. The silence hasn't worked. It's only made everything more difficult to bear. They have been left with nothing but a handful of unspoken words, insidious like poison, progressing a little more every day, encroaching upon everything, spoiling every last remnant of the honest intimacy they used to have. And they are both to blame. Together, they've destroyed everything beautiful they once had.

Sheida falters back to the sofa and catapults on it, wiping her tears. The screaming on the other side of the courtyard has died down. They are probably preparing for dinner now. Slowly, Sheida gets up and turns down the radio. She blows her nose and looks out the window. On the neighbor's balcony, the violets flitter in the breeze. A cat walks gingerly along the window ledge and jumps on the terrace of another neighbor. Sheida turns around and walks up to the phone. Her heart races at the prospect of hearing Valerio's voice. She hasn't seen him since Maryam's visit. She didn't feel ready to introduce him, dreading all of her mother's worried, annoying questions. *Maybe next time*, she told him.

Holding the phone to her ear, she curls up on the sofa, drawing her knees to her chest, and embraces herself as if wishing to gather the bits and pieces of herself strewn on the floor and suspended in the air and tugging at the corners of the window. Gather them and pile them back into a recognizable shape before she faces him.

Valerio answers. Hearing his voice, she closes her eyes and sighs with relief.

A starling perches on the railing in front of the window. Under the damp sky, the geraniums look out of breath. Dusk is slow in falling. Sitting behind her computer, Sheida takes a sip from the iced tea she made with the Iranian dry tea leaves Maryam sent her a few months ago. Sheida likes the smell of brown cardboard boxes arriving from Iran. They smell of dust and memory. *This is the smell of Iran*, she once told Valerio. She smelled the tea, the pair of green gloves her aunt knitted for her, the packet of barberries, and the note from Maryam reminding her to wash them several times before use, which Sheida has never been able to throw away.

Her computer purrs sleepily under her fingers. She scrolls down the page, skimming through the news on an online Persian newspaper. Since the uprising against the rigged elections in June and the government crackdown that followed, most of the news coming out of Iran is about the protests, mass arrests, attacks at university dorms, street shootings, torture in prisons, prisoners of whom no news has been given for months, and protesters whose lost lives are unaccounted for. There are also videos that have been uploaded by the protesters on the scene. Sheida has watched every one of them, of protesters running down the streets, some away and some toward the anti-riot security guards with their bullet-proof uniforms and batons, as they throw stones and shout out anti-regime slogans. The images on the screen fill Sheida with anxiety every time she sees them, as though she is late for something, or left behind, excluded. She is envious of the burst of energy in that young crowd, of the way it is all happening without her, of the way her place in that tide of history is unoccupied. At the same time, she is afraid of the bloody faces and the gunshot wounds and the baton-swinging security guards on motorcycles.

She clicks on a video of people chanting slogans on rooftops at night. *Allaho Akbar*, she hears from every side, *Allaho Akbar*. The buildings and the rooftops from which the invisible men and women holler are soaked in darkness. All she can see are the little lights shimmering behind closed windows. But their shouts and the furious strength ringing in them grow louder and louder, as if they are trying to reach the clouds and tear through them. Sheida watches, her heart beating so wildly that her eyes begin to hurt, as the night sweeps over the buildings, covering the shadows of the chanting bodies, entering the small vision of the camera. The ecstasy of it all, the pure harmony of it, baffles her. Women and men, young and old, feeble and strong, chanting slogans against the wrong done to them. Slogans for whatever memory of justice they can fathom. Behind her computer, Sheida whispers their words, their slogans, their cries of resistance. Their calling of God. Calling their God against the dictator. Her mother told her that going on rooftops and chanting *Allaho Akbar* was something they did during the revolution thirty years ago. It was a form of protest. It was safe, symbolic, something everyone could do. And now it has come back. *When all fails, shout Allaho Akbar*, her mother added with a sad, resigned shake of her head.

But Sheida does not feel sad. She feels exultant and small, unpardonably small, before the magnificence of these madly awe-inspiring and yet desperate chants. She can feel their chants surrounding her and their night penetrating her skin, their lovely, uncompromising voices swelling inside her veins, inside her lungs. She can almost see their God, can almost touch their voices that call upon Him as they straighten their backs, shout louder and louder, *Allaho Akbar*, shedding their fear into the blue night. She feels like they are becoming an irrevocable part of the rhythm of her breathing. Their voices calling out to her. She can almost see herself standing on a rooftop, her fist clenched in the air.

As the video ends, Sheida lets out a sigh. She feels light-headed and leans back in her chair. She takes another sip from her iced tea. The ice cubes tumble from side to side and against her lips. She clicks back on the home page, looking for other videos to watch, when a headline at the bottom of the page catches her eye. This is the second time in recent weeks that she has seen an article about the post-revolution imprisonments and executions. She does not know if it is a coincidence or if, with so many men and women twenty years later in prisons of Tehran and other cities, the past is resurfacing, almost as a premonition.

Yet something else draws Sheida to these articles and their tales of prison, violence, and death. They remind her of similar tales uttered by her grandmother those few times Sheida and Maryam went to visit her in Hamedan. The tales Sheida heard were in dribs and drabs, tumbling out of her grandmother's mouth when she did not know Sheida was eavesdropping, when Maryam and grandmother were alone in the room. Sheida watched through the keyhole as her grandmother turned into a different person. Her usual loud voice lapsed into a hushed whisper as she dabbed her teary eyes, which wavered from those of Sheida's mother, who sat there, her face closed like a rock. Maryam's silence and staring, vacant look made Sheida uneasy. It felt as if her mother concealed something in that silence, defended it behind her vacant eyes. At the time, Sheida wished more than anything to get away from that silence. It was suffocating. And yet the sorrow roaring in her grandmother's face kept her there behind the door, her ears attuned to her whispering voice.

Why is Grandma so sad? Sheida wondered. She tried harder to listen, to understand the words that she had a feeling she was not supposed to hear, for she sensed the evil in them and the pain. She picked them up like a bee flitting around forbidden flowers, sucking the sweet nectar. She wanted to hear as much as she could, wanted to understand whom these stories were about. It was hard, for no name was mentioned, and her grandmother's voice seemed to keep dying. Sheida knew that she couldn't ask her mother, or she would know the child eavesdropped. Later, when she asked her grandmother, a despairing look fell over her face, despairing and so devastatingly sad that it frightened Sheida. *I can't speak,* her grandmother repeated. *I can't speak.* And those were the only words Sheida was left with as she left her grandmother's room.

Only once did Sheida succeed in getting an answer from Maryam to the question about her grandmother's sadness. Maryam looked at her for a moment. Her gaze seemed to go right past her, as if she didn't really see her. *It's because of your baba, Sheida, Grandma's sad for her son,* she said after a few moments.

"But what does Baba have to do with prison?" Sheida asked, and as she did, she felt the heat running to her cheeks, for she realized she had given away herself and her eavesdropping.

Maryam glared at her, a glare Sheida would never forget. "It is all one big prison, Sheida. We are all in one big prison."

It was so immense, Grandma's pain, Sheida now thinks as she reads:

Approximately 4,000 to 5,000 young men and women were executed in July and August of 1988, the same year the war between Iran and Iraq was reaching an end. The government formed a three-person committee, what later on was known as the "Death Committee," to oversee the purge in each prison. Each committee comprised a prosecutor, a judge, and a representative of the Ministry of Information. The committee interviewed all political prisoners and ordered the executions of those deemed "unrepentant."

The prisoners were loaded on forklift trucks in groups and hanged from cranes and beams in half-hourly intervals. The others were killed by firing squads. At midnight, the corpses were carried away and buried in mass graves in the Khavaran cemetery, which used to be the cemetery for religious minorities. The bodies have been buried there in channeled routs and the soil has been pressed, rendering it impossible to recognize the graves. Any form of gravestones was repeatedly destroyed . . .

Sheida stares at the words, feeling the sweat working up on her neck and under her armpits. The word "mass" echoes in her mind. Corpse after corpse, bloody, shapeless, one on top of the other. The first article she read about the executions had not gone into such detail. She didn't know there were so many victims, didn't know about the mass graves. At the same moment, a memory flashes before her eyes. A memory she did not know she had. At the reawakening of this memory, a sharp pang goes through her. She sees her mother screaming, howling through the night, and someone appearing behind her, closing the door. The memory is vague, like a badly remembered dream. She can still hear the howling, the weeping. Was it her mother? Could it be Grandma instead?

She sets down the glass of tea. Her movements are measured, as if she's afraid of dropping something. She closes and opens her fist, licks her lips. Her throat feels dry and scratchy. From the neighboring apartment, the muffled hum of a television can be heard. Sheida's eyes return to the screen, and despite her efforts to calm down, her gaze rushes down the long columns of names of victims that have been included in the article, the age of each written alongside. Some are under eighteen.

The list continues, like on a memorial wall. She scrolls down the page, her eyes fogging over, transforming the names into staggering glimpses of a nightmare. *So many victims, so young.* The article has shoved Sheida into the wild torrent of her country's past. A raging torrent she did not know existed, not in such magnitude. Somewhere in that land, the bones of one young man have been crushed down by a thousand other bones. Somewhere in that land, thousands of corpses have been dumped into the sucking maw of the earth like mountains of refuse. *The cursed land,* that is what the article calls the area of the mass graves.

Sheida leans back in the chair, feeling exhausted, unable to tear her eyes away from the list of the dead, scrolling down the page. That is when the appearance of a name almost brings her heart to a stop. For a moment, everything around her seems to come to a breathless halt. The hum of the computer; the pale face of the moon; the particles of yellow light seeping into the room from the courtyard. She stares at the name, pressing her left hand against her throat, where a pulse flits and flinches. There in front of her, right in the middle of the page, is the name of her father:

Amir Ramezanzadeh, 27.

It is written clearly, as clear as a shriek piercing through deserted streets. Sheida feels her body go very still. Her palms are sweaty; she feels her limbs weakening. "There must be a mistake," she mutters to herself, her eyes glued to the screen. From outside, the grunt of a car parking in the courtyard fills the room.

Valerio opens the door and enters the apartment, which is immersed in blue darkness. Silence breathes around him, warm and ominous. He calls Sheida; there's no answer. He stands at the doorway and listens to a silence so pure, so deafening, that he doesn't dare venture forth. The warm air enters his eyes and fills him with foreboding.

In the living room, he finds Sheida on the floor, leaning against the foot of the sofa. She's holding her head between her hands, her disheveled hair flowing down her shoulders.

"What happened?" He turns on the light and walks quickly

over to her. He feels as though he's walking into something that will suck him in alive. Quicksand, without warning.

Sheida lifts her red-rimmed eyes and squints in the shock of light. She holds her arms out to him. He lowers himself to the floor and grabs her cold hands. She digs her head into the softness of his shoulder and stays there.

Slowly, after a few moments, she begins to speak. She tells him about the article; she gets up and shows him the name of her father on the computer screen. She gesticulates wildly, as if she has no control over her hands. Listening to her, Valerio feels bombarded by a flurry of disconnected thoughts. He watches her dissolving face, and his stomach churns with helplessness. He makes her sit down on the sofa and sits next to her. He strokes her hand quietly.

For a long moment, Sheida is silent. Her face is pale, her lips pursed. She looks somehow small, shriveled.

"What if it's just a mistake?" Valerio says.

She doesn't look at him. She shakes her head. Her face has hardened. "I don't know," she mumbles.

"You should talk to your mother. It could just be a mistake."

Sheida doesn't respond. Her gaze is lost somewhere below the curtains. She frees her hand from his and clasps her hands hard together. Valerio gazes at her and can't help but notice a strange look on her face. A look he didn't recognize in the beginning but that he realizes has been on her face all along: the look of a woman who is struggling with something inside. Something that is far bigger than she, bigger than anything he's ever known.

A few moments pass. The evening hum of the streets trickles into the room. From the corridor comes the hubbub of the neighbors descending the stairs, chattering loudly.

"Sheida, are you sure your father died of cancer?" Valerio doesn't know why he's asking this question and why his heart skips a beat as he does so. Perhaps he's afraid of what she might say. There have been very few times when Sheida has spoken about her father, and those few times always gave Valerio the impression that she was treading gingerly around an open wound into which she was unwilling to look for long. There was always an uncertain edge to her eyes, to her voice, that made Valerio think she was not comfortable with either the subject of her father or his death.

Sheida says nothing. She doesn't look at him. There's a tiny twitch at the sides of her eyes. She straightens her fingers and curls them up again. "That's what my mother told me," she says at last.

The unexpected calm in her voice takes Valerio aback. Her earlier panic, the alertness, seems to have ceased, her body to have settled. He stares at her, wishing he could read her thoughts. But he can't insist. There is something in her expression that doesn't give him the right to ask further questions. He doesn't know what to say other than "Then that must be the truth."

Sheida brushes her hands over her face. She lifts her eyes and looks at him. "I shouldn't have told you."

"Why?" Valerio cradles her face between his hands. "You can tell me everything. You know that."

She gives him a weak smile. "It's been so long," she says. "I missed you."

She sounds as though she'd like to move on, from this moment, from the tension tainting the air. He doesn't understand how she can move on so easily, so quickly. *Does she not trust me? What is she afraid of?*

Sheida wraps her arms around him and pulls him still closer, and Valerio knows that she won't tell him anything else. He gives up and fits himself into her embrace.

Her body expands and floats as he enfolds her.

A sob breaks somewhere. A voice crumbles.

Her fingers bore into the back of his neck with dazzling strength, receiving him with all that she can offer, the weight of history mounted inside her. His hands find the small of her back, and he hears a whimper, a smothered sob, a sigh stealing away through her lips.

Throughout the night, Sheida's eyes trace the cracks on the veined ceiling of the room. She can't close them; it's as if her eyelids have dried against her skull. She has never visited her father's grave. Maryam was always against it. She didn't want to be reminded of the fact that he was dead, she would say, it was better to remember him as he was. Sheida did not contradict her mother. She accepted those verdicts as general facts. Maryam's dread of the cemetery was contagious. Sheida was happy to be spared the gloom of the graveyard. But not going to the cemetery did not automatically mean one's father had been executed. *Does it?*

She fidgets nervously in bed. His first name, last name, age. They all correspond accurately with the truth. Tears drift back into her eyes. She is suffocating under an avalanche of uncertainty. She swings back and forth, reaching for the most impossible places. She cannot grab on to anything. Her hands grope around in the void.

She has only one clear memory of her father. Of when she was a child. She remembers being passed over a glass screen to the raised hands of a man who must have been her father. She remembers the black eyes, the rough, unshaved skin, and the black mustache. She also remembers his smell; it was the smell of staying behind, of not breathing fresh air. Where was her mother? she remembers thinking. Who would save her from this man? This stranger? She wailed as he held her up and kissed her on the cheek. He was warm. He laughed. And his laughter was sad.

Her mother never asked Sheida if she remembered anything of her father. As a child, Sheida waited silently for a sign that she could give vent to her terrifying need to know, to speak of her father. No sign was given. She suffered for not remembering, suffered for the emptiness. And her mother never asked why. She never knew. Then there were always those times when her mother sat silently, her head against the wall, lost in thought. Sheida had never been able to tolerate the long mysterious spells of silence that Maryam went through. She was jealous of the silence, of the thoughts forming in Maryam's mind, thoughts far from her. They were from a world to which she did not belong. It was a part of her mother that she never owned, a part of her that she knew she would never own. And that was where she would get hedged in, behind barbed wires of silent broken memories.

The worst was when Sheida would try to ask about her father. A few questions were enough to make Maryam spend the rest of the day in bed, engulfed in complete darkness with all the windows and shutters shut, moaning with what she called migraine pains. Sheida would quietly enter the room, where the smell of solitude and despair hung in the air as thick as dust. She would hold her mother's head over the toilet as she heaved. She would give her some painkillers, put her in bed, make sure all the curtains were drawn. The air around her mother was heavy with paralysis, with internal breaking, like a marble surrendered to the blows of a hammer. Most of the time, Sheida couldn't wait to get out of the room. The heaviness was unbearable, the pain unrelenting. That was when Sheida understood that no matter how many times and in what ways she tried to ask about her father, her mother would never speak about him. She would always cut her daughter off, would always change the subject. Sheida had no choice but to slowly resign herself to never knowing.

Sheida gets up from bed and pads over to the bureau next to the window. She opens one of the drawers. In the thin layer of light wafting in from the street, she rummages through papers, documents, photos, postcards. Half exhausted, half demented, she burrows through the papery tidbits of her life, digging her hands in. She turns on the table lamp.

Valerio wakes up and joins her by the window. Outside, the wind has picked up. It hisses through trees, buildings, and clouds.

"I'm looking for my father's picture," she murmurs. "My mother told me it's the last image of him. I have to find it."

They find the picture. A young man with full black hair, dark shiny eyes, and a mustache.

Sheida turns the photo around. There is nothing written on the back.

The coffee is boiling. Valerio turns off the gas and takes out two white cups from the cabinet. He pours the coffee while watching Sheida from the corners of his eyes. Sheida is embracing her knees, her feet on the edge of the chair. She doesn't look at him.

Her gaze reels away to remote corners, to the blue sky, where the sun hangs low.

What is Sheida going to do? Valerio wonders, placing the cup of coffee in front of her on the table. A terrible sensation bubbles inside him. He feels a strong urge to punch something. The wall, a tree, anything. *What if it's true?* A father executed, buried in a mass grave. There is such a weight of history behind this that it makes Valerio feel weak. He has never experienced anything of the sort, and neither has anyone he knows. For him, mass graves belong to the past, to books about the Spanish Civil War and films about the Fascist period. But not now, not in this life, not so close, not to Sheida; history is not supposed to come into one's house.

Sheida's father was three years younger than Valerio is now. He finds that mind-boggling, cannot get the thought out of his head. Did her father think death was nigh when he was twenty-seven years old? Or maybe he was so optimistic that he believed opposing a government didn't necessarily lead to being buried in a mass grave. The ignominy of mass graves! The humiliation! The disgrace!

He glances at Sheida, who looks exhausted and pale. The steam of the coffee rises and disappears somewhere between the white edge of the cup and Sheida's hands clutched around her legs. She looks at the coffee and unclasps her hands; her legs stretch out on the floor. Valerio embraces her, hoping to transmit some warmth to her body. He feels the coldness of her hands pricking inside him like the cold edge of a sword and struggles against the odd sensation of inadequacy taking shape inside him. He feels he has suddenly become a mere spectator, no longer with a role to play. Sheida has a world of her own to which he does not belong, and nor can he inveigle his way into it. He feels jealous of the mother, the country, and the unknown father that have taken his place, jealous and intimidated by just how much history Sheida has on her side.

He suggests a walk, some fresh air. Sheida doesn't need a walk.

"I have to talk to my mother," she says.

"Is that a good idea?"

She looks at him. "So many years have passed. If I don't do it now . . ." She doesn't finish the sentence; she waves a hand in the air. Valerio watches her turn around, walk into the other room, and pick up the phone.

Sheida trembles, hearing the warmth of Maryam's voice. She imagines being close to her. The scent of her mother almost fills her nostrils. She opens her mouth to say something and immediately closes it, trying to calm the beating of her heart. But on the other side of the line, her mother's sensitive radar starts picking up signals the moment she hears the tightness in Sheida's voice. She bombards her with questions. Is she okay? Has she had an accident? Has anything happened at work? Is she sick? There is anguish in Maryam's voice, the helpless anguish of a mother whose child is too far away for her to able to do anything if something ever went wrong.

Sheida is once again tempted to quell the words on her tongue, to not say anything, to continue living like before, keeping her mother on the safe side, the side of the unspoken. She closes her eyes and opens her mouth once again.

Truth cannot have so many sides.

"Did Baba ever go to prison after the revolution?" she asks, and as she does, she feels the dark ship of anguish and another feeling, almost like repentance, grow in her and sail off.

There's a long silence. The wires vibrate.

"Did he?" Sheida repeats, swallowing hard, for she realizes that she never truly believed the story of her father dying of cancer. In her grandmother's tear-filled eyes and her mother's stony face, there was something that went beyond a simple death of a husband and a son. Something disquieting. Something so large that it smothered everything else and left nothing but a shadow.

On the other end of the line, thousands of kilometers away, Maryam is silent. And then she says, "Why?"

"I've read something, and I need to know if it's true." Sheida's voice shakes.

"What have you read? What are you talking about?" The daughter can sense the mother's panic. She's seen it play out so many times.

"It's an article. It talks about the 1988 executions. There's a long list of names." Sheida's voice is unbearably high, almost a screech. "So was he in prison or not? Maman, you have to tell me the truth. Was he?" Sheida pauses. "You can't lie to me."

There is another long silence. Then Maryam's voice comes back very small. Sheida can barely hear her.

"What? I can't hear you."

"Yes," Maryam almost whispers then clears her throat. "Yes, he was," she repeats.

Tears rush to Sheida's eyes. She has not expected her mother to admit it so easily, so quickly. Her throat rattles, as if there is too much air in her lungs. She sinks heavily into the sofa, her fingers loosening their grip on the phone.

Has the moment finally arrived? Is everything going to crash down, spill over?

A few moments pass before Sheida can gather her bearings and speak again. "Why didn't you ever tell me?"

"There was nothing to say." Her mother speaks in a deep tired tone, as though her voice is coming out of an old, broken radio. "Your father died before you got to know him, and that's what you have always known."

"You told me it was cancer. You made me think he was ill."

On the other end, silence bobs up and down the line, mingled with her mother's heavy breathing.

"My father was executed," Sheida says. Her limbs feel like they are evaporating into thin air. "And you never told me. They killed him. His name is on the list. I saw his name on the list. It's all in the open, Maman."

She hears her mother let out a deep sigh, a sigh as heavy as an old secret.

"I know," she says, "I know."

Tehran, 1988

She was given the wrong bag; the wrong shirt; the wrong tooth-brush; the wrong pajamas.

She knew because she had bought the shirt, the toothbrush, and the pajamas for him. She knew because she had wrapped them herself, written his name and prison identification number on the wrapping paper, carefully, painstakingly, as if hearing the dictation of someone else's will.

She knew because she felt empty as a grave when she opened the bag. There was a hole in her. That was what death in a wrong bag could do to you. Dig a hole as big as your fist in your chest. A hole that would leave you numb for the rest of your life.

She trembled with fear and a feeling far more crippling, far more agonizing, as she touched the dead man's belongings.

The wrong dead man. The wrong belongings.

Someone else must have *his* stuff. Another wife, at that moment, was touching *her* husband's shirt.

She shivered, threw everything back into the black bag, and yanked the zipper closed.

Outside, tree leaves sprawled listlessly on the branches, underneath the sharp rays of the sun. The sky was clear, featureless.

Clutching at the bag, she ran. Down the busy street, where no one knew anything, saw anything, or heard her cries.

She ran past like a shadow that had nothing other than a bag with a dead man's belongings inside it.

With her other hand, she gripped her black headscarf to keep it from falling and revealing her shock of prematurely gray hair. She ran along the black water flowing down the wide drains, past newspaper booths, past a blind man selling contraband cigarette packets, past the grubby walls of schools, past the grubby walls of apartments, past the grubby walls of supermarkets and banks, past an old woman carrying heavy plastic bags with the side of her chador clamped between her teeth, past a long line of workers taking their lunch break at a construction site.

As she ran, she felt a sharp pain in her chest, an icy fist inside her, squeezing tightly. Her mouth twitched. She grabbed the coarse fabric of her manteau, clutching at her chest.

She was panting. Her mouth was dry, her face inflamed. Her lips felt swollen. Drops of sweat glided down her back. Her feet felt as if thousand of needles were piercing them simultaneously. But she could not stop. Her breath burned her throat. Her hand ran along the uneven slogans written on the walls. She stumbled. Her fingers scratched the thick skin of the city. She staggered; her legs bent when they weren't supposed to.

The bag in her hand fell on the ground, raising a sad vapor of dust.

Tehran, 2009

The gentle melody of Farsi wafts into the plane as mothers with thick waists tell their children to sit still. Fathers with clean-shaven faces and eyeglasses push handbags into the compartments while asking the restless little travelers if they need anything from the bags. The sound of laughter gyrates aloft and dangles from the miniature screens above the seats. Sheida closes her eyes. The tension of the past few days gradually sloughs off her body. Her thoughts drift to Valerio, to the heavy lull that fell on the apartment since her conversation with Maryam and her decision to go back to Iran. Valerio was unusually quiet, as if weighed down with emotions he did not know how to deal with and wished to speak, perhaps expecting her to ask him what he had in mind or confide to him what she had in mind. She couldn't bring herself to do it. She no longer felt interested in what was going on around her. Her grief and fury set alight a sense of spiritual detachment from the world. She felt estranged from the very air she breathed. She knew Valerio suffered as his attempts to bring her back to his world of diurnal struggle and nocturnal relax bounced off the misty wall of her detachment. She knew he wanted more from her, for her to involve him more than she had. But she felt like she had nothing for him, not now, not yet.

Slowly, as her thoughts meander away from her, something feels like it is unraveling inside her; a sweet numbness spreads down her arms. The murmuring hubbub of the passengers and the plane whizzing through space strokes her ears.

It seems like she has slept for only a few minutes when she is awakened by the crackling voice of the captain informing them that they're approaching Tehran. There is a slight commotion in the plane as headscarves and manteaus are slipped out of the compartments. The women need to prepare themselves before arrival. Scarves swing in the air, lie like a whisper on the hair, hiding thin highlights, accentuating the eyes, the arch of the eyebrows. The necks look shorter, the shoulders wider. The children laugh at their mothers' new looks. Husbands look on. Mothers smile. Their hands joggle around their scarves. For the first few minutes, it all feels like a game, light and fun.

Sheida looks out the window at the vast ocean of lights stretching into the distance. Tehran is under her feet, expanding as far as the eye can see. An anxious nausea rises up the column of her body in regular cramps. She feels sick to her stomach with excitement and anguish. She is approaching home, her city, her street, her house.

The plane makes a smooth landing, and a few people clap. After some long minutes, they slowly start getting off. Sheida's nostrils are filled with the pungent smell of smog as she crosses the threshold of the plane and steps onto the mobile staircase. She descends the stairs with faltering knees, clasping the railings, where the blue-and-orange twilight bounces.

A man in a yellow jacket and with a three-day beard directs the passengers to the bus.

"*Befarmaid khanoom*, the bus is waiting," he says to Sheida, who is looking around as if she doesn't know where she is. She turns to him, beaming. He looks at her perplexedly and says nothing.

The baggage claim area buzzes with the noises of arrival.

Throngs of women, uncomfortable in their new outfits; men afraid of being held up by passport control; children hanging like lonely keys on the huge parental key chain; porters with their yellow uniform and foreheads glittering with beads of sweat, running up and down the glossy floor, shouting to one another above the deafening, indistinct din.

At passport control, a man in a navy blue shirt buttoned up to his bulging Adam's apple scrutinizes Sheida's passport.

"Where are you coming from?" he asks in a flat voice.

"Italy."

"How long have you been away?"

"Eight years."

"The reason for your visit?"

The reason for her visit. She feels all the early excitement draining out of her. Why is she here? Why has she come back? Because her father was executed. Because her mother has been lying to her all her life. Because she doesn't know what to feel and what to think and what to do. Because history has finally caught up with her.

"To visit my mother," she says.

Outside, white and yellow lines of taxis straddle the pathway in front of the exit doors. The drivers rush forward as the glass doors slide open, disgorging nervous travelers and wizened porters. One of the taxi drivers grabs Sheida's suitcase. There is a tiny dot of hair below his bottom lip. The silver rings on his fingers glint under the fluorescent lights of the parking lot. She follows him out into the blue heat of the evening. He asks her the address.

As they plow through the clamor and smog, beyond the enormous chunks of concrete shaped into high buildings with small windows, Sheida catches a glimpse of the Damavand mountain peak. She feels a tightening in her throat at the sight of its sad, snow-covered glory. She lays a hand on the window as if she wants to grasp its image and imprint it on her palm. Her hand on the window, her breath caught in her throat, she holds on to that image like a remembered line of poetry.

The restless, sloppy traffic flashes past them, leaving behind a persistent nest of smoke. Women run across the street, the ends of their long black chadors sweeping the ground, grazing past car tires, whisking the fumes up along their bodies and into the air. Every time Sheida sees a black chador pass, her heart skips a beat at the thought of its long end getting stuck under the tires.

A motorbike whizzes past them, with two policemen riding. A man drops his wallet. A swallow perches on the branch of a mulberry tree. A child's laughter flies into the car. At the end of the street, Sheida spots another police jeep, three Revolutionary Guards standing outside of it. As the taxi leaves behind the green-and-gray jeep, the fear it has provoked in Sheida lingers. She feels like the city has turned into a military zone, eyes always watching, observing, guns and batons ready to pounce.

Gradually, the streets around her gain a familiar color. The coffee shop at the corner is still there, with its wide wooden doors and blinds on the windows. The hardware store next to it is closing for the night. An old man is pulling down the blinds. He presses on the blinds with one foot, lifting the other, letting it hang in the air. A woman is standing outside a clothing store, looking at the window display of dresses on mutilated mannequins, beheaded, their breasts cut off like unwanted lumps.

At last they reach the blue door of Maryam's apartment. Sheida gets out of the car and pulls her small trolley down the sidewalk. She takes a deep breath and rings the bell.

"Who is it?"

Sheida's voice trembles. "It's me, Maman, Sheida."

Silence and then a scream, "Sheida?" And the constant buzzing of the door, unlocked over and over again.

Sheida pushes the door open. Maryam's footfalls scurry down the staircase. One running up with her trolley, the other running down with bare feet and uncovered hair. They embrace as if clasping each other against a vile wind. Maryam touches her child's face in disbelief and holds her hands in her trembling fingers.

"What are you doing here?" she screams, laughing. "My God, what are you doing here?"

Sheida is crying. She didn't think she would, but she is sobbing so hard that she can't speak. Maryam wipes her tears with the ball of her thumb. "*Azizam, azizam,*" she repeats.

They go up, their arms wrapped around each other. Inside the apartment, nothing has changed: the brown couch, the photos of Sheida as a child on the wall, the wispy curtains, Maryam's red-and-white porcelain wedding mirror with its chipped edge. Sheida expected this. She knew nothing would be modified in Maryam's steadfast world. She knew Maryam would want her to find things exactly the way she left them if one day she decided to come back.

Maryam shows her the plants on the balcony. The sweetheart plant has grown; its leaves float down the table and onto the ground. When Sheida was a child, Maryam taught her how to clean the heart-shaped leaves: she held them one by one and wiped off the dust with damp cotton. The same way Maryam used to clean her face when she came back from work. She poured warm water in a saucer and sat on the floor, leaning against a cushion, dipping the cotton into the saucer. Stripes of water across her face. And Sheida watched as the cotton turned black.

Those were the most beautiful moments of their life together, when her mother would be at home with her, sit next to her, helping with her homework, a peaceful silence floating around them except for the hum of the heater where her mother kept their food warm until dinnertime. Then they would eat, watch their favorite TV series, each with a cup of tea and Grandmother's handmade quilt covering their legs. Sheida remembers the tired yet serene look on her mother's face that seemed to smooth out the wrinkles as she cuddled Sheida, looked deep into her face, and told her that her eyes were the most beautiful she had ever seen, that they flickered as if they had dragons in them breathing out fire, that she had not one but two rows of eyelashes on either side of her eyes. And Sheida would giggle, happy and proud.

Now, standing in this apartment where she spent both the saddest and the most joyful moments of her life, Sheida feels as if she never left. She is still the little girl whose mother, despite all her lapses and shortcomings, comprises the only solid center she has ever known.

There is a blue ceramic vase in the middle of the table with daffodils inside it. They are sold at the street corners, at traffic lights, in bunches, wrapped in old newspaper. Men with dark, dusty faces sell them, knocking at car windows with curved fingers, looping their way between cars. They rarely check the money they have been given in exchange for the tiny yellow flowers.

Mother and child eye each other across the daffodils, their thoughts roaming elsewhere. Each woman's gaze slithers through the delicate petals and has a yellow smell when it reaches the other.

Maryam talks and talks about the weather, Tehran's traffic, the daughter of a friend being accepted to the university, of another having a child. She flits from one issue to another, hoping to deviate Sheida's thoughts from the past, from the glaring pyre, from death, from the present. She is afraid of silence, afraid of Sheida's thoughts. She quickly changes the subject whenever she thinks she is losing Sheida's attention. Her words are as light as the rain.

Maryam never wanted to drag Sheida to the past. She wanted to keep her away from it and failed. Now Sheida is here, and Maryam can't pretend she doesn't know why. But she doesn't want to ask, does not want to initiate anything. She wants to keep death at bay as long as possible. There is much to talk about and yet nothing to say.

Sheida listens. She seems to be patiently waiting for the right moment to drop the bomb, burn everything down without looking back, ready to avenge herself on time and mother and motherland. Maryam takes a sip of water. She sees the blazing fire in Sheida's eyes and looks away.

"Aren't we going to talk about why I'm here?" Sheida says.

The daffodils are immobile in the vase. There is a drop of water on the tablecloth. It reflects the light of the lamp hanging above their heads.

Maryam lifts her gaze. She can't speak. She feels almost afraid of her own child. Realizing she has aged and Sheida has grown and nothing is the same anymore.

"Tell me."

"You kept Baba's death a secret from me."

Maryam does not respond or look at Sheida. Her gaze is buckled on an unknown point in front of her. Her heart bellows with pain. Her eyes remain dry. She has no more tears to offer the world.

These are exactly the words the child was never supposed to utter. These are the words Maryam dedicated her life to ward off. And now they are gliding in the air like hawks looking for prey. She has not been able to stop anything. She has been in agony, with her head crushed solidly between history's powerful knees. There are splashes of blood and brain everywhere. She has been defeated. *This is the end of the battle.*

"Were you ever planning to tell me?"

"I never thought it would come back to us like this."

"I had a right to know what happened to him."

"You couldn't do anything. It would've only ruined your life."

Sheida puts down her napkin. Her cheeks are flushed. "I couldn't do anything? What importance does it have? You've denied me my past. You've denied me my father!"

The glass trembles as Maryam lifts it to her lips and takes another short, staggering sip of water. Something hurtles down inside her. She feels bruised deep where the eyes cannot see. "I just wanted you to have a normal life. I wanted you—I wanted us to live like everyone else. I wanted to protect you." She pauses. "I was afraid."

Silence falls in the room like a curse. Maryam presses her hands on the table to keep them from trembling. She closes her eyes. *Laying it all down, every last bit and piece. Standing naked, waiting for the whip to flog down, surrendered.*

"Your father was executed." She opens her eyes and looks at

her daughter. "They came to our house and took him just a few months after I found out I was pregnant with you. They blindfolded him and pushed him into a car. I knew it was over. That day, I knew I had lost him. I knew I would never see him again in our house. He left me alone, with nothing in the world to replace him. Is that what you wanted to know? Is that the lie?" She is shaking. She feels like the floor has been pulled from under her feet. "I couldn't even mourn him. They called me, gave me his things, and said he had passed away. That's all. They told me I couldn't have a funeral for him. That's what he did to me. I was alone. I've been alone ever since. Can't you see it? I was paralyzed."

Her voice breaks off.

Sheida stares at her mother, dumbstruck. It is as though he has just died, as though decades have not passed. Maryam is still there in that old house, still watching her husband being blindfolded and taken away. She has never left that house, never left that moment. She has buried herself alive in everything that failed, everything that ended in annihilation.

"I can't move." The whites of Maryam's eyes have turned into seething pots of red. "I just stay and wait. I don't even know what for. That's all I can do. I lost a husband; I couldn't bear the thought of losing my daughter. What if she grows up and wants to follow his path? Look at what is happening now. Twenty years and nothing has changed. They've started it all over again, putting people's children in prison, killing them out on the streets. Haven't you seen it? I couldn't let that happen to you. I couldn't let them take you away from me!"

Sheida continues to stare at the tears rushing down her mother's face, at her face twisted with pain, with the jagged scars of memories. They terrify Sheida. Those tears. Those words. They crush something inside her like an empty soda can. She wanted to avenge herself. She didn't think of the tsunami breaking her mother's body open. She didn't think she would see her mother in shards and shreds, torn apart.

She wants to say something, but she can't. She wants to dig her nails into her thighs and tear the flesh out.

Outside, the clangor of running and jostling and shouting can be heard. Police sirens dovetail a woman's single scream. A helicopter roars back and forth across the silent sky.

Tehran, 1983

He said she was letting them plant fear in her. "If we let them scare us, then we will have nothing left."

She listened to him, standing by the window. She was watching the landlady on the veranda, picking stones from rice, with her floral chador sliding down her hair. She lifted a hand and swept it forward.

"They're arresting everyone," she said without turning around. "Why should you be an exception?"

"They cannot arrest everyone. There are so many of us."

He was sitting cross-legged on the ground. Next to him, a pile of anti-government leaflets he dropped into people's houses at nights. From where she was standing, she couldn't read what was written on them, but she knew this was not the revolution he had fought for. He held a cigarette stub between his fingers. The porcelain ashtray they had bought in Isfahan was next to his knee. The ash on the cigarette was so long it curved inward. She was afraid it would scatter on the rug.

He saw the worry in her eyes. He put the cigarette down on the ashtray. About her fear, he said nothing.

She placed a hand on her protruding stomach. She wanted to speak of her fear when she felt a tiny movement inside. She smiled and turned to him. "She's moving."

He scrambled to his feet and sprinted toward her. His hand on her stomach was warm. She felt the tears rushing to her eyes.

"I can't be alone when she comes. You have to be there. You have to be everywhere."

She knew he didn't like it when she spoke this way. But she couldn't help herself. She had fear growing thorns in her throat.

"I'm not going anywhere." He kissed her stomach and her hands and her neck. "I'll be right here."

The bell rang when they were putting the leaflets into piles. Maryam looked out. The sky that day was a different sort of blue, with the sun recoiling to the back, as if it were no longer watching them.

He said, *once the fear prevails, we will have nothing left.*

He was wrong.

She was left with nothing but fear.

Tehran, 2009

A mild breeze slithers through the mulberry leaves behind the window. White clouds float across the blue sky like a smiling dream. Maryam wakes up. Sheida is sleeping on the bed next to her. Her mouth slightly open; her eyes deeply shut. Maryam feels a rush of emotion, of pure joy, looking at her daughter, here with her. *At last.* She also feels strangely rested; not once did she wake up during the night. She cannot remember the last time she slept so deeply. There are two lines on the skin below Sheida's neck, like a necklace. Maryam would like to trace them with the tip of her finger. *Is this going to be a new start? Is this the first day of a new life?*

She gets up and casts a glance at her reflection in the mirror. Her swollen eyes sting. She peers into the mirror but can't see her eyes because of the fall of the folds. She runs her middle finger over one saggy eyelid and pulls it up. Scenes from last night pour back into her mind. She thought the anger had died down, and the pain. But nothing seemed to have changed. It was only waiting for the right moment to explode. She had not been able to restrain herself, to hold back memories, to continue bleeding inside. Amir's death is the greatest load Maryam has ever had to carry, his death and her secret, those lies she told Sheida, of tumors and hospitals. How ashamed she felt at times, how disgusted with herself and the way those lies disgorged from her mouth. So many times she wondered whether what she was doing was right. She had no answer, and as the years passed, she felt she had no other option. The secret had coiled hard and unrelenting around her and would no longer let a peep out of her throat. All Maryam could think of from week one, and all the weeks and months and years that followed, was surviving and forging through.

She remembers the day she moved back to her parents' house. She had lost five kilos in one week. She looked like a shadow of herself. *If you don't think about yourself, at least think about your daughter,* her mother had said as she packed Maryam's bags while Maryam sat in a corner watching her. Everything in the apartment reeked, not of Amir but of his absence, and Maryam did not have the force either to live with it or to let it go. Her mother packed all of Amir's things into a carton, sealed it with layers over layers of tape, and sent it to his mother in Hamedan. She then put Sheida in the stroller and took Maryam's hand.

It was strange to move back to that old house with its jacaranda tree whose sweet, dusty perfume woke Maryam up every night, gasping for air. The perfume of the flowers had never bothered her as a child. Now it clogged her lungs, pressing her throat as if it meant to smother her. *But you used to like it so much,* her mother would say in a plaintive voice. She did, she knew she did. Not anymore. *What is happening to me?* Maryam thought.

Instead, Sheida loved the tree. She would spend hours and hours under its shade, playing with her dolls or helping her grandmother clean the rice. As weeks and months passed, Sheida seemed more and more reluctant to stay with her mother in the room and instead preferred to stay with her grandmother in the garden. She had stopped coiling like a snail on Maryam's bed, with her elbows sinking into the mattress as she paged through a picture book, saying the names of each character out loud, almost shouting, trying to wake her mother from one of the long dozes that grew lon-

ger and longer every day. Maryam was, in fact, awake. She could
hear Sheida shouting, she just couldn't bring herself to get up. She
didn't have the strength. She felt like she had the world on her
shoulders, pressing her down. She just wanted to sleep and sleep
and never wake up. She appeared behind the white wooden lat-
ticework in the corridor only when she had to take Sheida to the
dentist or to get her vaccinations. Or when it was her turn to cook:
Tuesdays, Wednesdays, and Thursdays. *It is to get your mind off
things*, her mother had said. Or at mealtimes, when her parents
and her brother and his wife, visiting, all sat around the table, a
spoon in one hand, waiting for her. It seemed to Maryam, at the
time, that there was a deliberate rise in the volume of their voices
whenever she was about to enter the dining room. It was their
way of telling her that life had to go on. She found all the noise
irritating, as if she merely needed loud voices to forget her pain,
to forget that he was no longer there, that she was going to get old
alone, that she was going to get old with her life on pause. So she
preferred to stay in the room to sleep or look out the window or
knit one more scarf for her daughter, who hardly ever wore them.

But the day arrived when Maryam realized she had to put an
end to the long doze that was sucking her and her daughter in
alive. It was an insignificant incident, but it shook Maryam to the
core.

A year had passed. Sheida was going to start elementary school.
It was a cool and windy morning. Maryam neatly combed Sheida's
hair and put her bangs up with a small white flower-shaped pin,
getting her ready for school. But once they reached the school, the
principal wouldn't let Sheida into class. *Not without a* maghnaeh!
she said in a shrill voice. Maryam looked around. Sheida was in-

deed the only girl without a headscarf. She looked naked in the midst of covered little heads peering at her from a hole in white. Maryam felt a pang of shame, of inadequacy. She argued angrily, desperately, with the principal that her daughter was not nine years old, and according to Islam, you had to cover your hair only once you reached nine years of age, the age of *taklif*. The principal would not back down. Regulations were regulations, she averred, and nine years old or not, her daughter, like all the other girls, had to put on a *maghnaeh* when entering the school.

Maryam clammed up. She remembered that her mother had warned her about the *maghnaeh,* but she hadn't taken it seriously. She realized then that while she was wrapped in the shroud of her grief, the world had moved on, and now every little girl on the street had a headscarf on, and everyone seemed to know about it except her. She surely must have seen them. How could she not have paid attention?

She turned around to look for Sheida and saw her hiding behind the heavy iron door, holding on to the doorknob. She was standing rigidly, as if making an extra effort to keep her body whole. As though if she eased up for just a moment, her body and everything around it would crumble into pieces. There were no tears in Sheida's eyes, but it seemed to Maryam that her daughter was about to cry, that at any moment, hot humiliated tears would stream down her face. Maryam couldn't forgive herself for what she had done to Sheida, for the humiliation she had made her daughter go through. She couldn't go on like this. It was time to wake up from her sleep.

That was when she decided to find a way to leave the country. While waiting for the visa, which at the time she did not know was going to take ten years, she found a small apartment with brick walls and large windows and moved out of her parents' house. *It is time*, she said as she swooped Sheida up in her arms, her father carrying their bags behind her. Her mother waved at them, wiping her tears, pouring a bowl of water on the ground in their wake. As Maryam passed by the jacaranda tree, she inhaled deeply, filling her lungs with its fragrance; she no longer felt like suffocating.

Maryam steps out of the apartment, closing the door quietly behind her. Outside, the air is cool and fresh. It is still early. The air has not yet grown hazy with smog. The city is silent. It is this silence that, more than anything, gnaws at Maryam's nerves. She knows it, heard it thirty years ago. It is not natural, not an early-morning quiet. It is that of a city that has been beaten into silence, quickly, abruptly, without a moment of hesitation. And yet the city is still standing. A city that, although wounded and ravaged, has not backed down, a dormant volcano that could erupt at any moment. It is this standing, this resistance, that worries Maryam. Everywhere she looks, there are traces of last night's clashes: an overturned, burned trash can; broken asphalt, its pieces strewn along the sidewalk and on the street, with marks of dry blood visible on them; the writing in green on a wall, *Where's my vote?* Maryam knows there are more protests coming up, that the people will once again take to the streets. And with the protests, there will be more clampdowns and rampaging and arresting and killing. How many more victims? How many more dead? *When will the bloodshed ever end?* Maryam watches those few who, like her, are out on the street scooting past, a flux of ruffled blurry faces, cringing backs. *Will they once again succeed in draining us?*

There is a line outside the bakery. Maryam stands behind a woman wearing a white headscarf with pink flowers on it. She has a basket in her hand. Inside it are basil leaves wrapped in newspaper. The woman puts down her basket and turns to look at the sycamore tree behind them, then her glance falls on Maryam. "Another day," she says.

"And we're still here," Maryam responds.

The woman nods, gazes at the sycamore tree, and turns back to the baker, who, coated in dough powder, slides the *sangak* with a long spade out of the oven, tosses it on the counter, and flicks the stones out of its tiny holes. The bread is hot. The woman takes a sack out of her bag and puts the bread inside it.

Is Sheida happy? Maryam thinks as she watches the woman leave the line, her body slightly swaying side to side. Has Maryam been a good mother despite her frailty, her failings? She's not sure. With hindsight, she sees that she never had a clear plan about anything. She groped her way through Sheida's childhood, never knowing for certain what the right choices were. Amir had to be there. Maryam was alone and her heart was too ravaged for her to be able to focus. And all around her, it always seemed that the other mothers knew exactly what they wanted, what their children wanted. All the other mothers were able to sleep with their child in another room; Maryam did not. They knew when to cover the child's hair when going out; Maryam did not. They knew how to tell the child that everything would be okay; Maryam did not. It seemed to her that there were two types of mothers on earth: those who knew and those who did not. Maryam did not. She knew only how to protect her daughter from the secret. How to survey everything, sifting through it all, from Sheida's school courses to her father's death, before letting anything reach Sheida's mind. Maryam kept the unwanted residue to herself. The residue was everything that had gone wrong in her life. Sheida was best kept away from it, from the blood-soaked hands of history. Maryam had dug the foundation. She was the mother. She thought she knew best. But Maryam foundered, and there was no tree branch she could cling to.

Sheida is still curled up, asleep on the bed, when Maryam arrives at home. Maryam sits on the edge of the bed and strokes her daughter's hair. Sheida opens her eyes. Her sleep is as light as ever. That unchanged lightness brings the child home to Maryam. She bends and places a kiss on her cheek that smells of sleep. "Did you sleep well?"

Sheida nods and smiles. Her sleep-filled eyes are shiny. She brings her hands together and places them under her chin. "I remembered something a few days ago," she says, lifting her sleepy eyes to Maryam. "I remembered Baba all of a sudden. One of the only memories I have of him."

"What did you remember?"

"I saw him holding me up in his hands. I was really scared. That's all. I remember the fear perfectly. And there was some kind of a window."

"I took you to visit him twice. The second time, you were around three years old. I was able to pass you to him behind the glass screen, and he hid something in your clothes. I'll show it to you later." Maryam adjusts the blanket on Sheida's shoulders. As she speaks, she feels unexpectedly light and natural, as if she's been waiting all her life for this moment when she can let go. And surrender is as light as a raindrop.

"The first time, I wasn't there," she continues. "They wouldn't give me an appointment to see him. So I just took you there and insisted that he needed to see you. They finally agreed to take you in to him for a few minutes, but I had to wait outside. Your poor father didn't even know you were born. It must've been a shock when they just passed this little girl to him, saying that it was his kid."

Sheida smiles, though there is a sad look in her eyes. "What was he like?"

"Baba? Well, he was quite shy, kind of like you. But he was very determined, a bit stubborn, maybe—" She tries to laugh. Something catches in her throat. Nothing has become easier. Time does not heal wounds. It does not even overcome tears. When it comes to grief, time is nothing but a failed attempt at forgetting. "He was very kind, and he had a beautiful voice when he sang."

Sheida seems tense as she lies there looking at her mother. "I cannot imagine how difficult it must have been for you."

Is this a pardon? Maryam thinks. *Reconciliation?* She does not know how to respond. "I just wanted you to have a good life," she almost murmurs, as if no longer sure of its meaning. She has repeated these words so many times in her mind that they sound like nothing except a weak attempt to keep walls from crumbling.

"I've had a good life, Maman. I've had a beautiful life."

Maryam listens to her and thinks, *What about Italy?* She does not ask. She does not wish to open another wound. She knows she failed Sheida in Italy. She was the mother. She had to be strong. She had to protect Sheida, not the other way around. Maryam was not a reliable mother.

"I wanted your life to be full. That is, I tried to give you that life."

Sheida smiles. "Well, with all those courses you enrolled me in, chess and tennis and painting and English and calligraphy and gymnastics! Even gymnastics! I was stiff as an iron pole, and you still enrolled me in that terrifying course! So I can tell you, my life was full, all right." She laughs. Her face glows.

Maryam caresses Sheida's hair. Perhaps Sheida has indeed forgiven her. Perhaps what happened in Italy is no longer important, no longer hurts. Or perhaps Sheida does not mention it because she wishes to spare her mother. Maryam feels a lump in her throat, a lump of simmering gratitude.

"You were good at all those things," she says. "Now let's go have breakfast."

The sunrays trickling from the kitchen window into the cups give the tea a golden-red glow. Sheida places the cups on a tray and takes them to the table.

Maryam walks over to Sheida. She has a wooden box in her hand. "This is what I wanted to show you," she says, and opens the box. Inside is a bracelet made of date stones, enshrouded in pieces of white cloth, which she unravels carefully, holding it out to Sheida. "Your father made this."

Sheida places the tray on the table, looks at the bracelet. Her eyes are wide, her cheeks flushed. "This is what he hid in my clothes?"

"Yes."

They sit down. Maryam takes the bracelet out of its white shroud, out of its wooden tomb. She handles it carefully, like crystal.

"You've never worn it?"

"It's yours. I was only its keeper."

"It's beautiful," Sheida whispers.

Maryam looks at her daughter. She would like to sleep and wake up and find herself surrounded by green sparkling fields, the sunlight on her skin, the air scented with the perfume of wildflowers, the tip of the grass tickling her hands as she walks, arms outstretched, through the fields. She takes Sheida into her arms. She no longer feels like crumbling, like coming undone. For a long moment, she feels nothing. No anger. No sorrow. No shame. She turns to Sheida and clutches her daughter's face in her hands. In Sheida's eyes, he is alive, laughing, crying, hurling their unspoken words to the skies, like colored papers at a carnival.

"I'm sorry, Sheida," Maryam says. "I'm sorrier than you can imagine, for lying to you all these years, for denying you your father. But you have to give me another chance. Will you? We will begin anew."

Sheida nods, tears filling her eyes. Maryam picks up the bracelet. It's light and smooth. The date stones are so neatly attached to each other that her stomach quails.

"Let's see how this looks on you."

Maryam lays the bracelet on her daughter's wrist. She has to wait a moment for the tremor in her hands to pass before she is able to tie it. *Here it is, Amir. Here—I am giving it to her. You can rest now. It is over.*

·   ·   ·

Sheida watches her mother's slender fingers as they tie the bracelet around her wrist. She feels the heaviness and exasperation inside her slowly disappearing. She feels her heart swell with feelings difficult to describe. Joy comes close, but it goes beyond that. It inspires a sort of lightness, like the breeze, or laughter. It is liberating.

She looks at the faded, quiet bracelet on her wrist and touches it with the tips of her fingers. Tears blur her vision.

It is as though her father has at last embraced her.

Tehran, 1983

They were lying on a quilt spread on the tall grass. She could feel the grass's bouncy softness under her shoulders as it curled inward, bending to the pressure of their bodies. She stretched out a hand, reached beyond the mat, and touched its pointy head with the tip of her fingers. Somewhere beyond the sycamore trees and the dandelions, the murmur of a river filled the air.

He was propped on an elbow, the side of his head in his open palm. He held a tiny white flower. He tickled her nose with it while reciting a poem. She laughed, slapping his hand away.

He tickled her nose again. She rubbed her nose. She was about to sneeze. Her eyes were watery. Grabbing his hand, she sneezed and laughed at the same time. The crackling sound in her throat picked up and soared to the tree leaves above them. They too seemed to shake with laughter.

He laughed and threw the flower to the side, next to a packet of cigarettes, two used plastic cups, and an open book turned over on its wide, papery stomach.

"Let's have something to eat," she said, laughing her hearty laugh as she sat up and reached out for the sack. The quilt under her shoulders rose slightly, the grass straining to stand tall.

She opened the sack: boiled eggs, golden grapes, feta cheese, and olives.

He let out a sigh of delight. "You've thought of everything."

He cleaned the eggs as she watched. He had such small hands. At times, she wondered how he could do anything with those hands. They were almost smaller than hers. They were good for holding pens, or doing embroidery, or picking flowers, or caressing her, holding her like a secret. She had a yearning to bend and kiss them as they handled the white egg like a precious stone.

He handed her a skinless egg. She took it and bit into its softness. They ate quietly. Once in a while, they looked at each other and smiled. There was no need for words. They knew how to speak with their eyes. On top of the mountain, they each had come to know the cadence of the other's heartbeat.

A few swallows approached their quilt, bouncing lightly, pecking at the ends of the grass and the dry leaves strewn on the ground and in between tiny rocks.

After lunch, they decided to walk to the river. He folded the quilt and brushed his hand over the grass, as if trying to help the blades to unbend themselves. She led the way. He carried the sack and sang as they sauntered down a path looping around sycamore trees and raspberry bushes. His voice was warm, like the sunrays.

Soon the river's thunderous rumble rang through their ears and a fresh breeze spun through their hair. He stopped singing and inhaled a mouthful of the air sprinkled with river drops. They went down the rocky slope, holding hands. They listened to the tiny rocks crackling under their shoes, to the river carrying itself away.

There were tree branches in the river, half broken, half hanging on to the trees. A dragonfly flitted from one stone to the next. He tried to catch it. It flew away and landed on a glossy stone close to the riverbed.

He took off her hiking shoes and washed her feet in the cold water. Every so often, a piece of wood or a few strands of grass stumbled upon her naked feet, danced around her toes, pushed and pulled by the water, straining to free themselves. He flicked them away with the tip of his finger. She watched them float down over the rocks.

The cold of the water was numbing her feet. She slipped them out and placed them on the smooth skin of a gray-and-blue stone, warm with sun. She felt young in her feet, reborn.

She threw her head back and looked at the trees hovering overhead as if seeking to protect them from something. She placed a hand on her stomach and smiled. She looked at him. He was taking off his shoes, dipping his feet into the water, singing under his breath. She knew the song. She just needed the first hum slipping through his mouth to sing the whole song in her mind with him. But she never sang along, not out loud. She wanted to glut herself with the intimacy of his voice. She gently caressed her stomach. From the outside, she imagined caressing what was inside it.

When she told him the news, he laughed, almost cried. His eyes sparkled like raindrops in sunshine.

"You're the miracle," he said.

He tucked yellow flowers in between her toes, one by one, like a yellow crown.

The wind slowly roused itself, sweeping a few dry leaves off the ground, carrying them away, as if they were its lost, unborn children.

2010
Tehran, the Islamic Republic of Iran

Sara slips into the chair gingerly, so as not to upset the pieces on the chessboard. Her hands emanate a sweet whiff of coconut soap, which makes Donya feel like they are on a tropical island instead of in Tehran, with its frost-enameled streets.

"Whose turn is it?" Sara asks.

"Yours."

Sara runs her fingers through her hair, places her chin in her cupped hand, and observes the battle scene with the placidity of an experienced general.

They are sitting in the center of the lemon-yellow living room at a round glass-topped table. Olive-green velvet curtains have been drawn across all the windows but one. Through the mist rising, Donya can see the grubby wall of the Evin prison, running adjacent to the dust-ridden slopes of the mountain.

When she first arrived in Tehran a few weeks ago, she was startled by how close Sara's apartment was to the prison; she couldn't believe the city's expansion. Newly constructed buildings were springing up everywhere. The city had stretched its limbs, burrowed into the thorny edges of the mountain, and become neighbors with a once isolated prison.

"It's a city of seventeen million," Sara said, obviously enjoying Donya's surprise. "What did you expect?"

Donya watched a man climbing up the road toward the prison's entrance with flowers in one hand and a small bag in the other. She wondered what it contained. Warm clothes? Letters? Cigarettes? Dribs and drabs of a strangled life.

The hovering shadow of the walls was a weight he seemed doomed to carry forever. A hunched figure, he walked with difficulty, half limping, half hobbling to the gates. Like her grandfather must have done years ago, walking up the same road, carrying a similar bag, bent with the force of the same doom, in hopes of seeing his daughter, Firoozeh, behind those very same walls.

When she told her mother over the phone of the closeness between the prison and the city, Firoozeh remained mostly silent. Donya knew she was giving undesired information; her mother did not wish to know. Since their emigration to America almost fifteen years ago, Firoozeh had never returned to Iran, and she had made it clear that she had no intention of ever doing so. There was a tint of hatred in Firoozeh's refusal to return, which at times made Donya wonder what could have happened inside the prison that had thus traumatized her. Had they threatened her, tortured her? She wondered about this silently, for she was afraid of asking, afraid of the answer her mother might give her. What if they indeed tortured her? Or maybe forced her to do something she did not wish to do? Donya did not feel courageous enough to know.

As she stood by the window of Sara's apartment, Donya's gaze trailed the man until he vanished in the darkness that swept forcefully, quickly, across the prison, the slope, the thorns, and the ghosts of men and women who never returned from behind those walls. If she looked carefully, she could see lumps of shadow in front of the entrance, which seemed to have become one with the shadow of the man. At times, the shadows seemed to be moving, but it was too dark to tell what or who they were.

That was when Sara told her about Omid's return from a trip, first to Germany to visit Forugh and then together with Forugh to Italy to visit Forugh's cousin Neda. About Omid and his wife, Elnaz. Donya stood still as she listened, dazed, like a woman in an old photograph who didn't know how the camera worked.

"I've asked them to come over on Thursday," Sara said, her voice pulsating with a cautionary tone. She seemed to want to prepare Donya, to prevent accidents. Sara liked things to go as planned, like a stream that never changed its flow, never ran astray into unknown terrains in search of adventure. "Dante will be here too. You met him last time you were here, remember?"

Donya nodded, no longer paying attention to what Sara was saying about Dante. Hearing the name of Omid made something shake softly inside her. She clasped her hands and said, "Yeah, sure. That's wonderful."

Inside, it was as if her heart had been soaked in a pond of freezing light.

Now, days later, Sara wraps her manicured fingers around the head of a black bishop and slides it across the chessboard.

"Check," she says.

Donya presses her feet on the rug and folds her hands in her lap. Her feet are warm in her wool stockings. She's wearing a white dress with white flowers in green outlines that rustles as she moves. It took her a while to decide what to wear tonight. She leafed through her clothes hanging in Sara's closet over and over, unable to imagine how he'd like to see her, how she wanted to be seen.

What does love look like after six years?

In the end, she went with this dress. Elegant but neutral, she decided. The white of the dress brings out the black of her eyes and the olive of her skin. She refrained from wearing any jewelry, wishing to look simple. Not to look as if she wants to please; not to give herself away when there is the wife involved. It is odd, her lack of curiosity about his wife. She considers the woman insignificant. No, not insignificant. More like irrelevant. Irrelevant to the story that is hers and Omid's. The wife is the one who came after. After the end of the story. The territory has already been trodden, explored, lived by Donya. The territory of his body, his love. Donya is its true mistress. No land can be owned twice.

She checks the time on the numberless clock as Sara watches her with perfectly almond-shaped eyes. Donya smiles and averts her gaze. The ticking of the clock reverberates in her ears. She returns her attention to the game; she knows her next move. She knows that victory is nigh.

Even after so many years, she can't look at a chessboard and not think of those hot summer afternoons in the stuffy cultural center that her mother insisted on taking her to. The memories still fill her with anguish. The anguish of planning, of plotting, of reading the opponent's mind, of making the wrong move. The early awareness of that most cruel fact of life: you either win or you lose. There is no middle ground. There is no space where you can float, undisturbed. Hers was the angst of fatality.

She gives a last sweeping look at the chessboard. A complacent smile runs a soft wave over her lips. She picks up the rook from the far end of the board, flies it over the black and white squares, and knocks Sara's bishop over.

"Checkmate."

Sara frowns. She looks intently at her pieces, as if she means to pierce them with her gaze. The shriek of the doorbell makes them both jump.

"They're here," Sara says as she gets up.

He is here.

Donya watches Sara spring out of the room. She doesn't know what to do with herself as her heart hammers its way to the outer edge of her chest. She lives a few moments of agonizing quandary while she wavers between following Sara to the door and waiting in the living room, wringing her fingers until they're red. She walks to the window. A glossy layer of ice unfolds across the black-and-blue streets and on the long bent necks of lampposts slowly coming to light, white and yellow, mingling with smoggy twilight. The trees look asleep, a hazy halo of light around their scanty leaves. The prison is drenched in darkness. It can hardly be seen, both the prison and its shadows.

From the voices flowing into the room, she tries to decipher Omid's but can't hear it. Sara's high-pitched voice drowns everything out. Then she sees him walking into the room. Her first negotiation with happiness and loss. The same brown beard, the same warmth in his eyes, the same lean shoulders, the same nervous half-smile. His hair is much shorter than she remembers. Six years ago, his hair covered the sides of his neck. He looks tense, screwing his eyes the way Donya used to know so well, used to love so much. A tremble winds around her chest.

His tall wiry body covers the length of the room in a few long rapid strides. Donya has barely enough time to unclasp her pressed fingers before he grabs her hand and places two hurried kisses on her cheeks as he says, "You still kiss, don't you?"

"Yes." Her voice plows through the anxious knot in her throat. She doesn't really understand what he means by this question.

Behind him, his wife is standing. She raises her thin eyebrows as she shakes Donya's hand, slightly wrinkling her perfectly reshaped nose. Her mouth opens into a slow, lazy "Nice to meet you." With her other hand, she unwraps her headscarf, revealing shocks of silver highlights.

Donya is glad to avert her gaze from Elnaz; she turns to Dante, who embraces her in his strong arms. "Were you planning to come and visit us when we were all grandparents?"

"We're all well on our way."

Dante laughs as he opens the black bag in his hand and turns to Sara. "Look what I've brought." He smiles triumphantly, placing two bottles of wine on the table next to the chessboard.

Donya carefully moves the chessboard to the top of a small cabinet and sits down on the sofa.

"I don't know how you do it, Dante." Sara places five glasses on the table. "I'd be too afraid of driving around with two bottles of wine in my car."

Omid uncorks one of the bottles. The air inside is released with a gentle blop. "You should never be afraid of wine," he says.

The wine gurgles softly as it streams out of the long black neck of the bottle and into the glasses. As she watches him, an unexpected sense of calm embraces Donya. She wishes she could sit here forever, inside the carapace of an interlude, time standing at a corner, waiting for her to give it a signal to go on. It is as if, all her life, she's yearned for this peaceful moment of nothing and near, when he is with her in the same room, when she does not have to make a decision. When everything seems like a hallucination about which she does not need to worry, the sweet numbness spreading across her limbs. Not to feel excited, nervous, entranced; to be perfectly still in a moment of pause. Like just before a storm hits.

They were sitting cramped in the front passenger seat of a taxi; the window was halfway down. The streets were clogged with cars and buses and motorbikes and their diesel-drenched fumes. The tentative white lines on the asphalt demarcating each lane were ignored—simply overridden. Pedestrians and cars were all moving in the same space, with the same flow, looping around, circumventing, dodging one another. Cars honked, engines croaked, people shouted over the traffic. An all-encompassing, overpowering, window-rattling din that swept into the taxi like a sandstorm.

It was hot. The air-conditioning wasn't working. Donya stretched out a hand to roll down the window, but the handle was missing. The driver must have hidden it somewhere. It was the same in many other taxis on the ever-jammed streets of Tehran. The drivers hid the handles because they were afraid passengers would break them with the excessive rolling of the windows. Once in a while, a daring passenger would ask for the handle. The driver would grumble something about costs, the window being at its best height, too many demands. If the passenger insisted, he'd have no choice but to open the glove compartment with an exaggeratedly irritated gesture, extract the imprisoned handle, and give it reluctantly to his demanding customer.

Donya didn't dare ask.

"There are poems that would've been much better off written as essays," Omid said as he stretched his arm out behind her on the back of the seat and placed his warm palm on her shoulder. "If it's anything that can easily be articulated in an article, then it's an insult to put the same thoughts and ideas into the language of poetry. It sullies its essence, because poetry is there to say what cannot be said. It is there to speak of the hidden, the secret, the sacred."

He lowered his head and looked into Donya's eyes. His eyes shone with a particular light. His gaze had nothing to do with the words he was uttering. It spoke of other emotions, tacit, in flames, blazing away with desire so overwhelming, affection so penetrating, that Donya could only call it love.

They had known what they called each other's "adult version" for only two weeks. The last time they had seen each other, she was ten and he eleven, Donya's family was leaving the country, and Omid had come with his mother and Sara to say goodbye. Now each could not believe how the other had grown. They were curious about each other, eager to know who the other had turned out to be. Since meeting at his mother's house, where Donya was staying at Firoozeh's request, they had been inseparable. Donya felt mesmerized by him, by his knowledge of poetry, his passion for politics, his having read Karl Marx's *Manifesto* from the beginning to the end. He spoke and she listened, imbibing every word, absorbing with such fervency, such admiration that at times it shocked her. He spoke with the same vehemence with which she listened, as if there were nothing in the world as important as speaking to her, pouring everything he knew and felt and was, out and into her. She knew he was trying to impress her, and she felt inebriated with the sheer joy of it.

At the shrill of a honking car about to collide with the taxi, Donya jumped. The taxi driver angrily muttered something under his breath as he changed gears. He didn't even glance at the driver of the honking car, who waved his arm frantically in the air, yelling out some curse or other.

"Poetry has no mission beyond itself," Omid continued as the taxi stopped to drop off the passengers in the backseat and pick up new ones. "Don't ever listen to those people who ask what message your poetry means to convey. That's all nonsense. Poetry is poetry only when it reveals the depth of your soul. That's all. Not the reader's soul but your soul, the soul of the poet. The reader is secondary." He turned to the driver. "We get off here."

The taxi stopped in front of a recently built white condominium complex with a white cement fountain in front.

"*Parsi raa paas bedaarim!*" the taxi driver said with a smile as he took crumbled rial notes from Omid's hand.

Protect the Persian tongue!

Omid nodded. He looked annoyed, as if he had just realized that someone other than Donya had been listening to him.

In the ascending elevator, he pulled her close. She liked the touch of his beard against her skin and laughed. His hair and her fingers entangled.

"What?" he asked.

"It's strange. I'm so happy. It feels so easy to be happy."

Throughout the evening, they held on to each other while others stumbled around them, dancing, with tipsy smiles. A few started singing along with the song spurting out of the speakers. Their voices bounced against the thick layers over layers of curtains drawn to keep the noise from seeping out into the streets, where men with guns patrolled the nocturnal silence of the city in search of signs of happiness to repress, to flog silent the undesired laughter of a revolution.

Omid grasped Donya's hand and led her to the kitchen, where bottles of vodka exchanged hands. Donya watched as he poured the transparent liquid into two plastic cups and handed one to her. His smile spoke of growth, of exciting hinterlands.

"I've never drunk alcohol before," Donya shouted over the music.

"You haven't? Isn't there any vodka in California?" he joked.

"There is." Donya laughed. "I've just never had any." She was beaming. She knew that he found her unusual innocence enticing. "I'm not twenty-one yet. I had to come all the way to Iran to get drunk!"

He held up his cup. "Then here's to your first drink. *Salamati!*"

They gulped down the shots. A burning sensation hurtled from the tip of her tongue all the way down to her stomach. She gave out a laugh, joyful and untethered. He pressed his vodka-tasting mouth to hers.

"Next week is the anniversary of Ahmad Shamlou's death,"

Omid said as he pulled back without pulling away. "People gather at his grave every year to commemorate him, to read his poems."

"Are you going?"

"Are you coming with me?"

"Yes."

His face has matured. Vestiges of stories unknown to her are engraved upon the fair skin. He tilts his head as he speaks and holds his wineglass in cupped hands, with his elbows on his thighs. He is not wearing his shirt in that indifferent, rebellious manner of the past. He's tidier, more self-conscious, more in line with the demands of the world.

She watches him, her back basking in the warmth floating out of the silent heater. Her nerves are on edge. The first moments of excitement are wearing off, and reality has begun to settle in. The reality of Omid sitting only a meter away and yet blocked from her by years of separation, by a wife with a nose job, by her own inertia years ago, by having so easily run out of patience and letting distance and time conquer all. Six years ago, when it was time to go back to America, she had promised Omid that she would return the next summer. He was going to wait for her. *No matter how long it takes*, he said. They were going to live together in Iran. *Build a life together here, in this land. Why should we go anywhere else when this country needs us?* Donya accepted enthusiastically. These were the most beautiful words she had ever heard. To build their life and their country and finish everything their parents had left undone.

She promised to come back in a year, to come back and visit

him every summer until she finished university and she could move back indefinitely. For the first year, she was full of that promise. They spoke every day on the phone, sent letters, e-mails. She knew she could never find anyone like him; his dream was her dream. Their life awaited them. And yet as the months passed, it proved more and more difficult to keep her promise. Distance was gaining shape, solidifying. Donya felt alone and did not know how to handle her loneliness. At times she almost felt like not having anyone was easier than having someone so far away. *How am I going to do this? Month after month? Year after year?* She felt exhausted, like her life was nothing but a series of phone calls and e-mails. Omid did everything in his power to make things easier for her. He even arranged to pay for her airline ticket that summer. Then in the spring, Donya's grandfather fell ill. It was a painful day when she told Omid that she could not come. She had to stay with her grandfather. Omid did not protest. His silence was a tired, resigned silence. She knew he had already lost faith in her. After that day, their phone calls and e-mails became less frequent until, eventually, it all stopped without them ever saying goodbye.

Donya sinks deeper and deeper into the cushions of the sofa. She tries to straighten her back but can't. She feels pressed in by the past, by memories, by regret and other emotions she is too afraid to recognize. For a moment, the thought of Keyvon, her fiancé, the man she is going to marry in a few weeks, flashes through her mind. A clean-shaven face. Strong aftershave. Confident, easy, secure, there. The thought does not linger. It slips away and vanishes into the air like a cloud of dust. And instead of his face, another memory takes shape. Once, she remembers, after she and Omid made love, they wore each other's clothes and observed their reflections in the mirror. They giggled and touched and breathed into each other's bodies.

You make a nice woman.

You make a nice man.

There was something arousing in the novelty of the other's body in the familiar clothes. They pressed their palms against each other's mouth as they made love. Again.

I want to carry your breath on the palm of my hand.

Donya runs her fingers down the length of the glass, places them back up against the edge, runs them down the length, over and over again. She looks at Omid and resents the calm in his face, without a trace of reminiscence. She resents her own composure, the way she smiles at his wife. She resents all the mannerisms and placidity that come with the lull of time. They have both been behaving so well that Sara, who at first looked from one to the other with a gaze full of apprehension, is now tranquilly drinking her wine. She seems reassured that Donya and Omid have forgotten things that need not be remembered.

But Donya remembers everything. As clearly as the sheet of ice taking shape behind the window. She is hedged in by memories. She wishes she could look at him and see nothing.

I wish you were here so I could squeeze your hand. So that I would know there is something real around me. You're far. From inside the car, I hardly ever see the sky, he once wrote in a letter.

"I didn't expect to see so many Iranians in Turin," Omid says, looking around the table. Donya expects his eyes to settle on her, for his gaze to cross paths with hers, but it doesn't. It moves on. "Neda says in one year the number of Iranians has increased from a handful to more than fifteen hundred people."

Murmurs of surprise gyrate around the table. Sara takes a slow sip of her wine. She glances at Donya and gives her a smile. There is something exaggerated in her smile, as if she means it to break a spell.

"They're mostly students," says Elnaz, dragging out the words.

Why does she have to drawl that way and not speak naturally? Donya thinks, irritated.

"Since the crackdown and the mass arrests of last year, everyone is leaving Iran," Dante says to Donya by way of explanation. "Things have gotten much worse."

"It's like something heavy has fallen on top of us," Sara joins in. "Much heavier than before, smothering us little by little. We don't know whose words to believe, whom to trust. We feel as helpless as we felt powerful last year."

Omid places his empty glass next to Elnaz's on the table. "But the time just before the elections was beautiful, wasn't it? It now almost feels like a dream. The TV debates, the campaigning on the streets, all out in the open. It felt like any other country, like things were really changing."

Sara's face lights up. "I remember wearing something green every day, and I didn't even like green! But during the elections, it became my favorite color. It still is."

"Mine too," says Elnaz. "There were so many people. We were like a sea of green."

"What about the clashes?" Donya unconsciously lowers her voice, as if afraid of asking. "Weren't you worried about getting beaten?"

Sara laughs. "That's only the first time. Then you get used to it."

Donya gasps, clasping her hands in disbelief. "So you were beaten?"

"All of us were," Elnaz says.

"What happened before the elections was that they fooled us by opening up to us like that, and we fell for it," Dante says, not looking at anyone in particular. "They just wanted us to come out so they could identify us and see how many we were. It was only a trap. Once we came out of our houses, wearing our green shirts and scarves and waving banners around, it was more than easy to beat us into pieces. I still can't believe how we trusted them. We, of all people, should not have fallen for that sudden liberated air they made us think we were breathing before the elections. We should have known better."

No one says anything. From the quickness with which everyone lapses into silence, Donya understands that this is a discussion that all those present have had before, perhaps many times, repeating the same arguments, frustrated, unable to find answers.

She watches Elnaz cross her legs. She is wearing a short denim dress with a massive black belt encircling her curvy body. A row of silver bracelets on her solarium-tanned arms glints under the light.

"They might have identified us, but we also identified each other," Donya says in a low voice. She feels a bit shy to speak of "us" when she was not here, when she only watched everything on the news, thousands of miles away. "Now you also know how many you are."

No one says anything. Elnaz shifts on the sofa. Dante gazes at her with a sad smile. Donya never would have said anything if Omid hadn't been there. She wouldn't have dared. The tourist speaking of "us" and hope on her holiday break. But all this doesn't matter. Donya wishes to awaken something, to draw something from a world that's been lost, from her and Omid's world.

"And you were so many," she continues. "You were breathtaking."

Sara's eyes glitter. "We were, weren't we?"

"And we were on every television screen in every country of the world," Omid says, leaning forward, looking at Donya. She notices Elnaz's hand slink behind his back and tug at his shirt, as if she wants to stop him from speaking. *Does she know something?* Donya wonders. She can't repress the urge to interpret the gesture as a sign of Elnaz's jealousy.

Omid seems not to notice or, as Donya hopes is true, to ignore his wife's hand ever so stealthily tugging at his shirt. He continues. "We were a force that made them panic. They did not expect us to be so many."

Donya wishes he would speak more, venture further into what he thought and lived during those days. To argue with her, smile at her. She wants to see his eyes shine with that light he gets when he feels he's teaching her something.

The first time they made love, he held his head full of wild hair above hers and said, "You're a woman now."

"We might have frightened them, but they crushed us," Dante says, waving an angry hand in the air. "They left nothing of us. Most of the people I know are either in prison or have already fled the country."

Omid leans back, not responding. Sara looks tired. Donya does not know what to say. She gets up and walks to the window. The shadows are still there.

"What are those shadows?" she asks.

"What shadows?" Sara says.

"Come and see them. I've seen them before. I think there are people in front of Evin."

They all get up and join her by the window. She points at the shadows. "Those."

A flickering light can be seen where the shadows seem to be huddling together.

"They're there to celebrate a birthday," says Omid.

"A birthday?"

"It's the birthday of one of the students who was arrested last year during the protests. His family's there to celebrate it."

"They're not allowed to go in?"

"This is as far as they can go."

Pressing their faces against the window, cupping the room's light out with their hands, their breathing appearing and disappearing rhythmically on the window, they look at the motionless black lumps that are almost invisible in the cold night. As Donya watches the shadows huddling together, it dawns on her that what truly made her break her promise to Omid was not the distance. She had not been able to admit it then, even to herself, but she can see it clearly now that there was something else that had frightened her, intimidated her. The distance was merely an excuse. What made Donya recoil was Omid's dream of living in Iran. The prospect of living in this country where life overwhelms you, submerges you completely with its unflinching, unpredictable, ruthless reality. Donya was not ready for that. She did not have Omid's fortitude to live so intimately with nightmares of youth and prison and blood. And huddling shadows that carried so much pride and desolation and hurt. Donya could not handle that. She was not cut out for it.

She places a hand on the window, feeling a lump in her throat, as if the shadows are beginning to grow inside her.

"It must be so cold out there," she says.

For a long moment, silence holds sway as they stand there, watching the shadows and the wavering flicker of the candlelight.

"It's strange, but the shadows and candlelight remind me of wartime," Elnaz says. "At the time of the bombings, we used to pull the curtains and sit at the far end of the room, away from the windows, with only one candle burning."

Omid looks at his wife and smiles. "We always left the house. My grandfather would take us outside the city to the countryside."

"I don't remember that," Sara says.

"You were too young to remember. It was you, me, Forugh, Maman Zinat, Aghajaan, and Khaleh Leila. We would get into Aghajaan's car and drive out of the city. If I remember correctly, we would sleep in the space between two parked cars." Omid leans his shoulder against the window. Elnaz watches her husband speak. Donya watches the two of them and feels a squeeze in her chest.

"I remember once when Khaleh Leila was out and hadn't come back home when the sirens started ringing," Omid continues. "I was so scared I couldn't talk. I was just watching the sky and hoping nothing would fall on us until she came back. I cried so much I could barely see anything. And then, when I saw her through the door, it was like they had given me the world. I will never forget that moment when she appeared. It was one of the happiest moments of my life."

Elnaz stretches out her hand and caresses her husband's arm.

"Where was Khaleh Leila?" Sara asks.

"I don't know. She said she had gone to see her friend, but for some reason, I didn't believe her. I felt like she was lying. That was the first and last time I ever felt like she was hiding something from me."

"You were a clever little boy, weren't you?" Sara teases. "You even knew when people lied to you."

"I did. It's true."

"Well, I don't think that's too implausible. Like all of us, I imagine Khaleh Leila has many more secrets," Dante says.

"What do you mean?" Sara looks at him with a searching gaze. "Has Forugh told you something?"

At the mention of Forugh, something sparkles in Dante's eyes. A glitter Donya has not seen before. She wonders if there is something between them. She must ask Sara about it when everyone is gone.

"Forugh? No. Forugh would know less than any of us. Anyway, she's even more defensive than you when it comes to Khaleh Leila. It's as if Khaleh Leila has to be protected, kept away from the evils of the outside world or something. I don't know. Maybe it's different for me than for you. I just think there's always been a mysterious aura about Khaleh Leila." Dante pauses, lowers his voice a bit, seems to be trying to regain control of his emotions. "Don't you think?"

"I don't know. I don't think so." Sara seems disturbed, not enjoying this conspiratorial conversation about her aunt.

Dante smiles, perhaps to avoid further distressing Sara. "Well, I don't know. Maybe I just always imagined her having this incredible life outside of that house, a life to which none of us had any access. I've always enjoyed thinking of her like that."

"Well, whether she was telling the truth that day or not, we will never know," Omid says. "I just know that seeing her again after having thought I lost her was my first true experience of happiness."

Elnaz checks her watch, places a hand on Omid's shoulder. "It's getting late. We should be going."

Everyone turns and slowly walks away from the window and the shadows and the weight of those desperate hearts and hopeful candle flames and the lightness of memories rising.

Omid helps Elnaz put on her coat and turns to Donya. "Maybe we can go up to the mountains next weekend."

Elnaz looks on with uninterested eyes.

"I'm leaving in four days," Donya says. She feels the heat of regret rushing up to her cheeks. Four days. What are four days in the span of a lifetime? When it comes to Omid, time has never been on her side.

"Four days?" Omid's eyes widen in disbelief. His long eyelashes cast a shadow over the sadness of his eyes. Donya cannot withstand his stare, which makes her feel as if she's betraying something. She mumbles a few words about coming back again next year.

No one says anything. When he shakes her hand, she cannot hold his gaze. He flees her.

Back in the living room, Donya can't stay put. She feels disoriented and stands by the heater, holding her hands over it, and looks at the framed photo above it. It is of Sara and Omid and Forugh sitting on a bench, behind them a dark green screen. They're very young. Sara and Forugh look two or three years old. Omid, the eldest, is sitting in the middle, his arms around his sister and cousin. In his red-and-brown-checked shirt, he looks like a tiny adult, with his wide, innocent eyes. Through Forugh's parted lips, her tongue seems to be peeking. On Sara's white overalls is written: *My Silent Place*. Their three tiny faces stare blankly at the camera. Not one of them smiles.

"Isn't it a nice photo?" Sara asks as she comes and stands next to Donya. "I took it recently from my mom's album. I thought I should have it framed."

Donya continues to stare at the photo and nods.

"It was Khaleh Leila who took us to a photographer. She sent copies of this photo to our mothers in prison so they could see how healthy and unsmiling we were." Sara laughs.

"What's going on with Forugh's hair?" Donya says, forcing a smile. "Looks like she's been electrocuted."

Sara laughs again. "I know. Khaleh Leila says that it was because her hair was too fine. And look how blond I was! Now my hair is blacker than yours." She walks to the sofa and sinks cozily into it.

"Is there something going on between Forugh and Dante?" Donya asks.

Sara pulls a small blanket over her shoulders. "Yes and no. They say there isn't, but they write to each other, call each other all the time. Three years like this since my grandmother's death. So we think there is something."

"Why would they deny it?"

Sara shrugs. "I don't know. Maybe because they don't know what the future holds."

"What do you mean?"

"Well, Forugh won't come and live here. Dante doesn't want to go and live in Germany. So they're stuck, and we're all stuck with them." Although Omid told me that Dante is beginning to change his mind. He's been inquiring about visas for Germany."

Donya walks back and lowers herself onto the sofa. "Did Dante participate in the demonstrations?"

"He did. He even got arrested once. They kept him for a few days, but as soon as he came out, he started taking to the streets again. Maybe that's why he's so angry, so disappointed. He really believed something was going to change, and now with this decision to go to Germany, I imagine he's suffering even more. It's like he's putting a final closing point to all his hopes for change."

"Didn't you believe that something was going to change?"

"Maybe not as much as he did." A moment passes before Sara speaks again. "So does he look different?"

"Who?"

"You know who."

"He's cut his hair."

"His wife likes it short."

"It looked like he didn't remember anything."

"Don't be silly." Sara's mouth twists into a yawn. "Of course he remembers."

"There was really no sign that he did," Donya says as she fiddles with a piece of thread hanging from the hem of her dress. "He was so normal. Everything was normal. I really started to doubt that he remembers anything."

"What did you expect to happen?"

Donya leans her head back. Her gaze drifts away to the wet darkness outside. "I don't know. I wish there had been something. Some kind of an awkward moment, a glance, a smile. Something private between the two of us, some kind of acknowledgment of the past."

"And what were you going to do if there was a glance? Or a smile?" Sara looks at her, unamused, apprehensive. At times, Donya cannot tell if Sara is protecting her or her brother. Donya does not respond. She watches the reflections of the lights on the window, like eyes of sick pigeons staring.

"You're getting married in two weeks, Donya," says Sara after a few moments of silence. Her voice is aloof. She doesn't wish to be confided in any longer. She gets up, dragging the blanket with her. "And you're leaving in four days. I would focus on Keyvon if I were you, on your future together."

As Sara disappears into the bedroom, Donya listens to the last remnants of her voice lolling in the air.

Sara is right. Keyvon is waiting for her. She has to live with the past stored away somewhere in the back treasure chests of her mind. The past is slippery, unreliable, like melting snow on marble stairs. Donya closes her eyes. What has become of her that she can't even fight for her own happiness? Has she over time changed its definition, adapted it to her world, made of comfort zones and certainty and tranquillity like a huge calm blue lake?

She remembers the day she found out Omid was getting married. It was about three years ago. His mother, Parisa, had come to America with photos of family and friends, and Donya saw a photo of Elnaz. Until then, she knew nothing of Elnaz. She did not even know Omid was getting married.

"Who is that?" she asked Parisa, pointing at Elnaz, who looked thin and ill at ease standing next to Omid.

Parisa told her that was Omid's fiancée. Parisa's voice was low, as if she did not wish Donya to hear her. But there was a loud clank in Donya's ears, and for a moment, she could hear nothing more. She only continued staring at Parisa's hands, which quickly changed the picture. She then went to her room, locked the door, and from the bottom drawer of her wardrobe, took out a heavy folder filled with the printouts of Omid's e-mails. She went through them one by one, perusing them with dilated eyes, looking for something, she did not know what, until nightfall. It was then she realized that it was too late to turn anything around.

She opens her eyes. Outside, the tiny candle flames continue to burn into the night. How happy she would have been if she'd fought for Omid and was now lying next to him, falling asleep surrounded by the heat of his body. How happy she would have been if she hadn't let him go so simply.

She sits slumped on the sofa, watching the shadows, unable to move.

The overcast sky drops a pallor over the living room. Donya is sitting on top of a cushion on the carpeted floor, holding a cup of tea clamped between her fingers. The morning sun is veiled behind ashen clouds.

She is sore. She has not slept a wink, haggard with doubts, fears, the weight of a voiceless past. She sips the lukewarm tea as brown stains cling to the inside of the cup. She places it on the table and looks around her. Her gaze is automatically drawn to the sofa and the artifacts Keyvon has ordered for their summerhouse. There is Michelangelo's *Creation of Adam* on a handwoven silk rug. God seems to be frowning. Adam has a vine leaf covering his genitals. Donya is not sure if the leaf is there based on Keyvon's orders or if it's there to ease the rug's passage through Iranian customs; Adam cannot be seen naked when a woman is around!

Donya thinks of the hands behind the silky knots, with callused fingers. The unknown artists of an ancient land. What did they think of this rug? Did they like it? Did they enjoy stooping over knots in God's slanted hand? Did they giggle behind closed doors at that vine leaf?

At the foot of the sofa is a rug with the face of Keyvon's favorite actress smiling enchantingly. This was also a special order. On top of the rug, overturned, is a replica of the head of an Achaemenid king in a material that looks like bronze but is really brass. Next to it is a glossy painting of an old man with a white flowing beard, a long-haired young woman with protruding lips and a thin waist offering him a blue ewer of wine. Next to the two is a *ghazal* by Rumi, written in calligraphy. Keyvon didn't care which *ghazal* as long as there was the old man with the young woman.

As she looks at them, Donya's face grows taut with disapproval and an odd sense of exasperation. Everything looks so false, so self-indulgent. She bristles with the thought that soon she will have to surround herself with this kitsch and pretend to admire it. *How could Keyvon want any of these? He has never even read Rumi!* And yet she is not surprised. She knows Keyvon wants something convenient, something he knows others will recognize and admire. What could Donya say? How could she blame Keyvon for wishing to be sure of his place in the world? How could she blame his need of reassurance in a Michelangelo?

Donya places the cup back on the table, letting out a despairing sigh. Suddenly, she feels claustrophobic, her heart being squeezed in her chest. She needs to get out. But as she gets to her feet, she bangs her knee against the table. Paralyzing pain shoots from her kneecap up her joints with the speed of a bullet. Grabbing her leg, she thrusts the other hand out to keep the rattling cup from overturning. Her face is twisted with pain. Inside the cup, the tea is trembling, the brown stains fluttering like muddy butterflies.

Donya catapults back onto the sofa, rubbing her knee, muttering curses against the table, the weather, herself. On the other side of the window, the yellow leaves shiver under the onrush of rain.

She hoists her body up and hobbles to the bedroom, where she starts getting dressed, swaddling herself against the cold. What was it that Milan Kundera said about kitsch? She tries to remember as she buttons up her overcoat, but she can't think straight. An unfathomable anger is taking shape inside her. And sadness, acute and demanding. And pain, whispering.

Observing her face in the mirror, she applies the cold moisturizer to the bluish skin under her eyes. Her long nose is more pronounced than ever, as if someone dug out the flesh around it during the night. She looks at the tuft of hair peeking from underneath her scarf: black, simple, intact. *How could he marry a woman with such ostentatious highlights and a nose job?* She snatches her purse and the umbrella from the hanger and sprints out of the apartment.

Outside, the frosty breath of winter strikes. Shriveling inside her overcoat, Donya begins walking. The gray-and-white buildings look dismal under the rain. An old wrinkled man sells boiled beetroots on a cart, warming his hand on top of the steaming pot. A few women stand chatting at the doorway of a grocery store. Donya walks past them, past a long line of naked trees dying slowly, past a clothing shop not yet open, past dead flowers on the sidewalk, dripping.

Out of breath, she stops to look around her. Instead of the park she was expecting, she finds herself in front of the Evin prison. She takes a step back, flinching at the sight of its grubby walls, menacing, insurmountable before her. She has never been so near.

For a moment, she is unable to move, unable to take her gaze off the walls. The raindrops fall large and heavy on her umbrella. The violent battering and the silence of the prison make her feel jittery. The cold sneaks through the layers of her clothes and glides against her body. Her nose is running.

She turns around and begins walking away as quickly as possible, almost running, as if someone is after her. She keeps her eyes glued to the ground to sidestep the puddles on the uneven asphalt, orange and shiny with pollution. Sidestepping a puddle, she runs into another umbrella making its way along the wet street. She pulls her umbrella back to apologize.

It's Omid.

Looking as if he doesn't know where he is. His cheeks and the tip of his nose are red. He stares at her, stunned; he doesn't move.

"What are you doing here?" she asks, her heart racing.

"I was just dropping something off for work," he stutters, pointing at a building down the street. "And you? Where are you going?"

Donya thinks of lying, but she knows her eyes will give her away.

"I don't know," she mutters, dropping her shoulders in sudden relief at having seen him, as if she's just been rescued from a dangerous fall. "I was just taking a walk. Then I found myself in front of Evin. I don't know what happened. Being there frightened me. I wanted to get away as quickly as possible."

The rain drums against their umbrellas. Her shoes and the bottoms of her pants are soaked. The cold grips her feet in a fierce clasp. His eyes soften. She thinks he might embrace her.

"I have my car parked right here. I'll take you home." He points at her shoes. He doesn't stutter any longer. "You can't stay in the rain like this. You'll catch a cold."

His voice is warm, familiar, unchanged. Donya has to gather all her forces not to burst into tears.

His car, a red Peugeot, is parked a few meters away. They walk next to each other in silence diluted with raindrops. A middle-aged couple walks past them. The man's palm is at the woman's lower back, though it doesn't touch her. It's as if he's holding his hand there in case she falls.

Omid opens the car door for her, and Donya gets in. A whiff of old leather and cigarette smoke fills her nostrils. She didn't know he smokes.

For a fleeting instant, the thought of Keyvon invades her conscience. But it is far, a muffled whisper behind a closed door. Omid starts the car, turns the heater on full blast, and directs the heat to her face and feet. He avoids her eyes.

"I've never been there before," Donya says, looking at him. She revels in the safety of his presence, in the warmth embracing her feet and stroking her face. The sharp change in temperature makes her slightly giddy.

"It's not a very beautiful sight," Omid says.

"It's quite frightening. I thought my heart was going to burst when I imagined what it could be like on the other side."

Omid smiles sadly and begins reversing the car away from the curb.

"So what is work?" Donya asks after a few moments, realizing she does not know what he does. She never even asked Sara about it. She has never thought of Omid in terms of what he does but, rather, who he is: his words, his thoughts, his knowledge of poetry, his passion for photography, his dream of becoming a theater director.

"What?"

"What do you do? You said you were dropping something off for work."

"Oh, yes." He pauses. He looks distracted, nervous. His anxiety has an oddly tranquilizing effect on her. She rests her head on the slight curve of the seat.

"I work for a company." He sounds evasive, unwilling to pursue the topic. "Computer programming."

"Oh, okay." Donya loosens the scarf around her neck. Somehow his reply has no effect on her, does not surprise her or disappoint her. It has no importance. "You like it?"

He shrugs. "Sure. I like computers."

Donya looks at the windshield wipers swiping away the rain.

Omid never came to say goodbye. He left her a notebook in the mailbox instead. Their photos together were glued to the pages. Next to each photo he had written, in neat, careful handwriting, his favorite lines of her poems.

"Shall I turn the heat down?" he asks.

"Yes, thank you. I was getting roasted over here."

He smiles. He always liked it when she made jokes. He would laugh at all her jokes. He glances at her for a quick moment with the gaze she once believed was hers to possess.

Soon he turns onto Sara's street. He drives slowly. *I didn't go that far after all*, Donya thinks.

They pass by the clothing shop, now open. The bald manne-quins have tiny pieces of Scotch tape on their noses, as if they've just had nose jobs. The woman inside is wrestling with the cash register.

Omid brings the car to a halt in front of the black door of the apartment. Donya listens to the sound of the grunting engine, wondering if Omid is going to turn off the car. Her mouth is dry. She sighs with relief when the engine's croaking comes to an end.

The silence around them swells with confusion, with cautious feelings. Raindrops glide down the window, leaving smooth oily traces. A pigeon flies past, exhausted and wet.

"I haven't written a single poem in years." The words escape Donya's mouth. She is startled by the ring of sadness in her voice. She turns her face away from him.

A few moments pass before Omid speaks. "You wrote beauti-ful poems." She hears uncertainty bobbing in the cadence of his voice.

"I don't anymore." She turns to look at him. He doesn't say anything, his jaw set. He looks distressed, impatient to get away from her. She'd like to shake him, her hands clasping his shoul-ders. A rude awakening.

What was it that we lost?

"I work for a bank, and I'm about to marry a man who loves enough for both of us and has a summerhouse in Saint-Tropez," she plows on.

What is she saying? What is she trying to do? To save? To ruin? She can't stop herself.

"It's a beautiful house, really. Right at the beach, with a boat always waiting. We have to decorate it, so he's asked me to bring him souvenirs from Iran. But he's ordered them all himself. All I had to do was to pick them up. Replicas of Achaemenid kings, Michelangelo on a rug, a painting with a *ghazal* by Rumi." She pauses. A brown leaf is trapped between the wiper and the windshield. It shivers in the wind. "Even though he's not even once in his life read a poem by Rumi. I hate all of it, their falsity, and I hate myself for not being able to tell him that. As I collected them, one by one, I felt I was tearing something into pieces."

She tries to laugh. Her voice cracks between a smothered sob and a titter.

The top of Omid's cheek is brightened under sudden timid sunbeams. The light vanishes before Donya has time to reach out to it. His prolonged silence unsettles her as she continues nervously.

"This morning, I was trying to think of what it was that Milan Kundera said about kitsch. But I couldn't."

"About kitsch?"

"He says something about it, doesn't he? About kitsch being a self-congratulatory feeling or something."

"He says many things about kitsch," Omid says, looking out the front window as if seeking an answer out there in the cold. "I remember one in particular. He says something about kitsch being the stopover between being and oblivion."

A grateful smile unfurls across Donya's face. "I guess it has nothing to do with the gifts I've bought."

Omid fiddles with the key chain hanging despondently from the ignition. Once again, silence coils around them, pressing tighter, like a snake on the verge of breaking their bones.

"I'm sorry," Donya says. "I shouldn't have bombarded you with all this silliness."

"No, not at all."

She can no longer hold back. Her body is breaking open without warning. She lunges forward and buries her face in the collar of his coat. Perhaps if she had not given up so easily, had not grown tired of the distance so quickly, had not been so afraid of his dreams, something might have changed or, rather, not changed the way it had. They would have bucked each other up and faced it all together, all the disappointments, all the pitfalls. They could have saved each other.

She can feel his body stiffening against hers. He smells of the cold, of uninterrupted presence. He smells of not having the answers. Not any longer.

After a few moments, he places a tentative hand on her shoulder. She inhales his sweet, unscented aroma and wants to scream.

"I have to go," he says.

Donya lifts her head. Heavy as granite. A stifled sob jostles harder and harder against her throat. She looks at him. All he has to offer is a smile, embarrassed and quiet.

"It was really nice seeing you again," he says.

She pulls back, a broken wave receding to the sea, and opens the door of the car. Shame, regret, and grief gobble her up in unison. Something inside her shatters.

She climbs out with feet that feel no longer part of her body.

Outside, the only thing that awaits her is the lonely wetness of the air.

2011
Turin, Italy

They are sitting under the white umbrellas of the café facing the Verdi Conservatory. The late-afternoon light bounces off the creamy-colored walls of the buildings, grazing past the plants on the balconies. The fresh heat of spring comes up from the cobblestone streets lining the square.

Neda lets her eyes roll over passersby scuttling past and shop-owners standing still. A yellow scarf is wrapped loosely around her neck, touching her short black hair. The aroma of freshly sliced cheese floats out of the café and mingles with the fading sunlight and the sound of someone practicing the piano in the conservatory and the ever-present scent of exhausted history, working up sweet saliva in her mouth.

Reza is sitting in front of her at the round wooden table with his back to the square. His fingers are curled around his glass of beer, as if he means to keep it from escaping. His other hand lies on his knee and appears once in a while to brush through his dark hair, adjust the collar of his shirt, run over his oval face. The gaze with which he regards her is far, foreign. It is of someone who has left the worst behind and yet struggles to understand why, to decide whether it was the right thing to do. All the political refugees she has met through him have the same gaze, like survivors of an earthquake: safe, with nothing to hold on to, meandering on the ineluctable passing ripples of days and nights; the gazes of wanderers.

"It was during the protests on the occasion of Student Day," Reza says. His face has hardened. Neda sees something fanatic, almost inimical, flashing in his eyes. "My sister was with a friend, going to join the demonstrations. A crowd had gathered on Enghelaab Street. It was important to always be with the crowd to reduce the risk of danger and entrapment. My sister and her friend had only to cross the street to reach the slogan-shouting crowd. They were almost in the middle of the street when they were suddenly trapped by about ten anti-riot security guards on motorbikes, wielding large batons. They encircled my sister and her friend, their motorbikes roaring as they made perfect circles around them. They looked insurmountable in their padded, bulletproof uniforms, larger than life, untouchable, ready to pounce. On the other side of the street, the crowd of protesters, shouting slogans, throwing stones, was milling farther and farther away from them. Their backs were to my sister; none of them saw her."

Reza's voice comes to halt as if he's short of breath. Neda holds her hands very still in her lap, her eyes fixed on Reza, steeling herself against the story that is flooding her with a sense of nauseating premonition. A cool breeze rises through the square and glides past her face, carrying the hum of the streets, of women chattering and children laughing and dogs barking playfully, provocatively. Reza brushes a nervous hand through his hair before continuing.

At last, one of the guards came to a halt. He glowered at Reza's sister, gauged her, as if looking for the best place on her body for the first strike. He was young, perhaps not even in his twenties, his upper lip covered in silky down. His eyes glimmered with contempt, cold, eager, calculating contempt. The kind that had not had a chance to brew yet; it was raw and immediate. The kind that struck, that did not give a chance to react, to strike back. The kind that simply happened, that could not be grappled with. He raised his baton and, with one forceful, deliberate swing of an arm, struck Reza's sister on the shoulder.

That was the green light the other guards seemed to have been waiting for. They began closing in on her—they never got off their motorbikes—swiping at her with their batons, kicking her with their boots. Heavy boots. Boots made for kicking, for stamping, for trampling. They kicked her on the side, in the stomach. They snatched at her scarf, jerking her around, hitting her on the back, chest, shoulders, arms with which all she could protect was her head, hit her so hard that she began wobbling between them. Her friend began to scream, to cry, pleading with them to stop. But no one heard her. No one touched her. They seemed to be interested only in Reza's sister, going round and round on their motorbikes, kicking her in the belly. Her friend yelped, but his sister was silent. Not a sound came from her. Her friend shrieked, cursed, begged. His sister could not open her mouth. All she had were her arms wrapped around her head. Another swerve of the baton on her back, another kick to her side, and she went down.

Reza's head wags slightly back and forth while he speaks. His eyes seem to be filmed over. Neda's heart pounds hotly in her chest. The rest of her body is numb, motionless. She feels a gradual icy coolness stealing through her. She is covering her mouth with her hand. She feels like she has been kicked inside and has a painful cringing in her stomach.

Once his sister was down, the guards finally stopped hitting her, and her friend was able to take her home. Since her body was still hot, his sister didn't feel much pain in the beginning. She even told her husband that everyone had exaggerated the pain of batons. It didn't hurt so much after all. Even after a few hours, when the pain began to settle in, to encroach upon her body, which soon turned black and blue and purple, his sister didn't take the bruises seriously. She said it was nothing, she'd seen worse, the bruises would soon go away.

"But the next day, the bleeding began inside her, and it wouldn't stop. We took her to the hospital. There she found out she had been two months pregnant. The child had died inside her. She had to go through an operation to get the dead fetus out."

Heavy boots. Good for kicking, trampling, crushing. Good for killing a child inside a mother's womb.

"My God." Neda's voice stumbles through her lips as a moan. She puts her hands on her eyes and presses her eyeballs as hard as she can, thinking of his sister with the dead child, with the blood. "My God," she repeats. She is incapable of saying anything else. "Is she okay now? Has she—has she recovered from this?"

"She's fine now." He pauses. "It was hard in the beginning. But she is very strong. She has recovered, I think."

Neda finds she can barely breathe; her head throbs, and her

entire body is so sensitive that she'd wince at the slightest touch. "The poor, poor girl."

Reza fiddles with the edge of the table. "I have never talked about this story, this—this nightmare, to anyone. I don't know, maybe in a strange way, it feels personal. Also because it's my sister. But I can tell you nothing that happened in those days to me or people like me shook me like what happened to my sister. It was as if they were able to hurt not only us, our generation, but also the one coming after. And that was just too much to bear."

"You must have suffered so much."

"She suffered the most." He nods a few times as if trying to keep a feeling inside him from bursting out. "But she is much better now. Two years have passed. And who knows, maybe time does heal all wounds." He leans back against the chair. His fists are clenched on the table like he doesn't believe in what he's just said. His gaze is fixed on the table. Neda can see how he aches inside, how his body is giving itself up to the pain rising from the memory. She lays a hand on his clenched fist.

That is when the thought comes, unbidden, the thought of her own mother. She too could have had a miscarriage. It was just a matter of luck that she didn't, that Azar stayed alive, that Neda stayed alive.

Years ago, in Iran, Azar told prison stories as they all sat around a warm *korsi*, covering their knees with quilts and blankets. In the beginning, when Neda and her brother and her cousin Forugh were still young, Azar told fun prison stories: of the games she and her cellmates played, the jokes they made about the Sisters, the childishness of the newcomers, the brazenness of the veterans, of the funny haircut she once gave one of the prisoners. Neda remembers how she, her brother, and Forugh would giggle, hearing these stories, rolling about, competing to laugh the hardest, the loudest, gales of laughter spinning through the room. How fascinating they had found it all; how amusing. Neda especially loved the story of her birth, the way her mother told it, waving her large hands in the air, widening her round gentle eyes, telling Neda of her funny spiky hair, the big black eyes watching everything inquisitively like a school principal, dark-skinned *like a little ladybug*. Neda imagined herself bundled up, surrounded by women with eager hands and needy hearts. *You didn't have one mother,* Azar would say, *you had thirty.* And Neda would feel a joyful warmth in her stomach at the thought of how loved she had been, how needed. Neda thought she was a lucky child. *Such a fun birth story!*

And yet, as the children grew up, the prison stories gradually lost their color and warmth, as if her mother had decided that the children must now know the truth, or at least the other side of the truth. *For all the other stories are also true*, Azar insisted, *but they are not everything*. Her face no longer gleamed when she told these new stories; her hands didn't flutter in the air. They were stories about women who had lost their mind, those who became *tavaab*, those who never came back. Even the stories about Neda's birth were no longer fun. They were all about her mother's fears of losing her, keeping her, nightmares, guilt, anger, her paranoia that some of the women would try to trample Neda while she was sleeping, kick her in the head. The Sisters gradually lost their caricature-like quality and became overwhelmingly real, menacing, unpredictable, the Brothers, ruthless, sadistic, to be avoided as much as possible. During these stories, her grandfather would always leave the room, her grandmother would silently dry her tears, her father would remain quiet in the corner of the room, his face darkening, his entire being exuding such sorrow that it made Neda afraid of even touching him, lest he crack open like a broken pot. And the children only listened, struck silent by the power of that grief.

Then there was the dead uncle, Behrouz, her father's youngest brother, whose framed photo was on the wall of every house, of whom they rarely spoke. Not in the beginning and not after. This did not mean he was forgotten. None of that bygone history was. They could not forget even if they wished to *for the sake of the children, for the future.* It conditioned every step of their lives and every decision. It was always right there behind their eyelids. All they had to do was close their eyes to see it, to relive it. All they had to do was speak about it once, a question, an innocent comment over dinner, for her mother to grapple with nightmares all night long, for her father to smoke cigarette after cigarette in the backyard, swaddled against the cold of late hours. And so they knew: the future was marred long ago. And so were the children.

Gentle shadows of the falling dusk glide across Reza's face as he leans back in his chair to let a waiter with a tiny head and bushy eyebrows set down a plate of olives and cheese with small saucers of jam and honey.

"*Le olive*," Reza says, smiling, picking up an olive. He seems to wish to move on from the subject of his sister. "That's one of the first Italian words I learned. They taste different here, less bitter."

"The first word?"

"One of the first."

"That's funny." Neda too picks up on olive. "Mine was: *prendiamo un caffè?*"

They laugh.

"That's three words. You were already a step ahead of me."

"Two steps ahead," Neda says, and winks playfully.

Reza smiles, spitting the pit into his curled fingers and then opening them with a graceful spin and dropping it into his plate. The short cut of his hair makes him look younger than his age but gives a certain severity to his face, to his thin chapped lips with their soft corners. He looks formal in his dark blue suit, as if he's heading to a business meeting. She likes that he dresses up every time they go out together. She feels tenderness every time she watches him walking toward her, always neat, courteous, like a schoolboy. Taking those long, slow steps, his hefty arms swaying awkwardly by his sides, a wide yet hesitant smile on his lips, like he's never fully sure whether his mouth is capable of breaking all the way open. His steps solid, heavy, and yet they always give her the feeling that he's walking a tightrope.

That was the way he was when they first made love the morning he came over to her apartment for some books about Turin she had promised him. He had been in Italy for three months. He said he wanted to learn more about the city where he had ended up, its mysteries; he'd heard there were many. He had appeared in her doorway, wearing a long gray overcoat, smelling of wood dust and expectation. He was living in the back rooms of a carpenter's shop. To get to the street, he had to walk through the semi-dark storefront, among half-made cabinets and bed frames, the sawdust, fine and soft, settling on his skin. Just a few minutes through the shop and the smell stayed with him, sweet and pungent.

He was hesitant, standing in the middle of the room, his back to the golden glow seeping through the window. She saw the tension, the rigidity in the blurred outline of his tall, heavily built body. He waited for her to unravel him, watching her with his eyes bright like tree leaves under the rain, his nerves pulling at the corners of his mouth. And she did, slowly, feeling the sunlight warming her shoulders. Afterward, they lay side by side, she on the softness of his outstretched arm. Motionless, they lay, wordless. And they fell asleep in the scent of their bodies, serene, like children content, collapsing after a long day at the beach.

Ever since, something in her has gone out to him, a fearful, convoluted desire that took root inside her the very first time she saw him. It was his status as a political refugee that had intrigued her the night they met; that, besides his unhurried manners and long eyelashes. It was the Shab-e Yalda of last year. Reza was standing outside the Iranian restaurant where the gathering was held. Neda saw him looking at her from behind the window. She was sitting in a corner, alone. She didn't know anyone. In the three years she had been in Turin, she'd never hung out much with the Iranian crowd. She spent most of her time with the other students of the art academy. But as Shab-e Yalda approached, she felt homesickness mounting up inside her, unannounced, unexpected. She needed to spend some time with other Iranians, to swaddle herself even if for one night with the warm, melancholic, conspiratorial feeling of her mother tongue. She asked around about Iranian events and found out about this restaurant. Yet, once there, feeling solitary in her corner, she was already thinking of leaving. That was when she saw him, behind the window, smoking a pipe, its blue smoke blending with the fog and the night and the snowflakes ready to pour. She smiled but didn't know why. The pipe looked so old-fashioned. It matched perfectly the floating world of the restaurant with its floors covered with Persian rugs, the miniature paintings on the walls; a separate world, a suspended world, outside of time and space.

Now Reza leans his elbows on the table, tilting slightly forward, his chin dotted with sparse black hairs. He lays his large eyes, doused with an apprehensive melancholy, on her.

From the open windows of the conservatory, she can hear the music wafting out, caressing the air, majestic, accompanied by the voice of a soprano who seems to be undoing a knot in her chest.

"You hear her sing?"

"Yes," Reza says, smacking his lips. "It's beautiful. I like walking past the conservatory when I leave your house. You can never see who is practicing in there, but it's always bursting with music and life."

Neda tilts her head a little, gazing at him, imagining him walking away from her apartment in his blue suit, carrying his massive, loose-jointed body that still smells of her in the narrow, elegant, but bustling Via Mazzini, past the antique bookstores and sophisticated shops of design and small, low-ceilinged stores of up-and-coming fashion designers. A fugitive, with that distracted, dazed expression, like he doesn't know where he is.

"You like the opera?" he asks.

"I do, although I've never been to one."

"Me neither."

"We should go sometime. Get all dressed up. It'll be fun. But first we should start putting aside money," she says teasingly, giving him a wide smile.

He laughs, throwing his head slightly back and narrowing his eyes. He has a deep-throated laugh.

In his eyes, I am safe, she thinks. *I have always been safe, here, so far away from the havoc.*

She leans an elbow on the table, cradling her chin in her cupped hand. "I make you laugh."

"Yes, you do. You always make me laugh."

"Do you like how I make you laugh?"

He inclines his body forward. His knee underneath the table bumps into hers. "I do, very much."

"Why?"

"Why what?"

"Why do I make you laugh?"

He watches her. "Because it's easy to laugh when I'm around you."

She studies his face, thinking that it's true. When he is around her, his tight jaw seems to loosen up, his eyes brighten, and his laughter grows louder. He seems almost too eager to relax, to smile, watching her with an expectant gaze, as if waiting for her to say or do something to make him laugh, to make him forget, to make him feel new. He takes comfort in her, she knows. Breathing in her intactness, reveling in her quiet so as to forget his own anguish, his dither, the horror that still cleaves to his skin, the horror of the violence he has seen committed against ordinary people on the street, his days in solitary confinement, his horror of death that he faced alone, in prison, not knowing what would become of him. She has seen his eyes glisten many times with joy, with relief almost, at the sight of her, as if her very being, with her dainty Italian clothes that he never forgets to compliment, her confident manners, her smile, is proof that it's possible to reconstruct something beautiful out of devastated debris. And there it was again, just a few minutes ago, when she mentioned going to the opera. The glistening relief, the urge to believe that yes, life can be easy. It can be about deciding to go to the opera or not, about putting money aside; it can be fun, without dread, without horror, without always fighting, resisting, struggling, without always having to test the limits of one's bravery, of one's cowardice. Life can simply be about a spring afternoon, drinking a beer at a café, overhearing a soprano rehearsing for a concert.

I have become his protector, she thinks, *his amulet.* And she feels like she has grown strong, indefatigable arms that can pull him away from the undertow tugging at him and lead him through that inescapable world of moving on, of starting over. He can pour all his grief into her and walk away a free man.

"And that's good?" she asks.

He touches her cheek with the tips of his fingers. "Of course it is. It's very good."

From a church nearby, the echo of tolling bells swoops down on the square. The sound of children's laughter fills the air. A woman passes by, pushing a stroller. There is a hysterical flapping of wings and screeches as several pigeons fight to get the bigger share of a handful of seeds that an elderly man has sprinkled on the ground.

Reza looks at Neda with his dark eyes. He smiles, though there is something sullen hovering over his eyelids; he resembles a man wishing to liberate himself of a weight and stand tall. By now she has grown used to these abrupt attacks of gloominess when he looks as if he's drowning in a lagoon she can't see, to which she has no access. It is a lagoon of memories, of friends he has left behind, promises he has not kept, struggles that, at a certain point, he no longer pursued. Of these he rarely speaks to Neda, as though he doesn't wish to sully her with such compunctions that, in his mind, belong to another land, another time. Only when he's drunk does he cry, and then she knows. She is familiar with those tears. She has seen her father shed the same tears when alcohol loosens something inside him and he can't stop.

"In the beginning, when the protests started, there was a lot of enthusiasm," Reza says, picking up his story again. Neda sees that his thoughts never waver. That as much as he is here with her in this beautiful quiet square, he is also there, in that other world of bullets and batons. "We didn't know if we were going to topple the regime or not. In a way, it wasn't about that. It was bigger than that. We wanted the whole world to know that we were there and we were awake and we were not afraid. We wanted to show everyone that our generation had grown up, that we had a voice and we wanted to and could make decisions." He pauses, interlaces his fingers. His voice pulsates with fervor. "The most beautiful were the silent protests. It wasn't something planned in advance. It just happened. That's how much harmony there was among us."

Neda remembers watching the images of a vast sea of people walking silently down a wide bridge. So silent that, for an instant, she thought she could hear the sound of their heartbeats. There were women in scarves, men with green bandannas around their foreheads, young and old, passing in front of the awe-stricken eye of the camera. A long green flag floated on top, held up by the crowd. After a few moments, a thunderclap erupted as the demonstrators broke their silence by simultaneously clapping their hands. There was laughter as strangers united through its heart-lifting burst. Quickly, the clapping gained momentum, spurting out of the screen and into the room where Neda watched, like raindrops battering the roof.

"It was in one of those videos of the silent protests that I saw my cousins Sara and Omid among the protesters. Did I tell you? Well, they're actually my cousin's cousins," she says, beaming. "It's a moment I'll never forget. First I saw Sara. She was flashing a victory sign, laughing, looking triumphantly around her. It was almost as if all those men and women were there to accompany her. Then she turned around and called somebody. A few moments later, I saw her brother, Omid, catching up with her, grabbing her hand, and together they just strode out of the camera's vision. I couldn't believe it. I had to watch the video many times to believe it was really the two of them."

Reza smiles, leaning back in his chair, with a satisfied expression.

"They told me there were hundreds of thousands of people on the streets that day alone," Neda says, clasping her hands. "They couldn't believe it themselves; the sheer numbers shocked them."

"The regime was shocked too," Reza says. He draws his shoulders in, clenching his jaw, as he speaks. "It was like they suddenly realized that we, our generation, had not come out as they wished us to, that all their brainwashing hadn't worked. But that's when the crackdowns started. And it wasn't just about scaring us away and back to our homes. The forces were out there to kill us, to kill thousands, if not millions." Reza pauses. The muscles of his face are taut with emotion. He seems bewildered, in shock. His dark eyes widen as if in reawakening terror. Neda feels the goose bumps on her skin, all the way to the roots of her hair. "There were gunshots everywhere, yelps of terror, burning cars and black smoke rising to the sky, bloody faces and bodies. It was not a game. They were ready to kill as many protesters as possible without the blink of an eye. At the time not one of us imagined the regime capable of such brutality. Such violence, such a cold-blooded will to kill. Not even in our worst nightmares."

Reza falls silent. Neda stares at him without being able to speak. She remembers watching the videos. The scenes of the government forces' violence and the protesters' defiance imbued her with a strange, overwhelming energy. She remembers wanting to pick up a metal bat and break all the windows, to run until she collapsed, to set fire to everything around her, to jump down a cliff. And yet now, as she listens to Reza, watches the bafflement, the shock, in his face, something inside her stomach churns. She feels a shiver of rage, of repulsion, hearing him so astonished, boggled, as if any of what happened was not just as it always was. What was the difference other than now the killing had been transferred to the streets; that it was now bolder, in the open, the blood glittering under broad daylight and not behind prison walls, en masse, in the middle of the night? *Or was it always in the daytime, the sun catching the blindfolded prisoners full in the face?*

No, she had not been shocked. *They have already killed thousands, Reza,* she would like to shout. *Your worst nightmares came true twenty-three years ago.*

The waiter clearing away the empty beer glasses interrupts the conversation. *"Altre due?"* he asks, addressing her.

Neda and Reza look at each other, leaning back in their chairs. *"Sì, grazie,"* Neda says to the waiter.

After that, they sit silently, looking around, as if they both need a moment to deal with their emotions, to bring them under control by taking refuge in the life that is unfolding around them, in the square that has slowly filled with blue twilight, in the dawdling shadows that spread over the light green shutters of the conservatory. They watch as the café gets crowded. Groups of friends gather around tables. Couples seek to catch the other's voice over the din of glasses clinking, ice being hammered into splinters, the crushing noise of the martini shaker. On the opposite side, a man and woman stand in front of a perfumery, admiring the elegant bottles on display. In the middle of the square, a group of teenagers loll about on the steps of the bronze statue of La Marmora, one of the generals of Italy's War of Independence, inclining a bit forward on his horse.

The relaxed beauty of the place fills Neda with restlessness and wonder. *What are we doing here, in this city, in this country?* Just as a few moments ago, the setting seemed like the perfect surrounding for their intimate talk, making it easier for the words to flow out; now, suddenly, the simmering, bubbling life around them feels alien, unrelated to them, blurring out just as it gains life, as if it's a dream. For a moment, she is unable to tell which feels more unreal: the impervious hum around them or the conversation with Reza. It is as though, in a matter of moments, she has been launched from one world to another. From the weight of the past and present in a place where a blood-soaked dagger is twisting deep inside the heart of the country to a world where a girl on a bicycle pedals through the square, her pink-and-yellow scarf fluttering behind her in the wind. It feels as if Neda is two bodies in one. One that writhes and wriggles, one that lies still. Each world makes the other seem impossible, far, another reality.

From a table behind them, she can hear bits and pieces of a conversation about a cat that escaped the house after a visit to the veterinarian. The owner of the cat speaks in a plaintive voice. She is afraid the cat will never come back. It has lost its trust in her, she says, and now associates her not with food and shelter but with the traumatizing experience at the veterinarian. The conversation breaks off when a cell phone rings.

Neda's gaze turns to Reza, whose large body is slouching into the chair as though an unseen force is pushing him down. He looks strangely childlike, docile. Neda feels an urge to hold him in her arms. Who do they have but each other? She stretches out a hand and smoothes the few graying hairs on his temples. He takes her hand and holds it cupped between both of his.

"What tiny hands you have." He examines them almost perplexedly. "I could put them in my pocket and carry them around with me and no one would notice."

His eyes glimmer softly into hers. Neda smiles, liking the feeling of being wrapped protectively between his hands, so much larger than hers. His fingers are long and slender, the skin slightly rough, warm. She curls her fingers inside his cupped palms, pushes them open, and curls them again, playfully. She feels an urgent impulse to tell him more of what she experienced during those post-election days, sitting behind her computer, watching it all unfold. *It all feels so recent*, she thinks, *even though it's been over two years*. She feels a shiver of envy at the thought of him having been there, having partaken of that moment when history turned. He ran through those streets, threw stones, shouted slogans, was arrested, released, and arrested again until his last escape. He risked his life. How can she compete with that? How can she tell any story, speak of any memory, larger than that? For him, it was all immediate, intimate; he smelled the bullet smoke, the tear gas, and the blood that steeped the streets. He did what

her parents had done thirty years earlier. He is a constant re-
minder of her parents, of how her parents would have been if
she'd been able to see them. But in her memories, her parents are
much older. That was how Neda pictured all political activists
and refugees before meeting Reza, with the same shape, the same
composed, mature middle-aged faces as her parents when she was
a bit older, and they were with her, and she could remember them.
Not during the time when they were not there and she slept with
her grandmother, who enclosed her in her arms, her breath hot
on her face, nearly suffocating her. That image of her parents she
had never really considered, and it was not until she met Reza
that it occurred to Neda that her parents too were once young, as
young as Reza, when they were arrested. This simple discovery,
in all its apparent banality, had shocked her: imagining her parents scurrying through those hostile streets, throwing anti-regime
leaflets into people's houses, having underground meetings, just
like Reza, their young eager faces suffused with a single-minded
fervid light, their every movement dedicated to that ideal which
made everything else so insignificant. It almost took her breath
away to think that her mother had been even younger than Neda
when she gave birth, locked up behind brick walls. Then she remembered how Azar referred to some of her cellmates as very
young. *Too young*, she would say, *to suffer for their half-baked political ideals*. Her mother would speak of how those prisoners always wore black and gray clothes and sat in rows along the low
walls and pretended to be strong. But when she wore her white
shirt with its yellow and pink flowers, they couldn't hide their
joy. They forgot about their pretense of strength, as if remembering that they didn't belong to those barren walls and worn-out

carpet, that the prison was not theirs, that something had gone terribly wrong. Those confessions of her mother had at the time filled Neda with consternation, not so much for Azar but for those other "very young" prisoners. But now, as she looks at Reza, she sees that her own mother was one of those young prisoners, only she never mentioned it, never revealed it.

Soon the waiter appears with two perspiring glasses of beer, thick foam bobbing on top. They unravel their hands to let him set the glasses on the table and tug the receipt under the black plastic ashtray. For a moment, they look at the glasses, then at each other, pale smiles rippling on their faces as they clink their glasses and take a sip.

"It's good beer," Reza says.

"It is."

Reza hunches slightly forward, examines the plate of cheese, which they've barely touched. "So what can you tell me about the cheese?"

Neda too leans forward, pressing her chest against her clasped hands on the edge of the table, looking down at the plate. "Well, let me see," she says, disentangling one of her hands to point at the cheeses one by one. "We've got parmigiano, *raschera*, fontina."

Reza laughs amused. "How do you recognize them? When I'm at the supermarket and want to buy cheese, I just pick up something at random and can never remember its name."

"It was like that for me too in the beginning. Then I learned little by little."

Reza tears a piece of bread in half, places the cheese on top of it, and hands it to her. Just like her mother did a few years ago, making tiny sandwiches for Neda while asking how her painting courses were proceeding. Azar, who Neda knew wanted her daughter back in Iran and yet never allowed herself to say so.

Neda spoke to Reza only once of her mother and the story of her birth. They had arrived home after a night out. Dawn was yet to break over the hills of Turin. They were standing on the balcony where they had a better view of the pinnacle of La Mole Antonelliana tickling the sparse white clouds and the dashes of crimson and gold in the treetops that sealed off the street.

"I am a happy man." Reza enfolded her in his arms, his mouth near her ear.

She rolled around in the tightness of his arms. She smiled but was already selecting the right words for her story. He held his face so close to hers, as though he wanted to breathe out of her mouth. She wondered if he could feel the pounding of her heart, so wild she thought it might implode.

She then told him, first in a trailing voice that slowly began to gain strength as she undid the knots one by one. Reza listened to her. There was a weak, pained smile on his lips throughout, as if it had been etched into his face. She felt unease exuding from him as he listened with the obscure expression of a man who didn't know how to deal with an emotion. His face, aglow with the gentle light of the rising sun, looked fluid, unpredictable.

He never interrupted while she spoke, never asked a question or made a comment. Later, when she was done, he wrapped his arms around her again and held her tightly and made love to her quietly. It was their most silent lovemaking, as if the sky had landed on them.

After that, Reza never spoke of it again.

"There's something that I've never told you." His voice cuts through the flow of Neda's thoughts.

Neda lifts her gaze, somewhat startled, like she's been brusquely awakened from a dream. "What is it?"

From the buildings that drip of darkness diluted with lamplight comes the secret calling of birds, perhaps warning of intuited threats, perhaps bidding each other good night. *You are going to tell me a story,* she thinks. *Another story. But I am tired of stories. When will they ever end?*

"My father was a member of the Revolutionary Guards," he says. "In fact, one of its founders."

Neda looks at him, a shiver running up her spine as if she's caught a chill. It seems to her that his voice dips a little, like he's uncertain of what he's saying or wishes no one other than Neda to hear him.

"But he's no longer one of them. He left as soon as he realized they no longer stood by their principles."

Neda nods and continues staring at him, unable even to open her mouth. She is too shocked to think straight, to truly digest what he has just told her. Although in the beginning, his eyes wavered from hers, he seems to have regained his composure. He looks straight in her eyes while he speaks, like he means to show her he has nothing to hide, that he has a clear conscience.

"The Revolutionary Guards aren't what they were supposed to be—what they were founded to be. My father felt betrayed. His ideals were ransacked."

As she listens to him, a memory emerges in her mind's eye. She tries not to think of it, to focus on what Reza is telling her, but the memory keeps jostling its way through her resistance.

It was a day of bright sunshine. Neda and Forugh were playing in the backyard, at Forugh's grandmother's house, where Neda went every Friday to spend time with the three cousins. Forugh's mother, Simin, called them indoors, saying she had something to tell them. Her long, thin face was serene but haggard. She was sitting on the floor, leaning against a red cushion. As they came in, she watched them with her heavy-lidded eyes, clasping and unclasping her fingers. Forugh sat on her mother's lap. Neda sat down next to her, digging her knees into the tight knots of the yellow-and-blue rug.

Neda can't recall Simin's exact words. She remembers that Simin was not crying; in fact, she may have been smiling, a sad, lusterless smile, like wintery sunlight. The skin of her face was dry, with bluish shadows underneath her swollen eyes; her high cheekbones were gaunt.

Forugh was sitting very still, staring at her mother as she heard the news of her father's death. Her lively brown eyes went opaque, and a flush rose to her face, but she didn't move. It was Neda who broke into sobs and ran out of the room, to the basement, and hid inside an old wardrobe that Forugh once told her was the best hiding spot in the house.

They knew Forugh's father was in prison, but everyone else had come back, so why not him? It was unfair, Neda thought, for her to have her father back and for Forugh not to. It was only later that she found out there were thousands of children whose mothers and fathers had never come back. It was 1988, the last year of the war, the sacred war, the sacred defense, the best time to eliminate all dissidents without leaving behind a single trace.

The prison gates were closed, all visits were canceled, and the purge began.

Trials were conducted in which a Special Commission asked questions of every prisoner; they varied from "Are you a Muslim?" to "Will you publicly denounce historical materialism?" Based on the answers, the Commission divided the prisoners between those whose answers satisfied them and those whose answers did not. Thousands of *apostates, enemies of God*, were promptly executed. Some believe tens of thousands. No one knows the exact number. Forugh's father, like thousands of other fathers and mothers and daughters and sons, never made it home. The only reason Neda's parents came back was that they were lucky enough to have served their sentences and been released before the slaughter began.

Neda doesn't know how long she stayed in the basement that day, but Forugh and Simin came after her, speaking to her, consoling her, wiping away her tears. To lift her spirits, Forugh played the small colorful xylophone her grandfather had bought for her. Then she let Neda play the xylophone, and her mother watched them, smiling encouragingly, clapping for them.

Neda feels slightly faint. She realizes she has been holding her breath unconsciously. Under the table, her hands are cold. The violence of the regime has shocked Reza because he doesn't know. His father might not have told him that there are children who have never been able to grieve, who have grown into tall, confident adults and yet deep down are still little children, sitting in their mother's laps, unable to move.

Neda presses her palms against her thighs. Her throat is dry. Her eyes twinkle with angry unshed tears.

Did Reza's father know what was going on? How much did he know? How involved was he? Or was he involved at all? Maybe he wasn't. She hopes he wasn't.

Is there blood on your father's hands?

It would ruin everything if she knew.

She runs a hand through her hair and looks at Reza, whose large eyes are on her. *He is testing me*, she think, *wants to see my reaction, to see if I'm up to hearing the rest, to see if he can trust me with his story.* She must hear everything that he has to say. *Coming clean*, she thinks. She almost wishes he hadn't told her about his father, that he wouldn't try to explain, to lay it all on the table and expect her not to quaver inside. *What does he want from me?* For a moment, she decides to forget about it all, Reza and his father and his memories. *I don't have to sit here and listen to this.* And yet she can't stop sitting here, can't stop listening to him, can't stop breathing him in as if she wants to have him inside her forever.

"This was not what my father fought for, what he wanted to establish," Reza continues. "He wanted to protect the revolution. There were threats then, you know. Possible foreign intervention, the war with Iraq. But everything took a different turn. The Guards were taking too much power in their hands, and too much wealth. My father no longer felt like he belonged."

It is not Reza's fault, Neda thinks. How would the world ever continue spinning if every child were blamed for the sins of the father? She can't fall into the traps that history lays out in every corner. She must avoid them. She must listen to him, to his explanations.

But will this ever work? Is a relationship with a man who comes from the other side doomed from the beginning?

Neda shrugs as if to shake off the tension. She looks at Reza and sees his fingers locked around the glass. She marvels at him, at the reality of him. She wonders whether she would have sat at the same table with Reza, their parallel yet distant worlds meeting, if they were in Iran. She's not sure she would have, or whether she would have had the chance. She knows that in another lifetime, in another place, he could have been her enemy. He would have been as far from her as he is close to her in Italy, for here, thousands of miles away, history ceases to be so devastatingly personal. It becomes something you see on the news; it is less physical, sensorial, real. Words are easier to utter, lighter. Gestures become less inhibited, glances less instinctually cautious, feelings less grueling, less intertwined with guilt and blame and revenge and redemption of an entire nation. Every word is no longer an allegory, of either something higher and nobler or something vile and wretched; every action is no longer a symbol of defiance or conformism, every silence an opportunity to understand to which side one belonged, and every struggle for happiness an unfortunate distraction from the fight for the destiny of the country. Away from that land, eyes seem to have lost their constant flittering about, watching for possible dangers, their ears to have shrunk back to a normal size, no longer those large sensitive ears that strain because all they could hear were whispers. Here, they are able to take a step back, to observe and contemplate and draw conclusions, and to love, to love without fearing the worst, without pointing fingers, without incessantly fighting against the smell of blood clogged in their nostrils.

But do I love him? Neda wonders. *Is it possible?*

"Since then, my father always lived his opposition to the regime quietly," Reza says. "He never really spoke about it. He seemed to completely lose interest in politics. Even before the 2009 elections, when the electoral campaign was in full swing and everyone was so excited, always talking about the presidential debates and so on, Father seemed unaffected. But after the elections, when the protests began, especially after the crackdown started, it was like something burst open inside him, like it was the last straw. I tell you, he didn't miss one single demonstration."

Reza smiles as he recalls this peculiarity of his father. The courageous father, in his eyes, an audacious man. She sees his eyes scintillating warmly with pride. Neda smiles with him, but she can think only of time. When did his father leave the Guards? Over thirty years have passed since the revolution. Thirty years is a long time. When did his father decide it was all wrong? When did Reza's father decide there had been enough bloodshed? Before the bloodshed or after?

Although she tries to control it, to ignore it, she feels a squeeze in her chest as she listens to Reza, racked with an unfathomable sense of guilt and anger. Throughout her life, she has loathed the Guards, has been afraid of them. She can't bring herself to speak of them now, to ask questions as if they are just an interesting phenomenon to be investigated, understood. For years in Iran, the likes of Neda and her family lived separately, welded to that planet of memories where everyone knew what fear could be generated by the slip-slap of plastic slippers. Neda can still hear her mother's warning on the first day of school: *Never tell anyone where your parents have been!* There was a wide chasm between what could be talked about at home and what could be said outside, on the other side of the closed door. There were parallel worlds, one in which nothing was hidden, neither the memories nor the family's contempt for the regime; and the other, in which everything was prohibited, voices were hushed, and children inherited alertness against anything that could put the family in danger, carrying their parents' secrets with them, heavy as a sack of rocks that they could never set down. It became part of the way Neda regarded herself and her family: a family of secrets, of resistance, of defeat.

This is what we are, Azar once told her. *And you must know it, because you must know that your parents fought for a better life for you. But outside of that door, no one is to be trusted; no one. Not your favorite teacher, not the neighbor, not even your best friend.* Azar was afraid the regime's men would come after them again, come after her children, or deny them something other children had, or mistreat them. She believed that punishment could still befall them, that serving a prison sentence didn't mean anything; it did not exempt them from further suffering. She believed that *those others*, the guardians of the revolution, might not be done with them. For years, that is how they lived, in fear of further punishment, of a payback that was not fully carried out.

Then the protests began, and all the chasms grew hazy. Everyone was now on the streets. The children of victims as well as those of the perpetrators. Everyone palpitating with hope, anticipation, confidence. The children of all her parents' prison friends took to the streets. They had not been able to sit around, to be mere witnesses. They had not been able to accept their parents as the only historymakers. It had become their fight, all-encompassing, unbound, in which they were together in those uncharted waters and no one was left behind. The same waters that had brought Reza to her with a broken body and a battered soul, his hands as empty as her own, to this country miles and miles away, where looking back at history seemed to be so much easier.

Then it dawns on her, and the thought stops her breath. Reza did not want to hear her mother's story. His smile was that of a man who did not wish to know. She forced her story on him. He was its reluctant receiver. She feels the rush of blood to her throat. No wonder why he never broached the subject, never asked questions. He didn't want to look so far back. *He was afraid. He didn't want to carry the blame. He was fighting against it.* She had seen it in that glittering defiant scrim that came over his eyes while she spoke. Only for a moment, but she had seen it. She wasn't thrusting blame on him, a refugee who had lost everything. She wasn't blaming him. *Nor your father.* She just wanted him to know that the prisons were filled long before he began his protest, that under the ground, there were silenced voices.

Maybe he was just trying to remember. But what could he remember if he knew nothing? *How could he not have known?* Her head is throbbing. She rests her hands on the table, pressing her weight on them, writhing inside. She will tell him everything. She will no longer keep her promise to her mother. It's time to unravel everything. No more secrets, no more choking back. Everyone has to know. *To know, to know, to know!* Reza and all his friends who've passed over the issue in a silence similar to his, for the issue has been brought up, not by her but by others, news articles, interviews, letters. The spilled blood on the streets has made people remember things they thought had been forgotten. *Reza has to know. Above all, Reza.* For they cannot go anywhere if he doesn't.

"What's your father's name?" she asks.

Reza takes a sip from his beer. "Meysam."

Would her parents recognize this name? Did they know any of the names of their jailers, or did they call them Brother and Sister without ever uttering a name, or did they never call them?

She knows she would never ask her parents. A name has a weight, a reality, that is hard to ignore. *Meysam*, she repeats in her mind. Behind Reza, on the balcony of the conservatory, the Italian flags billow softly in the breeze.

"My father was the first in the family to join the street protests," Reza says. He sits up in his chair, tapping lightly on the bottom of his glass. "He would leave the house before all of us and come back later than everyone else in the evening, with his body bruised all over. He was always attacked. They beat him up with batons. Once he came back home with a bloody face. His right cheek had been smashed."

Reza raises his eyebrows, his face twitching into an uncomprehending, dismayed sneer. "In the beginning, my father tried to talk to those beating him, asking why they hit him, saying he could be their father. I couldn't believe he would say such things. How naive could he be? But he was always like that. He didn't seem to understand the gravity of the situation, of how far they were capable of going."

Neda fumbles with the olives. The one she picks up slips from her hand and falls on the ground. She is discomfited by the intensity in Reza's voice, by the vehemence with which he suffers for his father. There is a cold feeling in her stomach that quickly changes into a fury of heat climbing up the column of her body. As she takes off her scarf, the thought comes to her that perhaps Reza's father tries to reason with them because he was one of those who established them. He tries to reason with them because he thinks he can; they are his own creation. But then they beat him, and he realizes he has lost control. They have turned against him, gone beyond him, beyond his reach. They beat him along with everyone else. They're not afraid of shedding his blood, if necessary. Their training says nothing about second thoughts.

The thoughts disgorge into Neda's mind as smoothly and quickly as water out of an overturned glass. She is ashamed yet allured by these thoughts. Appalled yet enchanted by the ease with which they are unleashed inside her. She looks up at Reza and hopes he can't read her eyes.

"I would ask him: are you really trying to reason with them?" Reza continues, running an agitated hand over his face. "They're incapable of understanding anything. They're just violent wolves. Worse than wolves, they see nothing but blood."

"He was trying to change their minds," Neda hears herself say.

"But they would never change their minds. They wanted to get rid of us. We were too many, Neda. We were too strong, perhaps. Or they thought we were."

Neda drops her hands to her sides, her body slackening. She feels like she's being sucked ever deeper into the lagoon of her desperation. How can she tell her family, her brother, her cousin Forugh, especially Forugh, about the man she's seeing? Would it help that Reza is on the same side, that he has stood up against the regime, that he has lost everything, that his father has been beaten black and blue and purple, that his face was smashed with a baton? Would Forugh accept any of it? *None of this would resuscitate my father, would it?*

Neda looks at Reza and imagines his sister, with his eyes, his tiny teeth when she smiles. She thinks of her mother, of how Azar's stomach must have begun to show when the Revolutionary Guards came to take her away, heavy like the sea, her stomach and breasts laden with the preparation for motherhood.

These were the Revolutionary Guards your father helped establish. The unleashed monsters. The Frankensteins who imprisoned and tortured and killed and filled mass graves. The Guards whose even more ruthless protégés were now out on the streets, beating and killing and smashing. Those who had kicked the belly of his sister, kicked the child inside. His father founded the Guards and then pulled out. He believed that they no longer upheld the ideals he had fought for. But the monsters had been unbridled. It was already too late.

If not for my mother, then for your sister.

Neda feels a hard squeeze in her chest. She feels like crying. She wishes her mother were there so she could hide her face in her chest and feel her warmth and hear her heartbeat and lose herself and sleep and wake up with the sweet perfume of the jacaranda flowers and the sound of her mother's soft footfalls in the courtyard. Nothing like the unwavering certainty in those footfalls, like the nearness of the aroma of the jacaranda tree, has ever given Neda such a sense of peace.

They sit in silence. A tired, vacant look has come over their faces. They sit very still, as if all their memories are crushing down inside them. A few moments pass before they lift their gazes to each other. Reza takes her hand in his and gives it a slight squeeze. "Let's go for a walk," he says, and smiles gently at her. "I'll just go in and pay. This one's on me."

Neda nods and watches him walk away. She looks around at the square. The air shimmers with the light of lampposts illuminating the facades of the conservatory and its surrounding buildings, casting irregular shadows on the plants on the balconies. Two little girls in pink dresses are chasing each other around the statue.

The conservatory is quiet, its windows shut. A group of young men and women stands outside its closing doors, chattering, a few of them with cigarettes between their fingers, blowing waves of smoke over their shoulders, carrying their musical instruments in large black cases. Neda crosses her arms and presses them to her chest. She feels sore inside, shaken, exhausted. Her ears feel blocked, as if a curtain of silence has dropped over them, muffling everything else.

Once, when Neda shared her concern with her father about the prisoners languishing in the regime's prisons, their names, the pictures of their young faces going around Facebook, Ismael said, *At least now their faces are known, their names are on everyone's lips. We all died in silence.*

After a few moments, the door of the café opens and Reza re-appears. His blue suit looks slightly large on him, attenuating his straight back, his broad shoulders. He smiles as he approaches her, his face lighting up as if he's just seen her for the first time. She feels a rush in her stomach, almost gasps at the tender, welcoming, yet unruly edge of his beauty. She imagines her own parents in his place. She can see them walking next to each other under the effulgent light of pastry stores and shops of dry fruit and nuts pouring onto the sidewalk. Her father with his hands behind his back, her mother slightly shorter, a hand on her purse, the other curled almost into a fist. Her parents were not refugees. They stayed and went to prison and were released and raised their children defiantly in the same country where their own hopes and future were curtailed.

Neda wishes her parents had found their own protectors, their own amulets. She wishes they had not suffered so much, catapulted into another reality where they would realize that their fight had been taken away from them. At times, she wishes she could go back and lend a hand to her parents, help them cross over the shaky bridge that held the two worlds together, that of horror with that of hope. It is perhaps too late for her parents, but she still has Reza. In his eyes, she sees the same angst that she once saw in her parents' eyes, and she hopes she has the power to wipe it away. And that is why she can't let him go, no matter where and which side he has come from. She gets up.

"Are you tired?" he asks.

She shakes her head. Her mouth wobbles into a smile. She cannot withstand the intensity of his gaze. She places her hands over his eyes; as he closes them, his eyelashes tickle her palms.

Neda's mouth is dry. She has to swallow hard before she is able to speak. "I'm really sorry about your sister." Her voice seems to come from far away, and then it breaks. Her eyes swim with hot tears.

Reza slides her hands down his face. His shadowy eyes glisten kindly, sadly, full of thrumming sorrow. He draws her into his arms, holding her tightly, so tightly it almost hurts. But she likes the pain, the sensation of her bones being squeezed between his hefty arms and his chest. She presses herself against him, a tremor running through her body. Then he leans forward and places a tentative kiss on her wet lips. She breathes on him, warm, hesitant, as if testing the waters before sinking in. She kisses him back. Something inside her drains out and into him.

A few moments pass before she gently disentangles herself and digs in her purse for a tissue. She feels his eyes on her as she wipes her eyes and blows her nose, swiping it vigorously. She doesn't look at him but is acutely aware of his presence as he stands in front of her, hovering over her like a giant, as if he means to cover her whole. She can smell the wood dust on his warm skin.

"I didn't want to make you cry," he says.

She waves a hand in the air. She can't bring herself to look at him, not fully, lest she break into tears again. "Oh, it's not your fault. It's nothing."

"Was it because of my sister?"

Neda continues fumbling with her purse. "Your sister, my mother." Her voice falls, sinks deep into her chest. The menacing knot is climbing in her throat, the tears lurking behind hot eyelids. She waves her hand in front of her face to show that she cannot speak.

"Let's take a walk, huh? We both need some fresh air."

She laughs, her laughter clanking with a broken, choked-back sob. "Here's fresh air."

He laughs too. "Yes, but it's different when we take a walk. We can go to the river."

"Okay." She tucks a strand of hair behind her ear, straightens her back, and takes a sweeping look at the cobblestone street. She begins to regain her calm. The mild breeze that passes through her hair is laden with the smell of passing cars and something delicious cooking.

"I'm actually quite hungry," Reza says. "It must be the beer. Maybe also the cheese. What was the name of the cheese we had?"

Neda slips the tissue into her pocket. She still feels a prickly sensation in her nose, in her eyes. "Which one?"

"The one we had with honey."

She reflects. "Fontina."

"That was really good."

Neda smiles. "It was."

He offers her his arm. There is so much she has not told him, so many stories she has kept inside. *There is no hurry. There is time.*

She takes his arm, hard, unwavering in her grasp. Together they step out of the protection of the white umbrella and into the limpid night. They walk across the square, past the statue of the general on the horse, the elderly resting on the benches, the line of people waiting their turn for an ATM machine. Suddenly, in an act of elation, Reza throws his arm around Neda's waist, tugging at it, lifting her aloft. He twirls with her on his shoulder. Neda gives out a surprised shriek, then a gale of laughter, feeling weightless in his arms, the lights of the square spinning around her like lively scintillating butterflies. She continues to laugh, swatting at his arms playfully, asking him to put her down.

Her heart pounds in her chest as her feet find the solid ground. *He is like a child*, she thinks, laughing, running her hands over her dress, through her black silky hair, the echo of his laughter in her ears as he begins walking away with a light, confident gait, his solid, robust body loping into the shimmering glow of the square. More of a child than she has ever been, than her brother, her cousin, have ever been. For secrets steal your childhood away from you. Death stories, they were, of men and women hanging from the gallows. Childhood slips away when death settles in. Reza does not know that. There is so much he doesn't know. Reza perhaps doesn't know what jacaranda flowers smell like.

One day I will take you with me to the jacaranda tree, she thinks, matching her steps with his, fitting her hand into his. *Or perhaps—* she smiles—*we are already on our way.*

Acknowledgments

I am forever indebted to

my mother, for the night you came into my room and said, "I will tell you everything."

my father, for the letters you wrote month after month, year after year, so that it felt as if you were with me in all those seven years when you could not be, for answering all my doubts.

my brother, Navid, my best critic and friend, for always asking the right questions, for making one glance enough and words unnecessary.

my grandmother, Aba, for continuing to fill me with your love even from the other side of time. My grandfather, Agha, and my uncle, Ebrahim, for always being there.

my cousin Siavash, my first playmate and schoolmate, for taking that trip to Italy and bringing me the photo of the three of us together.

my sister in arms, Mehrnoush Aliaghaei, for being an ideal reader, for your friendship, for your passion and dedication.

Tania Jenkin, Tijana Mamula, Soheila Vahdati Bana, Marjan Esmatyar, Joy Lynch, and Maria Elena Spagnolo for your support and encouragement over the years.

Fateme Fanaeian and Sadegh Shojaii, for bringing the green breath of Iran to me.

Victoria Sanders, my brilliant agent, for taking a chance on me and on this book. And a heartfelt thank you to Chandler Crawford for believing in this journey.

Benee Knauer, for your meticulous guidance, for helping me pause and ponder.

Sarah Branham and Arzu Tahsin, my amazing editors, for your vision, your insights and enthusiasm, for your trust in me.

my uncle Mohsen, for the graceful power of your memory in our lives.

my husband, Massimo, for your love and strength, for listening to me, for having read everything from those first embarrassing stories, for having always believed in me. None of this would have been possible without you.